In
Secret Waters

Richard Weissmann

Llumina
Press

ISBN: 978-1-62550-448-7

I have heard the sweep of the offshore winds

And thresh of the deep-sea rain.

I have heard the song: How long? How long?

Go out to the sea again.

Anonymous

In Secret Waters

PART ONE

ATLANTIC OCEAN, EAST OF MONTAUK POINT, NY

CHAPTER ONE

I'VE DONE A LOT OF THINGS IN MY LIFE. SEEN A LOT OF THE WORLD. BUT, being an eighth-generation fisherman, here, on eastern Long Island, has finally brought me back full circle. Hell, I love my job. Getting out on the ocean on my charter boat a few days a week clears my head and feeds my soul.

Of course, even out here it's not always possible to get away from world-class idiots. This was one of those days.

My boat is the *Finest Kind*, a forty-two foot sport fisherman of my own design. There were four paying customers on board today. The biggest one, Derek Donovan, was fast into a good fish that had taken the deep-trolled bait and was keeping the fight deep, refusing to come up to the surface and show itself. We were fifty miles east of Montauk Point. The ocean was green with a gentle swell and the day was getting hot. I was watching the fight from behind the wheel up on the flying bridge. It was a billfish for sure. Probably a blue or white marlin. A damned big one, too.

Before we left Montauk this morning, I knew that Donovan was going to be a problem. The big man was the alpha male among the group of stockbrokers who had chartered my boat, and he wanted to maintain his "big man" image. He had been obnoxious from the time he had set foot on the boat, and now that he was half drunk and struggling to hold the bucking rod up as he leaned into the heavy fish he was becoming even more abusive. A real jackass, I thought, as I nudged the boat forward to help keep pressure against the fish.

"Hey captain! Whoa! Slow the boat down, you're breaking my fucking back," Donovan shouted. His partners whooped and laughed drunkenly.

"Hang on, Derek," one jabbed at him, "Keep your rod tip up and show that fish who's boss. It's probably a big sardine."

"My money's on the fish, Derek. Let me know if you want me to take over," another said.

Bill Lester, the *Finest Kind*'s mate, stood behind Donovan and offered advice. "Just pump and reel and keep facing the fish, Derek."

"Yeah, yeah, I know the drill, Matey," Donovan muttered.

Lester's broad face reddened and he turned to look up at me. He was shaking his head and clenching his jaws. "The name's Bill, Mr. Donovan. And, if you think you can do this all by yourself, I'll go below and have some lunch."

"Whatever," Donovan sneered. "I just want to whip this sucker's ass and hang his carcass on my office wall."

Lester shrugged and eased his big frame into a deck chair. He sat watching the action in silence.

I tried to smooth things over a little. "Bill's giving you good advice, Donovan. This fish isn't going to roll over for you. It still has plenty of fight. You're going to have to beat it or hand your rod over to somebody who will."

Donovan shut up and grunted with the strain.

The fish was still deep and not moving now so I gave the throttle a quick nudge forward forcing Donovan to bang his knees up against the port rail as he strained and cursed. I smiled, winked at Lester, then continued to use the throttle, easing in and out of gear to keep maximum pressure on the fish and to make Donovan sweat. Of course the big man didn't realize that the boat is what really beats the fish. If I sat back and let the boat drift the fish would drive Donovan to his knees inside an hour. Right now it was a big temptation to do just that, but I didn't have time to waste on assholes. I wanted to get the fish alongside as fast as possible so my clients could get their pictures before I tagged and released it.

Thirty minutes later, Lester began pulling on a pair of stout, canvas gloves as he stood up behind Donovan. "The fish is almost ready. When the leader swivel breaks the surface I'm going to grab it. But, stay alert in case he wants to make another run. Keep the rod up high until I tell you to drop it. And the rest of you guys, stand back from the rail and give me room."

Sweat poured down Donovan's straining face and his shirt clung to his brawny body like wet tissue. "Jesus! This sonofabitch is strong. Get out to the way, you idiots. I want this fish on the deck pronto."

Lester carefully slid his hand down the leader and began hauling. I slapped the boat in neutral and grabbed a tail-roping device. By the time I slid down the ladder to the deck, Lester had gotten a grip on the sword of the blue marlin and was holding him alongside the boat. The big fish was on its side. Its rows of lateral stripes glistened in the sun. It was a beautiful fish. Then I slipped the rope around the muscular base of its tail to hold it steady. Its enormous eye looked up blankly at me.

"Holy shit!" one of the clients shouted. "It looks like a fucking submarine. What'll it weigh, Captain?"

I did a quick calculation. "Probably seven or eight hundred give or take fifty. A big female. Damn big for these waters. You got yourself a prize Donovan."

Donovan shoved his way through the crowd, still holding the rod in one hand. "What the fuck are you waiting for? Haul its ass into the boat. I did my work for the day."

I looked up from the fish and fixed Donovan with a hard gaze. "Get out your camera and take all the pictures you want, Mr. Donovan. Bill and I will hold her steady."

"Pictures! What the fuck do I want with pictures? I want this fish mounted."

I knew trouble was coming. I sighed. "Yes, of course you do. And taxidermists now make beautiful reproductions from photographs and measurements."

The blood rose in Donovan's face until it looked like he would have a stroke. "Reproduction? I don't want no reproduction. I want the real thing. I caught it."

By now I had had enough of the guy and dropped all pretense of being polite. "This fish is going back where it came from, Donovan. You're not worthy of taking its life." I took one hand off the rope and braced myself. I'm not a real big guy but I can handle myself. Donovan had thirty pounds and two inches on me so I wanted to be ready if he made a move.

"This is absolute bullshit! We paid good money for this charter and I demand that you kill this fish." He looked around at his friends for support, but no one else said anything.

Instinctively I clenched my right fist and the sinews of my forearm must have sent a signal. Donovan took note of it and I saw some of the fire fade in the stockbroker's eyes as he considered his chances. I looked back at the fish. It was still lying quietly on its side as I quickly threaded a spaghetti tag through its pectoral fin and released the tail rope. Then I reached over with a pair of pliers and twisted the hook out of the bony mouth. Donovan shouted "NO!" and lunged to reach down over the side just as Lester let go of the sword. The big fish arched half its body up out of the water and caught Donovan on the side of his head with the full force of the scimitar-shaped tail. Then, with a mighty thrust of that tail, the big marlin disappeared into the green depths. Donovan would have fallen in after it had Lester not grabbed his belt and hauled him, sputtering, onto the deck.

"You can have your money back, less my expenses," I said as I climbed back up to the bridge. "This charter is over."

The four-hour trip back to Montauk was mostly in silence. The seas had built up with a strong S/W wind and two of the clients moaned with seasickness inside the salon. Donovan and the other executive sat morosely out on deck drinking beer, smoking cigars, and occasionally muttering into the wind.

Lester put the rods and reels in their holders, did a quick cleanup and climbed up to the bridge holding two long-necked beers in one hand. His wide face was permanently sunburned above a graying beard and behind the dark, wraparound sunglasses favored by deepwater fishermen.

"So, what do you think, Bub?" He said as he settled his bulk into the helm seat next to me. "Is this jerk going to make a big stink?"

Lester is a Bonacker just like me, descended from a long line of fishermen who came from England—some as early as the 1600's—and settled in the East Hampton area of Long Island, around Accabonac Harbor. "Bub" is part of the old language that we reserve for friends. It used to be that "Bonacker" was a term of derision, kind of along the lines of "redneck", "cracker", or "Okie". But, those days have faded now. The "correct" side of Montauk Highway—that is to say the south side, near the ocean beaches— has plenty of rich lawyers, stockbrokers, and even celebrities who dress down on the weekends, drive pick-up trucks, and are happy to be mistaken for natives like us.

I lifted my long-billed fishing cap and wiped the sweat away from my eyes; it was only early June but the mid-day sun was already heating up. "Frankly Bub, I don't give a damn," I said out of the side of my mouth in my best Rhett Butler imitation.

Lester brightened. "You know what they call a Wall Street guy on the bottom of the ocean, don't you?"

"I know. I know: A good start."

We both smiled at the old joke and then went back to focusing on our cold beers and the wide horizon. Behind us, the long wake of white, sea foam spread out in a V across the empty ocean. Lester and I have been friends since childhood and silence on the water comes as easily between us as conversation.

The rumble of the big Allison diesels was mesmerizing and Lester soon dozed off. I sat thinking about the big fish. I was glad we had set it free, something I would never have done twenty-years ago when I was fresh out of the Navy and running my first charter boat. Back then, it was standard operating procedure to kill anything that could attract customer attention at the dock or be sold to the Japanese fish buyers. Now, just the thought of that great fish swimming with the Gulf Stream, circumnavigating the Atlantic Ocean every year made me both happy and envious. I lifted my beer out of the gimbaled holder. "Here's to you, old girl," I said as I drained it.

Land was still too far in the distance to see, but a high formation of cumulus clouds marked its presence off to the northwest. I watched the slow mutation of cloud shapes through polarized glasses. Their abstract composition was like a Rorschach test, only a lot prettier. Below the bow, the water began changing hue from deep ocean aqua to a milky jade. Montauk Point was straight ahead, but the emptiness of the ocean was still broken only by a distant, outgoing cargo carrier off the portside. The GPS showed the *Finest Kind* moving slowly across its blue chart screen, though I didn't need it since I've been navigating these waters from the time I was a teenage deckhand on my grandfather's boat more than thirty-years ago.

By the time we rounded Montauk Point the sun was dipping low in the sky. The old lighthouse cast a long shadow that pointed straight out to sea.

The sight of home waters as I turned down the channel into Lake Montauk, coupled with the lowering sun, started to put me in a somber mood. Soon it would be the tenth anniversary of Kate's death. A decade was gone in a flash and the memories where still haunting me.

My thoughts were interrupted by the roar of a plane's engine a few hundred feet overhead. It was a yellow seaplane and as it swooped towards the harbor it waggled its wings. I looked up and waved.

"It's that crazy bastard Zeke Tredia," Lester mumbled as he came awake and squinted overhead.

"It's Zeke, all right. He must be running a charter. I don't know any sword fishermen who are using a spotting plane this early in the season."

"You're right, Erik. I can see people in the passenger seats."

The dock was pretty crowded with pale-skinned tourists waiting to see some giant of the deep tossed, dead, onto the planks. Once they realized there wouldn't be a show they moved out towards Gurney's Dock where the big, open boats were discharging passengers with buckets of bluefish and fluke.

Our passengers staggered ashore with their coolers of lunch and leftover beer. There were complaints about "bad treatment" and "Captain Bligh", even some lame threats about filing complaints with who knows who. But, most of the bluster and all of the fight had drained out of Donovan and he was happy to get a refund—minus my expenses—and be on his way. I handed the $500 expense money to Lester; he wasn't going to get any client tips today and he needed the money more than I did.

"Thanks, Erik, and good riddance to them," Lester muttered. "I think you treated them too nice."

I grinned. "Yeah, well, Bub. I guess that's why they call me Mr. Nice Guy. Besides, they have to go back to Wall Street tomorrow. That should be punishment enough."

"That's true," Lester nodded. "And we get to panhandle for another fare."

CHAPTER TWO

PANHANDLING IS NOT SOMETHING I HAVE TO DO. ONLY A FOOL OR A DREAMER would be in the charter-boat business for the money. Fortunately, I did well for myself when I left the Navy and took over my family's floundering boat building business. I had studied engineering and boat design at Annapolis so I had some ideas.

Up until then, Great Peconic Boats was barely staying afloat building traditional, flat bottomed skiffs used by local baymen. I took a different approach and designed a skiff that would have a wider appeal. Based on traditional designs with low freeboard in the stern, a high, flared, Downeast bow, and a raked windshield amidships, the thirty-footer moved fast and looked sharp. The boat's simple, clean lines first appealed to the weekend fishermen and, ultimately, to many of the Hampton "elite", who liked the idea of owning a piece of the real Hamptons. Before long, we were building bigger models tricked out with exotic woods, custom interiors, and faster engines.

Then Kate died and, as they say, my world came crashing down. Six-months later I sold out to a major international boat building firm. Now, there are Great Peconic Skiffs in places like Santa Barbara, the Virgin Islands, and the French Riviera. So much for the purity of form and function designed for local waters. But my accountant seems happy.

Just then, Lester, who had been swabbing the deck, jabbed me in the side and pointed up to the dock entrance. A very attractive woman was striding towards us while a chubby, older man with a full head of white hair struggled to keep up. Both of them were dressed in business clothes, he in a three-piece suit and wing tips, and she in a tailored silk blouse with a knee-length skirt, but wearing boat shoes. I couldn't help noticing that she had great legs, the legs of a dancer, and as the wind ruffled her short, dark hair she swept it back from her face languidly. I knew that these had to be the passengers from Tredia's plane.

"If this is our next charter, Erik, it looks to be a definite improvement," Lester winked.

Just as predicted, the pair stopped at the *Finest Kind.*

"Mr. Hazen?" the woman asked.

I pushed the faded cap back on my head and smiled at her.

"Captain Hazen," I corrected. "At least as long as I'm on board."

She looked slightly taken aback, but I guess my smile put her at ease. She beamed a smile back and held out her hand. "I'm Laura Morgan and this is my associate Marcel Feynard. We came to talk to you about a possible charter." I wiped my callused hands on the rag I was using to clean a fishing reel and reached out to shake hers. She had a firm hand with long fingers and no nonsense nails that spoke of a woman accustomed to the outdoors.

"Are you the folks who arrived on Zeke Tredia's plane?

She rolled her eyes and laughed. "Yes. We took off from the East River an hour ago. I don't know what's worse: three hours of Hampton's traffic or an hour of sheer terror with that maniac."

The lawyer nodded in agreement. "If I have to keep all the promises I made to God in the last hour I'll have to quit the bar and join a monastery."

"Zeke thinks he's still in Vietnam. Come on board. This is Bill Lester, trusty mate of the *Finest Kind*. He's the guy who'll handle the fish and pour the drinks."

The woman stepped gracefully across the transom. She stood looking around the boat as her associate struggled to keep his balance while Lester steadied him.

"Actually," she began, "we're not here to charter your boat for a fishing trip, Captain Hazen. That's why we came to talk to you directly instead of calling."

I raised my eyebrows and tossed my cap onto a deck chair. I could see both of them doing a quick assessment. At 46, I still pride myself on being in good shape with the lean, rangy build I inherited from my grandfather. With my khaki pants tucked into the tops of rubber fishing boots and an old tee-shirt that reads, "I fish, therefore I am", I hope that I look the part of a fishing captain, or at least somebody that knows his way around boats. I know from experience that for some clients that's important.

"Mmm. Not a fishing trip. Well, you don't look like drug runners or arms dealers and I'm not doing dinner cruises yet. So, what is you want my boat for?"

Laura looked around. The dock was mostly empty except for Lester, who was hosing down fishing equipment. "We want to organize a diving expedition to the *Andrea Doria*."

My smile faded and I could feel the white scar on my cheek redden. I looked at Feynard who stood silently, his hands in his pockets. "Please, sit down, both of you."

I glanced over at Lester, who just raised his eyebrows and busied himself with fishing tackle.

As they settled into deck chairs, I sat on the starboard gunnel. No one spoke for a few awkward seconds. The woman saw that she had hit a nerve, and she looked at the lawyer for support.

"Captain Hazen," Feynard began, "We came to you because you seem to be the leading expert on the *Andrea Doria* wreck. You even wrote the book on it. We both read it."

"Well, in that case you must have noticed that the book was written ten-years ago?"

The woman regained her composure and spoke. "Not much could have changed. We know that it lies in 240-feet of water about 100-miles east of here. We know that it's a dangerous dive—the "Mt. Everest of dives", as some have called it—and that more than a dozen divers have died on it over the years."

At the mention of diver's dying I felt my jaws tighten. "Mt. Everest? Yeah, well maybe it is. But, they haven't had much luck on Everest lately, have they? So, why would you want to attempt this?"

Feynard interrupted. "Oh, no Captain Hazen. We don't want to dive on it ourselves. We are looking for a team of expert divers— we are prepared to pay them well—to find personal property that we believe is on the ship."

"What kind of property are you talking about?"

"Property that was lost by my aunt and uncle," The woman said. "They were passengers on the ship when it sank. My aunt was killed in the collision but my uncle died only recently. He was 95-years old. I can't be any more specific than that until I know that you will accept our offer."

I paused and thought about the ship. It has been almost sixty years since the *Andrea Doria* was rammed by the *Stockholm*, just south of Nantucket Island, and sank with the loss of 54 lives. Amazing that there are still people who even remember it.

She was waiting for an answer. I saw that she was the type of woman who was accustomed to getting her way but my face felt like it had turned to stone and I didn't say anything for a good minute before I answered her.

"Look. I have a reputation for being a little abrupt—some people might even say rude. But I'm not a callous bastard. I'm sure that you're a sincere person, Ms. Morgan. I don't know what's motivating you to want to do this and I don't have to know. But if you accept my role as "expert" then let me give you some advice: whatever property you may be interested in has either been destroyed by more than half a century underwater, or it's buried under twenty or thirty feet of debris and silt. In other words, there's nothing down there that makes it worth risking a human life."

The woman leaned closer and spoke in a measured tone.

"Captain Hazen, I don't know if you're a callous bastard or not. But with you or without you I'm going to find out for myself if what I'm looking for is there."

Now this woman was getting my interest. Her smoky grey eyes were infused with determination and confidence. Maybe the hint of a smile passed over my face.

"And how do you plan to do that?" I asked.

The lawyer spoke before she had a chance to answer the question. "There are other divers who know the *Andrea Doria* well, Captain Hazen—but I don't have to tell you that."

I shot him an unfriendly glance. "So there are. Why come to me, Mr. Feynard?"

He looked nervously at the woman, who tried to smooth things over. "Because we want the best. We want someone who is not just a treasure hunter or a publicity seeker. And, mainly, we want someone that we can trust."

"What makes you think that you can trust me?"

"Call it intuition or call it a gut feeling, but everything that I've read about your knowledge of the ship made me feel that you could help us. I'm sorry if I was wrong."

"It seems a little ironic, doesn't it? A couple of treasure hunters who want the help of someone who's not a treasure hunter?"

"We're not treasure hunters! I told you that we're looking for something that belongs to someone else. Something important. We have every intention of giving it back when we do."

"I thought you said that it belonged to your uncle?"

The woman glanced at Lester who was sliding fishing rods back into their storage racks, and then back at me before she answered. "I said that my uncle lost it, not that it belonged to him."

"Ahh! This is beginning to sound complicated and a little mysterious. Was your uncle a smuggler or something?"

The lawyer started to protest but the woman held up her hand and cut him off. "In a sense he was a smuggler. But he was attempting to right a terrible wrong. Then the sinking put an end to his efforts. So I'm committed to finishing the job that he set out to do a very long time ago." She smiled again and glanced at the lawyer who just nodded. We all went silent for a few seconds. The high-pitched scree of an osprey drifted down from where it circled high overhead.

Lester's foghorn voice broke the tension. "Erik, I'm all done here. I'm going over to the Nor'easter for a beer. Nice meeting you Miss Morgan and Mr. Feynard."

I glanced at my watch. "I'll be over later, Bub."

I turned to the woman again. She must have thought I was sizing her up because she nervously fingered a gold earring and I could see her face redden.

I tried to clear the air. I knew I was being too much of a hard-ass. "If you have a little time there's something I'd like both of you to see."

She looked a little surprised as she glanced at the lawyer. "Of course. Mr. Tredia said he could take us back to the city anytime."

"Zeke? I might have to pry that old barnstormer off his favorite bar stool and dip him in the bay before I let him fly you anywhere," I smiled, then added, "Just kidding."

We walked to the parking lot where my Ford F-350 sat in the shade of Duryea's fish warehouse. Laura smiled as she watched me hauling fishing tackle, foul weather gear, boots, and coils of rope out of the truck cab and tossing them into the back.

"Sorry about the mess. I don't think there are any fish carcasses or leftover chum in here. Might be a little sand, otherwise the seats are clean enough."

She laughed. "My car is like this too. You never know when you might need an extra pair of shoes or an overdue library book."

She sat in the middle. I like to think that my truck cab smells of the sea; a not unpleasant fragrance of crushed shells and salty air. I didn't catch her gagging so I guess she saw it that way too. As I drove, she kept her hands folded over her bare knees like a schoolgirl and listened with what passed for interest as I pointed out some of the sights of Montauk.

Leaving the waterfront with its strolling tourists, we climbed a long hill lush with scrub oak and black pines. The imposing stucco and timber edifice of Montauk Manor stood high on a hill to the south like something out of a Bronte novel. Finally, we passed the train station, crossed over the tracks and pulled up to a series of warehouses that front on the little-used Nappeague Bay waterfront. A few rusty trawlers were tied to the docks and several derelict trucks were overgrown with weeds near a rusty railroad track spur.

"This is the Montauk most tourists don't get to see," I said, leading them across the crushed oyster shell parking lot towards a vintage Quonset hut. "This used to be the center of Montauk's fishing industry before they dredged the inlet into Lake Montauk and began to tame what was once a pretty wild place."

I guess my tour guide lecture gave her a chance to impress me, because she said, "You know, I spent six summers of my life—from the time I was sixteen, until I graduated from college—living in East Hampton, but I've never been here."

That took me by surprise. "What brought you to East Hampton?" I asked.

"My parents owned a house near the beach," she said almost as a question, then added "I was a lifeguard there for four years."

"Which beach?"

She looked at me a little sheepishly. "The Maidstone Club."

"Huh!" I said, raising my eyebrows, but not breaking my stride. "Nice spot."

In fact, Maidstone is one of the most exclusive beaches in the exclusive Hamptons. Mostly old money people with long pedigrees. It's named for a place in England that most of my ancestors came from. I don't know, maybe they once owned the beach, but, in modern times, the closest my family came to it was during the fall migration of striped bass. Then my grandfather's haul seining crew occasionally made a set or two for stripers in the pre-dawn hours.

She must have sensed my thoughts because I saw her face redden a little. "The house was sold years ago when my parents split up. I haven't been back since," she said.

"Don't worry. I won't hold it against you," I said jokingly, trying to lighten things up. "My family's beach was on the other side of the tracks. Louse Point. Plenty of gravelly sand, Zostera beds to wade through, and a great view of Gardiner's Island."

"What in the world is Zostera?" she asked.

"Eel grass. Scallops, ducks, and Bonackers all depend on it."

She shot a glance at me. "Bonackers? I remember that was the name of the East Hampton High School football team when I was a kid."

"It still is. We kinda take pride in it," I said as we skirted the crumbling bulkheads.

Feynard stepped gingerly over weed-grown patches while Laura matched my stride. "I'm surprised there aren't condos lining the shoreline here," he said. "Who owns all this?"

"Mostly a few old fishing families, mine included. Outsiders have been trying to develop Montauk since the 1920's but it's never turned out to be a very fashionable place. Between the changeable weather and the rough-hewn mentality of the full-time folks around here, we've been able to resist becoming a 'Hamptons East'."

I unlocked the Quonset hut door and turned on overhead florescent lights. The dark interior lit up to reveal a jumble of objects that looked like an unorganized garage sale. Several long wooden tables were heaped with various dinnerware, glassware, teapots and cups and a variety of kitchen tools. Scattered around were teak deck chairs, brass portholes, a section of anchor chain with huge links, and dozens of wine, champagne and liquor bottle, some with contents still inside. Against one wall stood a safe the size of a modern refrigerator. A large, ceramic mosaic leaned against another wall; it showed a pair of stylized, leaping dolphins. Above it, at least a hundred 8X10 color photos were pinned in a rough photo montage of a huge, underwater wreck site.

I registered the surprise on the faces of both of them.

"This is my little Andrea Doria Museum. At least it was going to be until my wife died."

Laura winced and turned away from the display. "I'm sorry about your wife, Captain Hazen; how long has it been?"

"A long time for you, yesterday for me. Nearly ten-years ago." And then added, "I rarely look at this stuff anymore."

She looked at me quizzically. "Why's that?" she said.

"Because she died on our last dive to the *Doria*."

"Oh, my god! I'm so sorry. I can't believe I've been so stupid. I heard a woman was among the divers that died on the wreck over the years, but I didn't make the connection, I didn't know it was. . ." Her face flushed. "Please forgive me."

"It's not your fault," I said. "I used to have a little pull around Montauk and I was able to keep the national media from sensationalizing the story. The local papers covered it, but it quieted down pretty quickly."

"It was a tragic accident," Feynard put in.

I ran my hand across the stubble on my cheek. "It was tragic and it was an accident. The point is it could have been prevented." I looked at Laura as I spoke.

"How do you mean?" she said.

"I mean diving to the *Doria* is one thing; the wreck is deep and it's cold but it's a nice challenge that lies right at the threshold of sport diving limits." I walked over to the cluttered tables. "The real problem comes with entering the wreck to find stuff like this, and that's what most divers want to do. I hate to sound dramatic, but that's the Siren Song that lures most divers--like my wife, Kate, and all the others who have died exploring it: sixteen at last count, I believe."

"But you have been inside the wreck many times," she said.

"Yes," I said softly. "More than two hundred dives in twenty years. But not anymore. The *Doria* has been on the bottom more than half a century and it's become a death trap. Too many people died because they got China fever."

Laura looked puzzled. "China fever?"

I picked up a cup and saucer from the table and held it out to her. She saw that it was painted with a blue crown and the word "Italia".

"That's the ship's logo. The Italian Lines. Finding ship's China became an irresistible lure for divers." I shook my head. "People risk their lives to get souvenirs."

She placed the cup and saucer on the table and began to speak. "I see what you're saying Captain Hazen, but...."

I interrupted her. "Look," I said, pointing to a photo on the wall of the ship on its maiden voyage in 1953. "That's what she looked like then. A beautiful ship, a work of art almost." I swept my hand towards the many underwater photos. "That's what she looked like several years ago."

Both of them walked closer and looked at some of the 8x10 photos, some of which showed divers shining lights into black openings bathed in the luminous glow of sediment swirling like blown snow.

Feynard looked bewildered. "But how can one tell what he is looking at? Everything seems so jumbled."

"That's the way a shipwreck looks. People expect them to be clean and recognizable—the way the old Hollywood movies made them. In fact, familiar features take on totally different shapes after time and nature has a chance to mold them."

"But I saw the photos of the *Titanic* and it was easy to see what it was like—even a crystal chandelier still hanging above the stairway—and that sank forty years earlier than the *Andrea Doria*."

Before I had a chance to answer, Laura spoke. "The *Titanic* is twelve-thousand feet down, in black water where most organisms can't live. The intense cold, the pressure, and the absence of life keep it nicely preserved. The *Doria* is in 240-feet of water. Well within the penetration of sunlight and the influence of corrosive agents."

"Very impressive, Ms. Morgan. I see that you've done your homework," I said. I looked at her and saw the intensity of her interest as she gazed at the details of the photos.

"Yes, I suppose I have done my homework. But I've also done a little wreck diving myself. Nothing that impressive, but I have explored some of the reef wrecks around Bermuda."

"Oh, good. Then you understand that diving to a hundred feet or so is what used to be accepted as the safe limit of sport diving. Unfortunately that limit still holds, but not enough people are willing to respect it now." And then I added, "Kinda like Mt. Everest." Again, I turned to the photo display.

"If you want to get a better perspective on the wreck, the photos are arranged from right to left and top to bottom showing sections of the ship the way they would be located if it were floating upright on the surface. The right side of the room is the bow and the top row is the boat deck—most of the superstructure has fallen off and lies in pieces on the bottom. The lowest row of photos shows the C-deck and cargo holds."

I pointed to the far left, bottom row at a photo montage of the huge blades of the ship's propellers looming above the gray bottom.

"A lot of the locations that you're looking at have been seen by only a few divers since the day of the sinking. I've been to some sections that are still so remote that I doubt that any other divers have been there yet. It took me twenty years of diving to do that. And, of course, there's still a good portion of the interior that's still unexplored—probably always will be. That's why I wanted you to see this stuff. The wreck is huge, cavernous, dangerous as hell, and getting more dangerous every year."

I strode to the midships section of the photos. "Do you see this?" I pointed to a large, dead codfish floating inside a tangle of barnacle encrusted fishing net. "This is only one of the hazards that a diver has to deal with: lost trawler nets are draped over the ship from bow to stern. They're ghost nets, still catching fish—or any diver unlucky enough to come up in the wrong place."

"Sounds like you're trying to scare us away," Laura said, looking up from the photos and smiling thinly.

"It scares me now. The ship is a trap. Besides the nets and the fishing line on the outside, the inside is a crumbling mass of steel partitions, plumbing and electrical wire. Just going in to take photographs is pushing the envelope on safety; looking for something in there is damn near impossible now."

I turned and walked over to the safe, spun the combination, opened it and pulled out several felt-lined drawers. "These are the only things of any intrinsic value that I've found in all my dives."

They both looked down at the array of old coins, some strings of pearls, a few pieces of gold and silver earrings, bracelets, and necklaces.

I pulled out another drawer containing similar items. "There wasn't much of value on the ship. Remember, it took ten hours to sink. Everyone who got off—all except the more than fifty who died—had plenty of time to gather up their valuables."

Laura looked up. "My uncle's property was quite valuable," she said.

"How could that be? I've researched insurance claims and so have a dozen other divers."

"There would not have been any insurance claim for this property," she said quietly. "You see, this property wasn't supposed to exist."

As she spoke she picked up an object that lay in the last drawer. It was a mother-of-pearl cigarette case and as she turned it over, she gasped, "Oh my God!"

"What is it?" Feynard asked.

She held it out. A small, gold plate on the case was inscribed with the initials "SCM". "My aunt who died on the ship? Her name was Sara Claire Morgan!"

I stood with one arm draped over the safe and scratched my chin. "Ms. Morgan, I'm not a big believer in fate, but things are getting a little weird? A diving buddy found that case on the last dive I made-- the dive that took my wife's life." My words had the effect of making her look a little less defensive and slightly more vulnerable. "So, I guess we've had a tenuous connection for a while now? You might as well keep the case. It belongs to you more than it does to me."

"Thank you. That's very kind." She paused a moment gazing at the case before slipping it into her bag. "Captain Hazen, I wonder if you are familiar with The Voyage Home Foundation?"

I smiled. "I think we can cut the formality. Call me Erik. And yes, I've heard of it. Returning money to families of Holocaust victims. Money stolen by the Nazis and hidden in Swiss banks, I gather?"

"That's right, Erik. However, what you might not know is that a great deal of that 'restored' money comes from the endowment that my uncle began with his own money. He was quite a successful investor and as his wealth grew he began to focus on philanthropy. Today, Voyage Home ranks among the greatest philanthropies in the country. We have gone beyond the original intent and now fund hospitals, schools, and medical research."

We stood facing each other across the showcase. Against my better judgment, I was beginning to like her. Something about the way she tilted her head as she spoke. Beneath the efficient businesswoman she had a fresh, outdoorsy look—only a subtle hint of makeup—and she exuded an athletic energy in the way she moved. She was also quite beautiful. "Why are you telling me this?" I asked.

"Because I want you to know that my uncle was an extremely good man. He always blamed himself for Sara's death. He apparently made one big error of judgment in his life, and he spent the rest of his life trying to atone for it. Believe me, there are not many men who did so much good in their lifetimes."

"Then this 'property' that you are interested in had something to do with your uncle's 'error in judgment'?"

Feynard in his lawyer role cut in at this point. "I don't think we're ready to discuss that until you have agreed to help, Erik. I'm sure you understand."

I nodded and looked back at Laura. "I don't know. I'm not sure that I'm ready to go back to the *Doria*. But, I have to admit, this is all becoming very intriguing."

"Suppose you give it some thought. Let me know before the weekend. We'll come back out on Saturday if you decide to help us."

"OK, I'll think about it," I slid the drawers back into the safe and led them out into the fading sunlight. "I better get you back to the waterfront before Zeke gets too comfortable at the Nor'easter Bar. I wouldn't trust him past the third beer."

Laura called Tredia from the truck and he was waiting at the dock when we pulled into the parking lot. She waved from the plane as it taxied out onto the bay and took off towards the setting sun.

I stood a moment thinking about the parallel that Laura had drawn- -indirectly but not inadvertently--between her uncle, Carl Ebner, and myself. Ebner had apparently made a mistake in judgment that cost him dearly—the death of his wife. Like him, I felt responsible for Kate's death. But at least Ebner had made some good come of it. Maybe it is time for me to stop beating up on myself. Maybe my long-standing obsession with the *Andrea Doria* does have a larger purpose. Maybe Laura Morgan's quest could bring me a measure of atonement.

All these maybes beat around in my brain as I turned and walked into the bar.

CHAPTER THREE

THE NEXT MORNING I WOKE UP LATE AND NURSED A HANGOVER FOR AN HOUR until the caffeine kicked in. By 10-AM I was in my little clamming skiff heading across the glassy bay to the eastern end of Hog Creek Point. My family cemetery sits high on a hill there overlooking a meadow and the blue bay waters beyond. I flicked a couple of mooring lines around the cleats of a dilapidated old dock, picked up a bottle of bourbon and a freshly picked clump of wildflowers, and headed up a trail through a break in the woods. Red-wing blackbirds trilled along the path that winds through bayberry and tangled catbrier, then opens onto a sloping meadow rank with newly mown rye, alfalfa and mint. A big, clapboard farmhouse with a wraparound porch had once stood here; built by my great-great-grandfather, Captain Elijah Hazen back before the Civil War. His success in the whaling trade represented the pinnacle of the Hazen fortunes. With the end of the 19th century came the end of commercial whaling and none of Elijah's children were able to maintain the house. It gradually fell into disrepair, was damaged by fire, and, by the time I was born, it had been razed. Luckily, none of my relatives ever sold off the land, so when I had some success with the boat building business I was able to donate the property to the Nature Conservancy. Now it's part of a National Wildlife Refuge.

Except, of course, the cemetery. Dozens of Hazen tombstones, all the way back to 1790, are enclosed by a split-rail fence. Children and women dead in childbirth. Fishermen "drownd" at sea. A few lived to ripe old age—including my grandfather who died at the age of 91 when I was in the Navy.

I stood in front of Kate's rose colored, granite marker, then kneeled and placed the wildflowers into a glass vase. A line from *Leaves of Grass* inscribed under her name says: "To die is different from what anyone supposed. And luckier."

I hope that Walt Whitman is right, I thought. Then I spent a few minutes trying to remember the laughing, athletic, sexy woman who had been my wife, and not the lifeless body—a strand of wet, blond hair swept across a pale cheek—lying on the deck of the *Finest Kind*.

I opened a bottle of bourbon and poured some onto the grave. Some high cumulus clouds were moving on the slipstream and had dimmed the sun. I muttered, "I hope you are in a place of everlasting luck, my darling." Just as I took a deep swallow of the bourbon the clouds parted, turning the bay into a shattered mirror of sparkling light—*the same kind of light that had danced on the ocean that day ten years ago...*

It had started with an early morning at sea when everything seemed right. A late summer day with the sky a dome of blue like lacquered porcelain and long, green swells sliding under the anchored boat with a monotonous rhythm. Kate on the deck, barefoot, wearing cotton shorts and a silky, pullover top. A couple of the other divers playfully flirting with her. Kate begging me to go on this dive, the last one of the season probably, because this was the kind of day that my grandfather—Captain Jack—would have called a 'weather breeder', and storms were not far off.

Now, I sat on the ground and leaned against the headstone as I took another pull on the bourbon bottle. The warm glow of alcohol felt good. Screw sobriety, I thought, as I heard my own words from ten years ago repeated...

'Sure, Babe. We'll go down this morning and wake up the ghosts.' Then the long decent down the line into the green-tinted twilight world and the dusky water below. Gradually the shadow of a massive presence. The sweeping curve of a vast wall of plated steel, abloom with sea anemones and outlined with a spidery railing. Stopping at the black hole cut into the ship by an expedition years before. Signaling Kate to stay there with another diver and her fluttering her eyebrows in a sort of goofy way and giving the thumbs up before I turn and disappear into the hole with my filming crew.

The sun was warming up now and I took off my cap and put it on the headstone. The bottle was half-empty. Or was it half-full, I wondered. Anyway, I raised it to my mouth and thought about how this ship had infected so many divers with heady thoughts of treasure.

Kate and the other diver had entered the ship to look for relics. Kate had watched as the other diver struggled to open a cabinet suspended overhead. The wall is the ceiling now. It all came crashing down in a cloud of silt in the blackness of 230-feet of water above.

Sunlight sparkled on the granite marker. The heat of the sun and the insistent keening of a lone osprey on a nesting platform brought me back to the present. I sat cross legged on the grave and looked down at the empty bottle in my hands. I struggled to my feet. My head hurt and I knew it wasn't only the bourbon. I had almost died that day myself from the bends. I paused for a minute, my hand on the warm stone, my mouth like dried seaweed. Then the final memory unwound in my brain.

Kate pinned under heavy debris. The cloud of sediment that marked her position in the vast darkness. Feeling her arms, weightless and limp. Her face with no mask or mouthpiece in place. Cradling her body and rising to the surface without stopping to decompress. Too late to revive her. The last view of Kate's slender body, clad in a blue and yellow dive suit, rising off the deck strapped to a stretcher in a halo created by the chopper's backwash in the vast blueness of the ocean. Too late to keep the Andrea Doria from claiming yet another soul.

I got up and walked unsteadily back to the dock. The sun was overhead now and a stiff west wind had built up on the bay. Damn! I don't want to wind up an old drunk living in the past like a lot of my relatives did. It's time to confront my demons. If that means going back to the *Doria* then so be it.

CHAPTER FOUR

I WAS STARTING ON MY SECOND IRISH WHISKEY AS I LOOKED ACROSS THE TABLE at Laura Morgan who was sipping iced tea. The nattily dressed lawyer completed the meeting over at the Blue Marlin, an upscale restaurant next to the Montauk Yacht Club. The summer season wasn't in full swing yet and only a few tables on the outside deck were occupied. Two older couples were laughing and clinking glasses just across from a muscular, young guy with a dark beard and long hair pulled back and rubber-banded in a knot at the back of his head who was drinking alone and looked a little out of place. At the far end a young couple were holding hands and talking quietly. Honeymooners, I thought. The Morgan woman was looking very good in a white summer dress with a halter top, short dark hair reflecting the sparkle of sun on the harbor, and a faint hint of lavender perfume.

So far, the conversation had been limited to a discussion of the Manhattan/Hampton scene and its slow but steady spillover into Montauk. I told them about my house in the Springs--on the unfashionable side of East Hampton—that had been built by my grandfather Captain Jack after WWII. I did a quick bio about being the first Hazen to break from the tradition of fishing for a living, and of graduating from Annapolis and spending six-years in the navy with a stint as a training officer for Navy SEALS. Finally—maybe it was the booze or maybe just the fact that she seemed interested—I mentioned my former boat building business, and I spoke about my gradual return to the older way of life after the death of my wife. Not many people understand that part of me, but I sensed she did.

It was the lawyer who finally turned the subject to the real purpose of the meeting. "So Captain Hazen, have you thought about our proposal?"

"Yes, Mr. Feynard, I have thought about it. Unfortunately, whenever I think about the *Andrea Doria* my thoughts aren't pleasant ones."

I saw Laura measure her words before she spoke. "Erik, we realize that the wreck holds bad memories--I can't even imagine the loss you suffered. But, what we are searching for also has many bad memories connected to it."

I sat back and looked across the bay where a school of bluefish were feeding on menhaden while gulls dove for scraps. "Then why look for it?"

"Maybe it sounds pompous but I think I have a moral duty to find it. I can only tell you that it's important. Not just to me and to the Voyage Home Foundation, but to thousands of other people." She looked carefully at me to see if I was going to respond, but I kept my poker face. She went on, "I think I can promise you that the good that will come of finding it will help ease a lot of memories."

I swirled the ice in my drink and focused on her eyes. They were intelligent and warm but they also flashed an intensity of no-nonsense business. "This sounds like some type of quest, Miss Morgan, er, Laura. How will you finance this project even if you find someone interested in running the risks?"

Before she could answer the question Feynard did. "The Foundation is quite capable, and fully willing to support the project, Captain Hazen. Of course there would be a liberal bonus in it for you if we achieve our goals."

The lawyer couldn't help himself but he was beginning to annoy me. "Money is good, Mr. Feynard. But I'm not as needy as I look. If I agree to help you it will be for other reasons."

Laura leaned forward and put her hand on my arm. "Please don't misunderstand. We aren't trying to buy you, but we do need your help and we are willing to pay you well for your time."

I looked down at her hand before she pulled it away. Slender fingers, short polished nails: feminine but strong. Just then the waitress came by beaming an Irish smile. I ordered a dozen oysters for the table, and caught the fleeting look of disapproval in Laura's eyes when I knocked back the last inch of Jameson's in my glass.

"Don't worry. I'm not driving home," I said and gestured toward the *Finest Kind* out on the dock.

Laura's face reddened. "I'm sorry; I didn't mean to be judgmental. Please forgive me."

"Forget it. You're not the first person who's told me that I drink too much. Which brings us back to the question at hand. Why do you think you need me? If you have the resources of a big foundation backing your project, why don't you just go and hire a commercial salvage company to help you find what you're looking for?"

"Because we want to keep this search quiet," Laura answered. She kept her eyes focused on the table and twisted a plastic drink stirrer into a knot. She knew by now that I'm not the type of guy to be disingenuous with and she was trying to be as forthright as possible. "We can't afford to attract any attention to this project. Not until—and if—we find what we're looking for."

"I'm sure you can appreciate the need for discretion, Mr. Hazen," the lawyer said. "We mustn't compromise our chances for success."

Laura was more composed now and spoke clearly to the point. "We were counting on your knowledge of the ship to keep the search as simple as possible. We don't want any heavy salvage equipment sitting out there attracting publicity. I was hoping that we could recover the property with simple diving gear. Your own collection of artifacts proves that it can be done."

I lifted an eyebrow and squinted skeptically at Laura and Feynard but didn't say anything because the waitress brought the drinks and the plate of oysters. The alcohol was helping my mood. I was actually beginning to enjoy myself.

"Are you sure you don't want a bottle of wine? The local vineyard puts out a beautiful sauvignon blanc," I said, and, smiling, kissed my fingertips to ease the tension.

I could see the Frenchman in Feynard come awake. "Why not?" he said. "It would be unthinkable to eat these wonderful fruits de mer without an accompanying vin du pays."

"Excellent choice, Monsieur," I said affably, as the waitress took the order and left.

"Now, let's get back to what you were saying about finding this property of yours. There are at least two major problems with your plan. One," I held out a hand and extended my thumb. "This is not like diving for old bottles in the Caribbean. As you well know, the *Doria* is 240 feet down at a place in the North Atlantic where the weather is unpredictable, the water is always cold, and visibility and currents makes sport diving, not to mention salvage, difficult and dangerous. The artifacts that you saw in my collection were incidental finds that were discovered during hundreds of dives over a period of almost twenty years."

Both of them started to say something but I held up the index finger of my extended hand and continued. "Two: the wreck is deteriorating rapidly now. Everything is collapsing inward. Almost anything of value is buried under the debris field that's piled up on its starboard side, which is now deep in sand and silt. I doubt that you could find anything without using cutting torches, cranes, and suction equipment. That means a major salvage operation to me," I said and shrugged my shoulders. I sat back and spooned some vinaigrette onto an oyster. Then I broke off a piece of warm French bread and waited for a response. I suspected that she was not a woman who allows emotions to control her reactions.

She sighed, then sat up straight and looked at me. "I'm sure that all of what you say is true, but I'm not going to accept defeat without even trying. If you're not willing to take us there then we'll have to find someone who will. I understand that there's a boat out of Montauk that makes regular weekly runs to dive on the *Doria*. They've had a lot of success bringing up artifacts. I'm sure that they could put together an experienced dive team." She smiled as she lifted an oyster neatly out of the shell and into her mouth with one motion.

"We haven't met with Captain Manson yet," Feynard added. "But he seemed most helpful on the phone when I broached the subject."

"And did he happen to mention how many divers he's lost on the *Doria* in the past dozen years?" I couldn't help feeling my face hardened and my jaws tense as I thought of Hank "Blackbeard" Manson, captain of the *White Shark II*, a 75-foot, steel hulled, commercial fishing stern dragger that he converted into a dive boat. With twin 750-hp diesels, it's the fastest dive boat for its size on the east coast. He operates out of Miami in the winters and Montauk in summer. Manson is a self-promoting treasure hunter whose record of putting amateur divers onto the *Doria* includes six deaths. He is a flamboyant showman who once specialized in shark fishing charters which involved him killing every shark that he could find for his clients. He likes to play the part of a pirate, including gold hoop earrings, flaring black beard—sometimes with gold tinsel tied into it—and his red, boozy face. When shark fishing became more regulated in the new century he bought the dive boat and billed the *Andrea Doria* as the "Mt. Everest of wreck dives." He was also a guy who'd do anything for money and fame—or even infamy—including take chances with people's lives. I was so pissed off with the mention of Manson that I almost forgot that the lawyer was talking.

"We realize that diving can be dangerous and accidents do sometimes happen...," he was saying, as I interrupted him.

"I don't call six dead divers—there were three in just one summer—'accidents sometimes happening'," I snapped.

"Look, Erik. In case you haven't noticed, I'm a big girl and I don't need any man watching out for my safety. I will be going out to the *Andrea Doria* just as soon as I can find a willing guide and put together a small team. I want it to be you, but if not it's sure as hell going to be somebody with experience and knowledge of the ship. So quit trying to influence my decisions. I'm quite used to making them myself." She sat back in the chair and looked out at the harbor.

I sat studying the bottom of my empty glass. The lawyer just shook his head but decided to keep his mouth shut.

Finally, the ice was broken when the waitress appeared with lunch. For the next half hour there was no more discussion of diving, only some comments about the grilled bass, the state of commercial fishing in local waters, and the quality of local wines.

Over coffee I made a proposal. "Okay. Since you're so determined, this is what I'll do. I'll take you out for a few days and make some exploratory dives. It might take me a week to get my boat outfitted for diving and supplied for several days offshore. I'll also need that much time to get together some of my old diving crew. I may even have to scare up some new divers."

Laura's face brightened. She smiled and put a hand on my elbow across the table. "For a while there I didn't think that I was going to convince you. Thank you. A few days should give me enough time to prepare. I'll have to take some time off from the Foundation."

"Also, take a good look at my boat. It's not a cruise ship. Are you prepared to spend maybe a week at sea in pretty close quarters with five or six men?"

She looked amused. "I spent a year in the Peace Corps living with a family of nine on a remote island in Malaysia. I think I know about close quarters."

"Just checking. At any rate, I want to be finished by the end of June. The main diving season runs from mid-July to mid-August. If we have to dive during that time we're going to have too much company out there."

"So that gives us a window of about two weeks?" the lawyer said.

"Maybe. Depends on the weather and on the likelihood of success—which has to be my call," I added with emphasis. Laura nodded.

"Another thing that we have to agree on. There will be no diving by anyone but my divers, and myself. Absolutely no amateurs in the water. Including former lifeguards." I looked directly at her as I said this.

"Don't worry. I'm strictly a warm water diver. I won't make any trouble for you Captain Erik." She laughed and held up her hands in a mock surrender.

"OK, so far I've been making all the conditions. Before I can draw up a rough estimate of expenses and fees for the expedition it might help if I knew what it is we are looking for?

She glanced at the lawyer who just nodded his head. Then she leaned in close and spoke softly. "Diamonds," she said, and added, "Quite a large quantity of them."

I raised my eyebrows and sat back in my chair. A few more table were occupied now, the honeymooners were gone, the older couples were laughing a little louder, and the muscular guy seemed to have his attention on a smart phone. I leaned forward again.

"This sounds like something from an old Heraldo Rivera stunt from the 1990's," I said. "How did they get there and how large a quantity are we talking about?"

Again, she spoke softly. "It may sound that way, but I have good reason to believe that this is real. I'm not sure just how many, but a lot. Maybe enough to fill a suitcase. The whole story—as much as I know, anyway—will have to wait until we meet again; it's a little too complicated to go into now." She paused to see what my reaction would be, and pushed a dark strand of hair over one ear from which a simple gold hoop earring dangled.

Things were getting curiouser and curiouser. I had a bunch of questions but knew it wasn't the time or place. The lawyer paid for the meal and was busy writing me a retainer check and I didn't object to either one. When I looked around, the party of four was also leaving and the muscular guy was in the parking lot getting into a black, Mercedes SUV, still looking at his phone.

"Things are moving quickly now and I'm going to have to get back to the city," she was saying as we stood up from the table. "I know you have a lot of preparing to do, but do you think it possible you could come in to meet at my office—say on Wednesday?"

I hesitated and the lawyer spoke, "There is quite a story to tell, Captain Hazen, and it would be best to tell it there."

"OK, I'll come in to hear your story. I'm going to need a little convincing that there is more to find on the *Doria* than ghosts.

We shook hands. I noticed that she let her hand linger a moment more than it had to and the warmth felt a little less businesslike.

Interesting woman, I thought as I watched them get into a late-model Volvo with the plates reading: GDL2571. No vanity there.

I like that.

CHAPTER FIVE

MONDAY MORNING THE FINEST KIND WAS HAULED OUT ON THE RAILS IN THE Eastbay Boatyard and Lester was working below with a couple of mechanics who were attaching the diving platform that I had removed years before to streamline the boat for fishing. I was cleaning out a closet in the biggest of the three staterooms below that I thought would suit Laura. If the weather was good most of the guys would sleep up in the pilot house and out on the deck. The whole boat would be crammed with plenty of equipment: dive tanks, dry suits, spools of rope, underwater gauges, cameras, tool bags, and giant compressed air supply tanks filled with tri-mix—a mixture of regular air, oxygen, and helium, needed for working at depth. Of course there would have to be enough food and drink to last up to ten days.

This particular closet hadn't been opened in years and had the rubbery smell of old foul weather gear hanging inside. On a shelf underneath was a stack of neatly folded tee shirts, each one embossed with the words "The Finest Kind Divers" arranged in a circle enclosing a diver's name. I held one up and looked at the name: Kate. I resisted the urge to press my face into it, and, instead, folded it back on the pile and loaded all of them into a carton.

I starting thinking that the whole project wasn't such a good idea. The next shelf held a couple of bottles and some glasses in a teak rack. They were full bottles of Macallum Scotch and I hefted one. It was 9 AM. Maybe just one drink to kill this feeling? I thought, just for a moment, and quickly recognized the old con, the cool reasoning that could sound so logical to boozers like myself. When did it ever stop at one drink?

A raspy voice came from somewhere outside. "Hey! Captain Hazen. You in there?" I put the bottle back and snapped the cabinet shut.

"Yeah, who wants me?" I shouted over the wind and the clatter of tools coming from below.

"Hank. Hank Manson. Can I come aboard this fine yacht, or do I have to be piped aboard like a bloody admiral?"

"Come on up, I forgot to bring my boatswain's whistle today." My mind raced as I tried to think of why Manson would be here. We aren't exactly mortal enemies, but our mutual dislike of one another is no secret around the Montauk docks. Almost from the beginning, back in the late 90's, when Manson retired his legendary shark fisherman image to run dive charters advertised as "Deep and Dangerous", I had been publicly critical of his operation. After three of his clients died in a single season while diving on the *Doria*, I had lobbied the Montauk Captain's Association to bring formal charges against him and press to have his Captain's license suspended. But, Kate's death had put an end to all that. Afterwards I felt that I wasn't any better than Manson.

"Goddamn fine boat, even if it is plastic," Manson's voice rasped as he stepped onto the boat's transom "Named for what you Bonackers call 'the finest kind,' I guess."

I hadn't seen Manson up close for a few years and his looks were a little startling. His head was mostly bald with a stringy fringe of grizzled black hair joining a widely flared beard of the same color. All the hair framed a long, angular, hatchet face dominated by a hooked beak of a nose and close set, hooded eyes the color of a shark's hide. As he dipped his head to swing his lower body up onto the deck a large gold earring flashed in the tangle of hair. He was about six feet tall but slender and wiry looking for a man of sixty. For a moment, I could imagine that I was back in the 18th-century watching a boarding party. All the man lacked was an eye-patch and cutlass.

"We Bonackers are a dying breed, Hank. Kinda like the sharks you used to hang on the dock."

"Yea. Hell, I'm just an old Brooklyn boy. Never could get you East End natives straight." He reached out a hand that was missing the pinky and ring fingers plus half of the middle finger. I shook it and felt a surprising strength in the older man's disfigured hand.

"I bet you didn't come to talk about local history, did you Hank?"

Manson just grinned. "You never know, do you? It depends on how local you consider the *Andrea Doria* is."

He caught me off guard with that and I felt my face flush. I fixed my eyes on him and watched his grin fade. But, I kept my voice even and friendly and even managed a smile. "Since when do you need to consult me about the *Doria*?"

"Just thought I'd ask, seeing as how you're suddenly getting ready to take a charter out there after all this time."

"Now where did you get that information?"

Manson laughed. "Hey, Captain Erik, I'm always tuned in to the idiot network."

'Idiots' to Hank were just about everybody who didn't make their living from the sea—and even ninety percent of them qualified.

"Ain't nothing happening out here that I don't get wind of in a New Yawk minute."

I put one foot up onto the boats rail and leaned into my knee. "Yeah, well you know how sea stories pass for information out here."

Manson smiled but his eyes darkened. "Look, I'm not trying to butt into your business. I just thought you might know something about this spate of interest with the *Doria*."

"What 'spate of interest' are you talking about?"

"I got a call yesterday asking if the *White Shark II* would be available for a diving charter before the season begins. Some guy who sounded like a bad actor in '40's spy film. Anyway, this guy said that he wanted to charter the boat for an extended trip to dive the *Doria*. Said he was getting a team ready to go and they were going to do some salvage work. Might last a coupla weeks, he said."

Manson squinted at the leading edge of gray cloud that was slipping under the blue sky like an envelope. "I told him my boat was still down in Miami and it might take 8 - 10-days to run it up to Montauk and get it ready for the summer season up here. He didn't like that. Said he wanted to get an early start. Offered me some big money if I'd be ready by next week." Manson spit over the side of the boat and stuck a ropy looking cigar in his mouth. He lit it with an old Zippo.

"So, what'd you tell him?" I asked coolly.

"Said I'd do what I could. Told my Captain down there to pull the plug on the last overnight charter—just a bunch of idiot college kids that wanna blow some weed, screw the natives and dive on the reef. If I push it I can have the boat back here by the middle of next week."

"Why'd you come over here to tell me this?"

"Hell, I wanted to get your take on this thing." Manson held the cigar with the two good fingers of his right hand and blew a stream of foul smelling smoke into the wind. "Why all this rush, rush business about getting out to the *Doria* before the regular dive season in July?"

"I'm going to have to disappoint you Hank. My charter is just a couple of photo journalists. They're doing an independent film about the *Doria* that they hope to sell to PBS. I've been hired to help them do it; me and a few of my old dive partners." I leveled my gaze at Manson and smiled faintly—I'm not a great liar but I think I sounded convincing. "I have no idea who your clients are. Probably just another bunch of hopeful treasure hunters with a crack-pot theory about treasure." But, even as I said this, I had a bad feeling about what the other party might know about the diamonds—and how they know it.

"Yea, maybe." Manson clenched the cigar in his teeth, grinned theatrically, and flung his leg over the side to step on the dive platform. "I guess we'll be seeing you and your, ah, film makers out there. Hope it don't get too crowded for all of us."

"The ocean's a big place Hank, and the *Doria*'s a big wreck," I said as I watched the back of Manson's shaggy head behind a puff of lingering cigar smoke.

His raspy voice drifted back through the smoke as he stepped off the ladder, "Big, yeah. But not so big when you're looking for the same thing," he said, ominously.

CHAPTER SIX

Wednesday morning I drove into Manhattan on the ill-named Long Island Expressway, where the closest I came to "express" was written on the back of a FedEx truck as I inched along towards the Mid-Town Tunnel. By the time I got across town and down to the TriBeca area, the day had gotten hot. I actually found a parking spot on Greenwich Avenue, right outside the converted warehouse that was now headquarters to the Voyage Home Foundation. I took the elevator up to the second floor and stepped out onto the wooden floor of a large space with high ceilings and windows that looked out towards some old docks and a new park along the Hudson River.

I was glad I had dressed in a clean pair of khakis and a new, white Orvis fly fishing shirt when I saw Laura Morgan walking towards me wearing an above the knees skirt, a silky, short sleeved blouse, and high heels. In the heels she almost came up to my eye level. She must have noticed me sniff the air because her first words were, "It's coffee. This used to be a coffee bean warehouse, all the way back to early 20th century. We never have gotten the odor out."

"One of my favorite odors," I said as we shook hands. Her hair was pulled back and clipped on each side with a tortoise shell pin. She also had the same faint fragrance of lavender that I had noticed the week before and her skin had a healthy glow that didn't come from a tanning parlor.

"I'm glad you could come, Erik. I've got some actual drinking coffee in my office if you're interested."

I followed her past people working in cubicles scattered about the cavernous room and into a private office that has a good view of the Hudson and a few sailboats in the distance. The lawyer, Feynard, sat in an armchair. I sat in a similar armchair and there was a brief exchange of pleasantries as Laura placed some coffee mugs and sugar and creamer onto a serving tray on top of her chrome and glass desk before settling into a swivel chair behind the desk.

She glanced at Feynard and then turned to me. "I hope you don't think I'm being distrustful by having my lawyer in the room? Marcel has become a dear friend in these last several months as Uncle Carl deteriorated. He helped me provide some of the care giving that became necessary towards the end," she looked affectionately at the lawyer.

"I was only trying to be helpful," Feynard said modestly.

"You were more than helpful, Marcel," she said, and then turned back to me. "You see, Erik. Marcel takes care of his elderly father. Actually a year older than Uncle Carl. He is quite the devoted son."

Feynard squirmed a little in his chair and looked uncomfortable. "Please, Laura. I just do what anyone would do for family and friends."

"You are too modest, Marcel. Your father is lucky to have a son like you," she said, smiling. Feynard continued to look embarrassed as she swiveled in her chair and poured a mug of coffee for me from one of those insulated carafes.

But, let's get down to business." She unlocked a cabinet next to the desk and removed a sheaf of paper. "You already know that my uncle, Carl Ebner, founder of The Voyage Home Foundation, came to America on board the *Andria Doria,* and that he lost his wife, Sara in the tragedy. She was my mother's older sister; she was only 22 at the time of her death in 1956."

I nodded and waited for her to go on. I saw her glance at the lawyer before she did.

"My grandmother and grandfather—Sara's parents—were French Jews. The three of them survived the war due to the efforts of friends in the French Resistance, who kept them hidden in a series of safe houses in Paris for more than a year, until the allies liberated the city. After the war, they stayed in Paris and my mother was born there in 1949. Two years later they immigrated to America, all except Sara, who was attending the Sorbonne, studying journalism, and starting to write a book about the Holocaust—a term that had just been coined at the time. In 1955 she met Carl in a bookstore and they were married soon after."

She paused and took a sip of her coffee.

"Up until three months ago, when my uncle died, that was about all I knew about his past. Then, after his death, this letter came into my possession," she held up the few sheets of paper. "It was in his safety deposit box, clearly marked with my name. Even Mr. Feynard knew nothing about its existence."

The lawyer crossed his legs and spoke. "Apparently, Mr. Ebner wrote that letter shortly before his death and wanted Laura to have it as she was going to be the official successor to the foundation at that time. I had no clue it existed."

I nodded my head at the papers in Laura's hand. "Well, I guess it says something about diamonds?"

Feynard sipped his coffee and spoke before Laura could respond. "Let me fill you in on some WWII history that hasn't been given much play in the history books," he said. "Soon after the war ended there was rumor of an enormous cache of diamonds, and, perhaps, other precious jewels that Hitler had amassed. Think about it, everyone knows about the gold bullion and stolen artworks that the Nazis hid in caves during the war. We've all seen pictures of the piles of gold wedding rings and dental fillings taken from the murdered Holocaust victims. But what became of all the precious gems that we know were looted? The diamonds from perhaps hundreds of thousands of rings and personal jewelry belonging to wealthy and middle-class, mainly Jewish families—coupled with the looting of major centers of the European diamond industry—must have resulted in one of the largest concentrations of precious gems ever assembled." He paused and looked intently at me before continuing.

"But, out of all these, there was rumored to be a collection of only the finest examples. Newspapers of the day dubbed it "The Fuhrer Gems". Perhaps a bit melodramatic, but not necessarily inaccurate," the lawyer said and then added, "Up to this day there has been no record of what happened to them!" He finished his coffee and sat back to watch my reaction.

I began thinking that both of them might be delusional. "Then, if I'm hearing you right, you're telling me that a cache of Nazi plunder has been sitting out there on the *Andrea Doria* for almost sixty-years?" I shook my head and must have telegraphed my skepticism.

Laura pushed her hair over the ear with the gold hoop earring. "That's exactly what we are telling you."

"So you're saying your uncle was a Nazi?"

Laura flushed. "No, of course not. He was Swiss , not German." She shuffled the papers on her desk uneasily. Feynard looked uneasy again and he turned to glance out the window.

"But, how did the diamonds get on an ocean liner more than ten years after the war ended?"

Now she flattened the papers on the desk and tapped them with a manicured index finger. "That's where this letter comes in." She looked at me and said, "Have you ever heard of Albert Speer?"

"I remember he was a Nazi. One of Hitler's top lieutenants, wasn't he?"

She tapped an Ipad and handed it to me. It showed a photo of a handsome, clean-cut, intelligent looking man in a grey business suit. More like a professor than a Nazi.

"Yes. He was the architect who was supposed to design a civilization that would last a thousand years. Hitler considered him a good friend.

"I seem to remember from history class that Speer was also the head of Nazi armament," I said.

"You're right about that," she said. "But, he was also a man who gradually realized that the Fuhrer was insane. Towards the end of the war, he was probably involved in the plot to assassinate him. At the Nuremberg Trials, in 1946, he was sentenced to twenty years. It's not clear why he escaped the death sentence; possibly because of the twenty-three men who were tried, he was the only one who expressed moral responsibility for his part."

"OK, you have my attention. What does the letter say about Speer?"

Laura sighed. "My uncle was an official with the Basler Handelsbank in Switzerland. It was a bank favored by the Nazis. It sounds ridiculous to say it, but Speer was a cultured man who struck up a friendship with my uncle at the Basel Opera House before he realized who Speer was. Uncle Carl agreed to handle his account at the bank—he was quite a good money manager. Speer always insisted that the money was his own family fortune. And it probably was."

Feynard broke in. "Albert Speer came from an aristocratic family and was a wealthy man in his own right. I'm sure that Mr. Ebner was doing nothing wrong by managing his investments."

"Some people might not agree with that, Mr. Feynard," I said.

The lawyer began to protest but Laura held up her hand to silence him. "You are right, Erik. There are some people who might think that my uncle was a Nazi collaborator. They might even think that the foundation's money came from the plunder of Europe." She shook her head in disgust. "Maybe you remember that back in the 1990's a senator from New York was trying to track down Nazi loot in Swiss banks. He investigated Voyage Home, implying that it had a connection. Luckily, the Jewish Defense League came to the foundation's defense and the investigation was dropped. But not before the publicity hurt Uncle Carl. "It's for that very reason that I need to recover the diamonds and see that their value is returned to the families of Holocaust victims throughout the world. That's what my uncle wanted. He tried and failed, but now I have a chance to finish the job."

I nodded my head. "Fair enough, but you still haven't told me how your uncle came into possession of the diamonds."

"It's all in this letter," she said, turning a few pages of it on her desk. "The relationship between Uncle Carl and Speer began to cool as the war dragged on. He still managed the Speer family's account, but they rarely met face to face. Towards the very end of the war Speer rented a safe deposit box. Uncle Carl knew nothing about it at the time."

"And I'm guessing that this is where he hid the, so called, 'Fuhrer Gems'," I said, watching Laura nervously twisting a paper clip as she looked grimly at the letter.

"Yes. But Uncle Carl knew nothing about them."

The story was becoming more intriguing by the minute. "When did he know about the gems?"

"More than ten years after the war ended. In 1956, just months after he met and married my aunt in Paris." She paused and flipped through a few pages of the letter.

"But I'm getting ahead of myself," she continued. "Go back to 1946. Albert Speer is sentenced to twenty years in Spandau Prison. But, another man, who happened to be Speer's driver, and, who had been captured by the Russian Army, was also sentenced that year: to ten years in a gulag. His name was Werner Hutt. He was an SS Colonel." Again, she tapped the Ipad and handed it to me.

"Whew! This looks like what a Nazi is supposed to look like," I said. "It appears that his mother mated with a lizard."

Laura continued. "Yes. Hutt was a rabid Nazi who hated Speer for rejecting Hitler and the party. He knew that the gems were in the safe deposit box. More importantly, he knew where the key was hidden."

"Wait a minute," I interrupted. "You're telling me that he could just walk into the bank and open the box?"

The lawyer broke in to answer my question. "Remember, Erik, this is a Swiss bank. Everything is numbered. Names mean nothing; all that's required is an access code. Hutt was Speer's personal driver—in a sense, a servant. It's very likely that he could walk in and open the box."

"At least that's what Speer feared," Laura added. "That's why he contacted my uncle from prison. It was the summer of 1956—half way through his sentence—and he wanted one last favor. He told Carl where to get the key and asked him to get the gems out of Europe before Hutt could get to them. He was afraid that if they fell into Hutt's hands they could become an enormous advantage for the reformation of a Nazi party—something that was already happening at the time."

"What did he want him to do with them?"

"To bring them to America. To trust the American authorities to return them to their rightful owners. You see, in the end, Speer regretted all he had done and just wanted to make his peace. He even donated the profits from the books he wrote to Jewish charities; anonymously, of course."

I handed the ipad back to Laura. "Did Hutt ever try to get to them?" I asked.

"He was killed in the collision and sinking," she said.

Now she really got my attention. "You're saying that he and your uncle were both on the *Andrea Doria*? What happened?"

"I'm not sure about the details. The letter says that Hutt apparently followed Uncle Carl onto the ship and laid low until the night before they were due to arrive in New York. When he did make his move he was going to steal the gems and then kill my uncle. Instead, he was killed in the initial collision. Uncle Carl tried to save Sara and failed. The ship, the diamonds, and his wife went to the bottom," she said, shaking her head and glancing out the window where a little sailboat regatta was taking place in the distance.

"So, the rest of the story is, as they say, history. But, in this case, a secret history," I said.

She placed the letter back into the file drawer. "Yes. But I don't want it to remain a secret. Now it's up to us to finish what he was trying to do."

"We are counting on you to help us accomplish that," Feynard said.

"It's a fascinating tale," I said. "And, assuming it's all true, it's going to take more than my expertise as a diver and expedition leader to find the gems. It's going to take a hell of a lot of luck and a miracle or two. Do we even know how he carried what must have amounted to a suitcase full of diamonds on board the ship without being detected?"

Laura shook her head. "Unfortunately, that's a big question mark. There is nothing very specific in the letter about their location on the ship."

"We'll have to start with his stateroom."

"Well, I know that he travelled first class, and that my aunt was killed in the collision, which means it must have been in the impact area, right?"

I grimaced and nodded. I hate to give nice people bad news. "Those are the starboard cabins—at the very bottom of the wreck which lies on that side. It's the deepest part of the wreck and the part most obstructed by debris and silt."

I could see in her eyes that she wasn't going to be swayed by defeatist talk, so I added, "But I should be able to find out the cabin number; I have a copy of the original passenger manifest at home. It may be the proverbial needle in a haystack search. But, there's a chance. There's definitely a chance."

For a moment, both Laura and the lawyer sat quietly just looking at me. Finally she simply said, "Thank you Erik. That's all I want to hear."

"You know," I said, "I'll always remember a woman that I once saw in a documentary. She was a Holocaust survivor who told the story of how she had been taken to one of the death camps—I forget which one—and stood in a line of people who were told to strip down as they passed by a checkpoint. The woman had the diamonds from a necklace her husband had given her hidden in her mouth. As she got closer to the inspection table, she saw that the Nazi guards were looking into each prisoner's mouth so she swallowed her diamonds. A day or two later she recovered them when she went to the bathroom. Then she swallowed them again. She did this every few days for the entire year she was in the camp. When the Allies liberated the camp she still had her diamonds." I paused and looked at Laura. She had closed her eyes as I told the story.

"But, you know," I continued, "the thing that impressed me was when she said that saving the diamonds had saved her life. It gave her a reason to live. A purpose. Not for the value of the diamonds, but to keep the Nazis from winning another victory. To beat them."

"That's exactly it. A long fought for victory. That's what I want." Laura said smiling once again.

CHAPTER SEVEN

THE SCUPPER, DOCKSIDE BAR AND GRILL, WAS NOISIER THAN USUAL ON THURSDAY night. The crews of two local long-lining boats were in after a week's trip to the Hudson Canyon, and a trawler crew from Rhode Island was gathered under the big TV near the front of the bar. A Yankee-Red Sox game was on, and from the old-fashioned juke box Willy Nelson was rasping out *On the Road Again.* I could see the fishing had been good by the way the men were spending freely at the bar.

I was off the sauce, for the moment, anyway, and nursing a tonic and ice with lemon as I sat in a booth across from my old diving partner, Mike LeClair, who was on his second bottle of Rolling Rock. It looked like the lights went out for a minute as Booker T. "Book" Johnson squeezed his Homeric frame into the seat next to me and got me in a bear hug that nearly dislocated my shoulder.

"Goddamn, brother! You are one hell of a sight after all this time," he bellowed.

I grinned and pumped Johnson's oversized hand. "I see you haven't grown old and feeble yet, Bub. I figured those muscles would have turned to flab by now."

"You ought to know by now that the flab is all between his ears," LeClair said.

"Hey, I hear the brain is eighty-percent fat. I'm just an intellectual heavy weight."

We all had a good laugh before the barmaid came over to take our orders. It felt good to have some of the old camaraderie back again. I hadn't seen either of them since a couple of years after the accident. When I contacted them at the commercial dock on the Brooklyn waterfront where they run a salvage company, they were two years into a five-year project to remove old docks and clear underwater obstructions for the completion of the West Side Highway Park along Manhattan's Hudson River shore. Both of them were happy to take a break and come out to Montauk. When the waitress came back with a rum and tonic for Johnson, we all held our glasses up for a toast.

"To old friends and new adventures," I toasted.

"I couldn't have said it better myself," LeClair said. "Man, I want to tell you, your phone call was like getting a governor's reprieve from death row. We've been working in that big old muddy river for so long I'm starting to get the urge to slither around on my belly. Book here's dug through more Manhattan mud than his clam digging ancestors did in all the years before they sold the island to Peter Minuet.'"

"Mud, sewage, and a lot of nasty stuff," Johnson agreed. "We could both use some blue water and sunlight for a while. A little working vacation is fine with me."

I chewed on a swizzle stick and got serious for a minute. "This may not be a vacation. You probably are going to have to paw through some more mud. But, there will be lots of fresh air and watery horizons, not to mention the chance to make some good money. If we are real lucky we might even be able to bring some long overdue justice into the world."

LeClair leaned in close. "Money's always good. But the justice thing has me kind of intrigued. Could you be a little less mysterious with your old partners?"

"I wish I could. My clients are concerned with security. You guys will just have to trust me for now. I'll explain everything once we get underway on Saturday." I shrugged. "That's just part of the deal."

"Why the early season start, Erik?" Johnson asked.

"Two reasons: first, I want to do this before the sport diving boats start coming out to the wreck, and, second, there's a chance we're going to have some competition with another crew that might be after the same thing. I could be wrong about what they're after, but, the fact is, they chartered the *White Shark II.* The boat is due up from Florida next week, two weeks earlier than usual."

"Hank Manson's boat? That old pirate is still around?" LeClair asked.

"You haven't heard?" Johnson said with disgust. "He gave up hauling dead sharks to the docks for fun and profit—not enough of them left anymore. Now he runs wreck diving charters every summer even though he knows jack shit about diving."

"Oh, yeah," LeClair said. "I read about those accidents that seem to follow his boat around. Weren't the newspapers calling it the "death boat" a couple of years ago?" He stopped when he saw me wince. "Shit, I'm sorry Erik. Are you going to be OK going back to the *Doria*?"

I looked at the ice cubes in my empty glass as I swirled them around. "That's one of the reasons that I took this job. The *Doria* has been haunting me long enough. I've been in limbo too long, I need to get some closure."

No one said anything for a minute. Then the waitress came over and we ordered burgers and fries and more drinks.

"Plain tonic water, eh?" Johnson said. "Looks like you want to face your demons sober."

I smiled and nodded. "Probably a good way to face them," I said.

LeClair was staring at the bar and Johnson nudged him. "You see something pretty over there that I ain't seeing?"

"Just the opposite," LeClair muttered. "You see those two guys ordering drinks on the right end of the bar? The ugly ones with the shaved heads and the black sweaters?"

We both nodded and Johnson said, "Yeah. There's some ugly people at that bar, but those two about wrote the book on ugly."

Johnson was right. Both were short and squat, almost ape-like. They didn't look like fishermen to me, and they didn't look too happy either; everyone at the bar seemed to be having a good time except them.

"That's the Shoup brothers," LeClair said. "They're twins from Baton Rouge, Louisiana. I had the displeasure of working with them on an oil rig job in the Gulf of Mexico several years ago. They're fucking neo-Nazi, white supremacist shits."

Just then, the brothers left the bar and walked towards us. They had the bow-legged swagger of rodeo riders.

"Looks like they are going to pay us a visit," I said.

As they slipped into the booth behind us the Charlie Daniels band was playing *The Devil Went Down to Georgia* and the amplified sound of fiddle music made it hard to talk. But, there was no mistaking the voices I heard behind us.

"Hey Burris. What's this I hear about there being some badass divers in this town? There's no oil rigs in sight—what do you suppose they dive for?"

"Maybe they dive for change that the tourists throw in the water, brother."

"You mean like them nigger kids down in the islands?"

They both guffawed at that. I felt Johnson begin to shift around in the seat and I heard myself mutter, "Ah, crap."

"You got that right," the first voice said. "Only it seems like up north, here, the niggers are bigger."

"Oh, yeah. And they smell a lot more....."

Before he could finish, Book Johnson's huge arm came across the back of the booth and his baseball mitt of a hand clamped around Burris Shoup's neck, pulling him halfway over the partition. Shoup kicked his feet knocking over the beers on their table as his brother started to jump up. Before he could, LeClair was on his feet and caught the chopping punch that Russell Shoup aimed at his groin. Then, he twisted the arm like a crank handle, pushed Shoup down and pinned him against the seat.

Burris was sputtering and gasping, and Russell was cursing, but the music had built to a crescendo and no one at the bar seemed to hear anything.

"You assholes haven't got any smarter as you got older, have you?" LeClair hissed as he tightened the arm lock.

Book had his face a couple of inches away from Burris's upside down, choking face and he was grinning like an alligator.

"Probably no one taught you manners when you was a little child," he growled. "So, this is lesson number one: don't get close to this native son again 'cause I'd hate to see your cracker organs donated to any good people." Shoup's legs were wedged under the table so he couldn't kick much. He was just gasping.

I stood up just as Johnson released Burris and he dropped down onto the seat of his booth wheezing between gasps. LeClair let go of Russell and looked down at the brothers.

"I hope this has been a learning experience for both you boys," he said.

Johnson slid out as I signaled the waitress and slapped down more than enough to cover our unfinished meal. As we walked to the door, I heard one of the brothers choke out, "F-fuck you!"

"Brilliant repartee," I said to no one in particular as we stepped out into the chill night air.

CHAPTER EIGHT

THE NEXT MORNING A RED SLASH OF SUNRISE SLICED ACROSS THE EASTERN horizon out beyond the Montauk Coast Guard Station. The *Finest Kind* was back in the water bathed in the glow of yellowish halogen dock lights reflecting off the opaque waters of the marina. A small craft warning flag was snapping in a stiff breeze out of the northeast; not a good weather sign for this exposed tip of Long Island.

I left LeClair and Johnson sleeping off their hangovers and stepped down onto the dock. Hector Gonzales was already up and sitting on the bridge sipping a huge cup of coffee. Hector is a great boat handler and an even better cook. He had worked for me before on overnight fishing trips. We exchanged good mornings and I walked down the dock past some charter fishing boats that were loading up on ice and bait for another day. The low rumbling of their idling engines blended with the mewling of gulls, and the salt air was scented with diesel fuel mixed with the pungent odor of thawing chum buckets. Nailed to the dock poles are the remnants of past fishing adventures: the scimitar tails of swordfish and giant tuna, the withered carcasses of striped bass, the bleached and gaping jaws of blue, dusky, and tiger sharks—noble, ocean creatures reduced to desiccated, gull picked remnants fluttering in the wind.

Sometimes I feel like a traitor to my heritage when I have such thoughts. My ancestral history and all the blood that flows through my veins is wrapped up in fishing. As a kid, each season had a different meaning, but each one began and ended with the water. Spring was netting in the rivers for herring, and setting out fyke nets in the bay for returning flounder and weakfish, just as the Montauk Indians did way before my ancestors. Summer was gill netting for bluefish and striped bass inside the ocean bars that shifted with the returned of warm weather. Fall was haul seining along the ocean beach for schools of stripers following the shoreline as they migrated into warmer southern waters. Winter could be clamming or winkling in the shallow bays, or, even gigging through the ice for eels dormant in the muddy bottom.

My grandfather, Captain Jack, was the finest man that I ever knew, yet, his favorite memory before he died was the day that he and his haul-seining crew pulled 9000-pounds of striped bass out of the surf in East Hampton in one set of the net. Of course, by the time he got it into the city market the price of bass had dropped by half. That kind of fishing wasn't sustainable even then, and I think Captain Jack knew it, though he would never admit it.

Anyway, those days are gone now and a lot of the old way of life has gone with it. But, there's still an awful lot of waste and disrespect shown to the wild creatures that swim in our waters. At least that's what I was thinking about as I passed the city fishermen arriving bleary eyed with their coolers of beer and salami sandwiches for a day at sea.

Gosman's Coffee Shop was already bustling with fishermen as I entered. I waved to a few people I knew and sat at the counter next to a tall, thin, young guy wearing a yellow slicker, which contrasted with his fire red hair.

"Sean Roebling?" I asked.

He stopped shoveling pancakes into his mouth and wiped some syrup off his chin as he turned to me. "You must be Erik Hazen," he said, sticking out a pale hand with the slender fingers of a pianist. "Glad to finally meet you, Captain. I'm looking forward to this trip."

"From what I hear, this should be a piece of cake for you"

"You mean because I spent two years on a nuclear submarine? Yeah. But I've been out of the Navy for a few years now and things are getting a little boring," he said, then added, "You were in the Navy too, weren't you?"

"I was a combat swimmer back in the 1990's. It's been a long time now." I said as I tried to size Roebling up. He is your classic computer geek, but with a harder edge from being in the military. His reputation as an expert in underwater, 3-D imaging led me to hire him for the expedition. He is also an experienced underwater photographer whose images have appeared in several national magazines.

"I realize that it was pretty short notice, but were you able to get those plans and photos that I sent you transferred to a computer model?"

Roebling resumed his attack on the breakfast, but paused to reach over and pat a laptop case next to him on the counter. "Right here along with back-up discs," he said.

"Great. I'll depend on you to make everything work. I suffer from A.D.D. when it comes to computers," I said signaling the waitress to bring me his check. "Also, I don't know how much action you like, but I understand you're also a good diver and I might need another man in the water. Depending on how things go in some exploratory dives, this could be just some interesting wreck diving or a full-blown expedition. You interested?"

Roebling swung around on his stool. His eyebrows are as red as his hair and they almost connect when he smiles. "Hell yes, Captain. I was hoping you'd ask. My gear's packed and ready to go. You know, once, when our sub was going to Groton Connecticut for maintenance, I picked up the *Andrea Doria* wreck on our side scan sonar, but there weren't any windows to look out of and see her.

"We'll change that for you soon enough. You're going to see parts of her that haven't been seen by anyone except fish for over half a century."

As I paid the bill at the register, I couldn't help noticing someone I had seen just a few days ago. The muscular, dark, bearded guy who had been hanging out at the restaurant. He was getting into a black SUV out in the parking lot. I thought it a little strange the way he averted his gaze when he saw me.

CHAPTER NINE

THE WEATHER WAS A LOT BETTER AS SATURDAY MORNING DAWNED. THE WIND had died down enough so that the small craft flag was lowered and the temps were in the high 50's. Laura was wearing a Yankees baseball cap, white cotton Irish sweater, khaki fishing guide pants, and leather topsiders as she half sat, half stood with one leg up over the coaming on the low gunwale near the boat's stern. She seemed comfortable and relaxed, talking and joking with the crew. I was up on the flying bridge with Bill Lester letting the two big diesel engines warm up. I was drinking another cup of coffee, and watching the scene below. What I was thinking was that she didn't look at all like Kate but somehow she reminded me of her. Maybe it was just the youthful freshness of a pretty woman. Maybe it was a certain way the soft curve of her neck met the determined line of her jaw; I'm not sure what it was. But, then I smiled. One thing that set them apart was the hat: Kate had been a confirmed Mets fan.

The racks built along both sides of the working deck were filled with dozens of SCUBA tanks, and a pair of ten-foot long supply tanks filled with helium and oxygen were chocked and lashed down along the bulkheads on either side of the main cabin. Cases of underwater camera and lighting equipment were stacked neatly inside as well. Gonzales had enough food stocked in the galley to last a couple of weeks. Even the wine rack had a few bottles in it, though I tried not to think about that too much. I hadn't had a drink since the night at the restaurant. I felt good. The *Finest Kind* was alive again, rumbling beneath my feet.

"Well, what do you think? If we leave now we'll be anchored over the wreck by tea time. Maybe even get in a dive before dark."

Laura looked up and smiled. "Say the word Captain Erik. I'm feeling a little like Ishmael; I need to sail about a little and see the watery part of the world."

Lester scowled. "No Ishmaels on this boat, please," he said aloud, and then mumbled under his breath, "Tough enough having a woman on board."

I just grinned at his comments. "Don't mind Bill. He's just a superstitious old Bonacker." Then I looked out at the breakwater where there was still enough of a breeze to pile up four-foot seas.

"She may quote Melville," I said to Lester. "But I hope she has the stomach to match."

Johnson stood up in the bow and cast off the lines and Gonzales tossed off the stern lines. I threw the twin engines into forward gear. The boat surged forward and headed for the channel.

It had gone about a hundred feet from the slip when it jerked to a stop as though it had hit a wall. The entire hull groaned and shuddered while the dock vibrated on its pilings like an earthquake had passed beneath it. There was the sound of gnashing metal and the engine pitch changed to a wail as I jerked the throttles back into neutral.

"What the Hell?" I shouted as I turned and saw Laura sprawled on the deck and Johnson untangling himself from the bow rail which had prevented him from being thrown into the water. Roebling came charging out of the cabin, his slicker dripping with spilled coffee and was nearly knocked over by LeClair, who shoved him aside as he raced to the stern.

"Some fuckin' thing's holding us to the dock underwater," LeClair cursed as he and Gonzales peered into the turbid water over the stern.

I quickly shut down the engines and hurtled down the ladder into the cockpit. "Is everyone OK?" I asked. I know my face was pale, my cheek scar standing out in scarlet relief.

"I'm OK," Laura said, rubbing a red welt on her leg where it had struck the winch stanchion as she fell. "Is the boat damaged?"

"I don't know," I muttered, trying to keep my voice under control as I took a few deep breathes to calm down. "We'll have to go down and see what the hell happened. This is not exactly the way I was hoping to start this expedition."

LeClair and Gonzales worked with boat hooks to keep the *Finest Kind* from ramming other boats at the dock while some dock workers tossed lines out to Johnson. After a lot of hauling and maneuvering we finally got the big boat tied up back in its slip. Johnson and LeClair were in the water minutes later wearing masks and snorkels. They dove under the the *Finest Kind* and quickly came up sputtering and cursing.

"Sonofabitching pair of steel cables are wrapped around both shafts and clamped to the dock pilings," LeClair spumed in disbelief.

Johnson held onto the dive ladder and looked up at me and Roebling. "The props are pretty bent up. I don't know about the shafts yet, if they're bent we'll have to have the boat hauled. We'll use scuba gear and some tools to unwind this mess. Whoever did it used half-inch cable. Someone doesn't' want us to leave this dock, for sure."

"You mean somebody sabotaged the boat?" Laura asked incredulously.

I nodded and helped the divers back onto the boat. "Professionally done!" LeClair said. "Looks like somebody really wants to slow us down."

My mind was racing as I stood scanning the parking lot. The lot was almost full with weekend fishermen cars. Then, as I watched, a black SUV pulled out and sped away. Maybe just a coincidence—plenty of black SUVs around, I thought. But maybe not.

Laura looked pretty shaken. "Who would want to stop us from going to the *Andrea Doria*?" she said.

I helped her into a deck chair. "I don't know. But, we met some pretty bad characters a couple of days ago, and some mysterious party has chartered Hank Manson's boat to go out the wreck next week. Do you know anything about that?"

"No, of course not. Marcel and I were just using his name as a bluff when we mentioned him."

"Well, somebody's not bluffing. This is going to set us back a couple of days."

"At least they didn't punch a hole in the damn bottom," Johnson drawled.

PART TWO

OUT TO SEA AGAIN

IT WAS **9:00 A.M.** MONDAY MORNING AS I STEERED THE FINEST KIND PAST the eastern breakwater and into Block Island Sound. The wind was blowing out of the west at ten to fifteen knots. Block Island was a distant mole on the sea's surface ten miles off the port bow. To starboard, the Montauk lighthouse rotated its warning beam from atop the old glacial moraine's pile of boulders that marked the end of land, just as it has been doing since George Washington commissioned it two hundred years ago. With the vast improvements in navigation technology, it's now more of a tourist attraction than a working lighthouse, but I still liked to think of it as a guiding light for ships at sea. Beyond the lighthouse, the long swell of the Atlantic looked like wrinkled foil as it rolled out to the horizon under a cloudless sky.

The sabotage had cost us two days. The steel cable was wrapped so tightly around both shafts that we had to use a cutting torch to free them. The boat had to be hauled to remove the starboard shaft which was badly bent. Both props had to be pulled and sent to a machine shop to be repaired. Only my connections with the boat yard helped us to complete everything by Sunday night. Laura Morgan stayed up at the old hotel until the repairs were complete. She was shaken by the incident but determined to follow through with the expedition.

The sabotage added a new, and dangerous element to what had been just a near impossible task. We all agreed that although we couldn't be sure who had been behind it, the field of choices was certainly limited. The unsavory characters in the bar were high on the list. It couldn't be just coincidence that oil field divers were in town just when somebody was chartering Manson's boat to dive on the *Doria*. It could have been Manson himself looking to slow things down until he was able to get his boat ready, or it could have been whoever Manson's charter was—the muscular, dark haired-guy came to mind. Maybe it was a combination of both. There weren't any other choices.

I was betting it wasn't Manson. The man has been known to be unscrupulous, but he's not a criminal. I remembered a story that had happened years ago. A local diver had spent two weeks preparing to salvage the bronze propellers from a sunken freighter. It was a risky operation that involved clearing debris, cutting through the shafts, and rigging lift harnesses. Just before he was ready to retrieve it, Montauk was socked in with fog and he couldn't get his boat out for almost a week—this was in the days before GPS. By the time the diver got back out to where he had left it marked with a lobster buoy, the propellers were gone. About two tons of bronze worth almost a dollar a pound, back when that was big money for a freelance salver. No one could ever prove that Manson had taken the props, but he had run his boat out in the fog the day before, and the next week he had been spending pretty freely at the bars. Technically, there was nothing illegal about it—just unscrupulous. That's just the kind of thing Manson would do, I thought.

Bill Lester came up onto the bridge at 10:00 A.M. balancing two cups of coffee and a pair of bacon and egg sandwiches. The day was getting warm and since we were running with the wind the sun was beginning to feel hot. I was wearing my long-billed fishing hat and I already had to take it off and wipe the sweat away.

"We're making good time," Lester said as he settled into the padded bench seat and looked at the dual tachometers on the control panel.

"Yep," I agreed. The engines are running smooth and this following sea is surfing us along pretty nicely too."

"We should be on anchor by late afternoon, don't you think?"

"I think so—if everything goes smoothly."

"You anticipating more problems like the one we just got over?"

"Hell, I don't know what to think. It's bothering me that somebody messed around with my boat without us ever suspecting anything. It's pretty clear that they're trying to scare us off—give us a warning. What comes next is anybody's guess."

"Yeah, well you and me have been through more shit together over the years than most cats have lives. But whoever's playing this game is just gonna succeed in pissing me off." Lester's muscular arms strained the sleeves of a cotton pullover as he wolfed down the bacon and eggs.

"Come on, Bub, I've never seen you hold a grudge." I said, my voice full of sarcasm. I took a gulp of the hot coffee. "Come to think of it, maybe they did us a favor. At least we know that we have competition, and that they're not too scrupulous about how they compete. Knowing your enemy is a basic rule of survival."

"Maybe. But what do we really know about these people? There's got to be a connection with this Morgan woman. It's not just coincidence that two salvage expeditions are racing each other to dive on a ship that's been laying out there since before we were born."

"Well, if she knows anything she's not telling us she's putting on a pretty good act. The way news travels around Montauk it's no surprise that somebody figured out we're being chartered to dive on the *Doria*. But she claims no one else knows anything about a salvage operation."

Lester shook his head. "Somebody must know more than I know, but that's not saying much seeing as I don't know shit about what we're going for. But it must be big for somebody to try keelhauling the boat."

"As soon as we get on anchor there'll be a briefing." I felt my craggy features soften a little as I sympathized with my old friend's consternation. "I'm sorry Bub. I don't like this any more than you do; it was her idea to keep the lid on this thing as long as possible."

"Yeah, well it looks like her secret keeping has some limitations, doesn't it? I'm going to go down and take a nap, if it's ok with you?"

"Go ahead. I'm feeling pretty supercharged right now."

It was true, an hour later I was still feeling the exhilarating sense of freedom that I always get running a fast boat out in the open ocean. I didn't want to call Lester up to the bridge, or set the auto-pilot and busy myself down below. I was just enjoying the ride.

The earthly curve of blue water extended from horizon to horizon with only a few distant fishing boats and an occasional incoming freighter to break the two-tone composition of sky and sea. Most of my life I've spent at least part of every day on the water. Maybe it's my Bonacker heritage, maybe just a condition of being human, but I feel alive, recharged by the salt air. I looked at my watch—almost noon—and wished I could celebrate with a drink.

"Can I come up?"

I turned and looked down at Laura, who was standing on the rear deck. She wore khaki shorts and a white tank top that hugged the curves of her athletic body. I smiled and nodded. "Sure. The view's a lot better from up here." So as not to be misunderstood, I quickly added, "I mean of the ocean, of course."

She laughed and climbed the bridge ladder.

As if my words were calculated, a pod of glistening dark backs with high dorsal fins appeared on the surface a hundred yards in front of the boat. A fine mist of miniature geysers drifted above them.

"Pilot whales," I said, as the little whales sounded then reappeared moments later off the starboard side. "Local fishermen call them blackfish. They're like overgrown dolphins, but not as playful."

Laura shaded her eyes in the morning sun. "Fantastic. There must be at least twenty of them."

"Probably. Sometimes they run themselves up on the beaches—no one's ever figured out why. But fishermen know them as an indicator of big sharks in the area. White sharks especially like to feed on them, and they'll follow them like wolves after a herd of caribou."

"Oh. Thanks for the encouragement Captain," Laura said as she watched the pod move off to the south. "The whales are beautiful. But I'll be sure to remember what you said about sharks tomorrow when you're dangling at the end of your decompression line."

I grinned. "That's the least of our worries. But the wreck of the Doria has always been a magnet for sharks. It's like a reef on an otherwise featureless plain so its home to a lot of sea life. Back in the early days, lots of divers refused to go into the water when they saw all the shark activity. Most often they're blue sharks, which are kinda like the Labrador retrievers of the shark world: mainly curious and don't bite."

"And how do people feel nowadays?"

"Most of us are more sophisticated about sharks. Maybe all those nature programs on TV? We know they're big, potentially dangerous creatures that deserve our respect. But they rarely bother divers."

Laura raised her eyebrows and looked skeptical. "Maybe so. But it's the word 'rarely' that I'd be worried about."

I laughed and lifted my cap again to let the wind cool my head, then ran a hand through my mop of hair before pulling the cap back down.

"You really love it out here, don't you?" Laura asked.

"It's in my blood. Maybe that sounds sentimental, but to me the water—especially the ocean—is a part of life that I wouldn't want to live without. It's what we Bonackers call, 'the finest kind'."

"Hence, the name of your boat," she said, tapping her head. "But it doesn't sound sentimental. I think I know what you mean."

I glanced at her as she sat next to me, her knees up, the wind ruffling her black hair where it stuck out from under the turned around baseball cap. A city girl enjoying the country. "Yeah, I'm sure you do." Then I added, playfully, "It'd be kind of like living in a New York neighborhood without a Starbucks."

She turned and gave me a goofy, cross-eyed look. "Very funny. You must think that I'm some kind of snobby uptown girl who can't live without designer boutiques and coffee bars. You really don't know me very well."

"You're right, I don't. Believe me, I respect anybody that could be an ocean lifeguard—even if it was on a beach full of celebrities and hedge fund managers."

She looked askance at me to see if I was breaking her chops.

I grinned back. "No. Really," I said.

"Yeah, well they don't drown any different than poor people, you know."

"You got me there," I said, then turned serious. "Are you sure that no one else knows about the diamonds?"

She didn't seem surprised at the question. Her face remained composed and open. "No one at all. I've been wracking my brain about this since the incident and I can't think of anybody."

"Except Feynard?"

"What of it? Marcel has been with the Foundation for several years. He was probably closer to my uncle than anyone. He's not just my lawyer, he's my friend." There was no mistaking the annoyance in her voice. "Are you insinuating something about him?"

Obviously, I had hit a nerve but I pressed on anyway. "Look. I'm not accusing anybody but I had to ask. Someone might know what we're after because that someone damn near sank my boat! Do you think it's going to just end there? Because I don't."

She stood up abruptly and it was clear that she was annoyed. As she turned to climb down the bridge ladder she gave me the kind of disapproving look that a school teacher might give to a bad student. But, coming from a beautiful woman made it worse.

"I don't know why anyone would want to sink your boat, but being paranoid about it isn't going to help us. I think we should focus on finding what we came to recover." Her voice had lost its friendliness and become all business again. And not very friendly business.

Okay, I thought after she left. It looks like we have differences to get through before this trip is over.

Suddenly the *Finest Kind* seemed like an awfully small boat.

CHAPTER ELEVEN

BY LATE AFTERNOON I EASED THE THROTTLES BACK AND LOOKED DOWN AT A featureless spot in a great circle of ocean with no landmarks or features to give it a sense of place. It was as though the boat was pinned to the sea like the bulls eye on a target, delineated by a compass line of horizon and a blue dome of sky. I remembered the opening line of a favorite ship wreck story, by Stephen Crane: "None of them knew the color of the sky." No, of course they wouldn't, I thought. The tossing waves and the awful slant of light into the impenetrable depths below was enough to keep the eyes of most men on the water, not the sky.

But it's not totally true that the sea is featureless. Ancient navigators in the South Pacific sailed from island to island by subtle changes in current and in the color of water, and even by the types of fish, birds, and floating weeds in some places. Even my grandfather, Captain Jack, and plenty of others like him, knew certain spots on the ocean long before GPS and LORAN had made drawing an X on the sea's surface nothing more than the push of a button.

Maybe it's in the blood, I thought as I eased the throttle to trolling speed and began circling an acre of ocean while Lester appeared on the main deck grinning up at me. Maybe it's like the homing instinct of salmon and birds, or, maybe even the anonymity of the sea can't hide a place of such tragedy. Of course, Peter Gimble—the late film maker and adventurer who made his first dive on the Doria twenty-four hours after it sank—was said to have located the wreck site when he spotted a cocktail olive pop to the surface.

At any rate, I just knew without checking the bottom recorder or the GPS that we were over the *Andrea Doria* wreck at 4:45 P.M.

After twenty minutes of maneuvering Lester called out as the grappling hook snagged the midships of the ghostly wreck which clearly showed up in bulky profile on the digital recorder screen in front of me. It was ten years ago that I last saw it. A general cheer went up from the deck, but I only stared into the green water below, mumbled a brief prayer, and once again wished for a drink.

As soon as the motors were shut down, the vast silence of the ocean enveloped the boat while it rolled gently on the swell. I gathered everyone on the rear deck where we set up deck chairs in a semi-circle around a folding cocktail table.

It was time to let everyone in on our mission.

I noticed that Laura remained unsmiling and business-like since our earlier run-in. She was avoiding eye contact, but when she finally glanced at me I removed my fishing cap and smiled at her. My hair was matted and pressed tightly against my head as I ran a hand through it, pushed my dark green Polaroid sunglasses up and squinted in the slant of early evening light. I guess I looked harmless enough, so she cracked a grin and eased the tension. Only Gonzalez stayed inside, working on dinner down in the galley.

Roebling set his laptop on the table while I started the meeting. "I realize everybody wants to know more about the objective of this trip, so before I talk about the technical aspects of the dive I want Ms. Morgan—Laura—to clear up the secrecy about our mission." I sat down and stretched my legs out like a man getting ready to watch a show.

She sat up stiffly. She flashed me a politician's forced smile before she began to speak. "Thank you, Captain Hazen. I will keep the story brief so that you can get to work as soon as possible."

But, the clipped civility of her voice began to fade as she unfolded the tale. By the time she was finished telling the story of Carl Ebner and the *Fuhrer Gems* it had become urgently passionate in defense of her late uncle's actions. By then the sinking sun had dipped behind the flying bridge and the deck was in cool shadow. No one spoke for several seconds. The only sounds were the lapping of water and some discreet salsa music from inside the boat.

Book Johnson was the first to say something. "Woo-wee, I've heard me some treasure tales before, but this one about takes the prize. This is no four hundred year-old pile of gold doubloons. This is a treasure that belongs to people that could still be alive—or at least to their children and grandchildren."

"That's exactly the point," Laura said. "If we can recover this property it may be the last chance for making reparations to the families of people who are fast becoming extinct. My uncle set out to do it almost sixty-years ago; I only hope that we can succeed now."

I noticed the determined set of her jaw and the confident way she swept her eyes around the little group. She definitely has the inspirational qualities of a great leader and teacher. No wonder she was the head of a major organization.

"Help me out a little here," LeClair said, "If all you say is true—which I'm sure it is—there's still one glaring problem here—how do we find it when we don't know where on the ship to look?"

I sat forward and spoke. "Now you didn't expect this to be easy, did you Bub? Nothing ever is when it comes to the *Andrea Doria*." I paused for just a couple of seconds but long enough for everyone to get my drift. The *Doria* didn't give up her secrets easily.

"Since we don't know the exact location," I went on, "we'll just have to search several spots on the ship that would be the most likely locations. We're going to start with the first class cabins."

Now I signaled Roebling who started the laptop with a remote. He scrolled open a program, and an intricate, 3-D collage of the wrecked ship appeared on the screen. He handed the remote over to me and I used it to point to a rectangular black opening in the side of the ship.

"This model is based on my own photos and videos taken over the years. Sean, here, has done a damn fine job of setting up this simulation. It's about as life-like as you can get without making the dive. Since I haven't been down to the ship for a while, I've used some educated guesswork to add to the deterioration and the depth of the debris field. So this is not going to be exactly how it will look now, but I wanted everybody to get a general orientation before we dive tomorrow."

"Mike and Book already know the wreck, but this should be a good tutorial for everyone else. That opening you see in the hull on the mid-ships is known as 'Gimbel's Hole'. For those of you who don't know, Peter Gimbel was heir to a department store fortune but focused his life on underwater filmmaking. His most famous film was about white sharks, called 'Blue Water, White Death', which was an inspiration for Peter Benchley's book 'Jaws'.

"Anyway, Gimbel was the first diver to reach the wreck—only a day after it sank! Then, in the early eighties, Gimbel's divers returned and cut this access door when he filmed a television documentary about the sinking. I was just a kid then, but I was hired as a deck hand on the research ship that summer and Gimbel let me make a dive with him to see the ship--but not go inside. I was just blown away by the sight. That's what got me hooked on the *Doria*," I paused momentarily lost in the memory.

"Most divers use that entrance to get into the first-class lounge and dining room areas. If it's still there, we can use it to access the starboard side cabins, which, when the ship was floating, were directly below the lounge but three decks down. Now, with the ship lying on its ruined starboard side, the cabins are three decks in to the left as you face the bow. Very confusing and very dangerous." I handed the remote back to Roebling who zoomed in on the access hole and dropped down through it. The 3-D effect simulated what a diver would be seeing as he entered the hull.

Roebling used the remote like a game stick and moved the cursor through the black hole and dropped it down vertical walls, which were actually decks on edge. The way down to the starboard side where the gaping wound was now buried in the bottom silt was a maze of half standing bulkheads, collapsed stairways, corridors with piles of fallen steel panels and twisting electrical and plumbing conduit, all simulated by the 3-D model.

Johnson spoke up. "You say the target area is a cabin on the starboard side of A-deck?"

"That's right, just on the spot where the cursor is hovering now. Records show that this was Carl Ebner's cabin."

"But the debris on that side of the ship must be twenty feet deep. How do we get through that to the cabins that are underneath?"

I looked up at the big man and around at the others who were silent. The boat continued to roll and the sucking sound of water coming from below the transom each time it dropped in a trough stood out in the silence.

"That's just what we're going to have to figure out in the next couple of days," I said matter-of-factly. "Look, we've got some options. When Gimbel was filming his TV documentary he found a way through the generator room right down into the crack through the hull that sank the ship. He was able to swim to the outside of the ship through it. If the bulkheads along the A-deck corridor have held, then the debris will be lying on top of the row of cabins we're interested in. We may be able to make our way down to it by finding a way around and under the debris. Maybe through the crack itself."

Le Clair spoke up. "Of course, Gimbel was last here over thirty years ago. If those bulkheads have collapsed then the cabins will just be pressed into the bottom by a thousand tons of junk," he muttered.

I nodded. "If that's the case then nobody is going to get to the cabin without an enormous salvage operation to excavate below the hull, cut away the two-inch thick keel plates, and haul everything out with giant surface cranes. Not only would that cost millions of dollars, it might also be too heavy handed to recover anything. If the cases or containers we are looking for were to be broken open, the gems would be scattered and lost in the silted bottom forever."

"That is, if they haven't already," LeClair added.

Roebling had remained quiet, but now he blurted out another concern that was on everybody's mind. "We don't even know if the gems are in the cabin. Couldn't they have been anywhere on the ship."

"That's true," I said. "We don't know anything for sure."

"So you're telling us this is a WAG-OP?" Johnson muttered.

"I guess you could say that," I smiled and nodded.

"Can someone interpret for me," Laura said, raising her eyebrows and looking quizzically at both of us.

"During Navy search and rescue missions that acronym stood for 'Wild Ass Guess Operation'," I said, still smiling. "But the value and the danger of what your uncle was carrying would probably eliminate the cargo holds. Why would he entrust baggage handlers with that kind of luggage? Also, I doubt that he would have let it out of his sight for the time it would take to cross from Italy to New York."

By now I could see that the enormity of the mission was beginning to have an effect on Laura. Her confidence had waned a little but her face stayed determined. "Let's not talk about launching a salvage circus. It's not going to happen. We'll take this a step at a time and try to stay positive," she said.

I glanced at her. She had guts and I wanted to succeed for her. "I couldn't agree more, I've been on this wreck hundreds of times, Mike and Book have been on it dozens of times and Roebling here is one of the best divers and electronics experts on the East Coast. If anyone has a chance at finding the proverbial needle in a haystack, it's probably us."

"So when do we get started," Laura asked.

"Early tomorrow morning," I answered. "It might take us some time to tie into the wreck at our point of entry. We only have two more hours of daylight today and everybody needs a good rest, so we might as well relax, and wait for dinner. Hector promised us one of his Caribbean specialties tonight."

•

The last smear of fading sunlight was tinting wisps of fog the color of smoked salmon by the time dinner was finished. Everyone had eaten Hector's seared tuna with coconut-ginger sauce, curried rice with fried bananas and collard greens sautéed in garlic in oil. For desert there had been a thin-crusted sweet potato pie topped with cinnamon honey.

Afterwards, I stood in the stern drinking tea—of all things—as the western light was squeezed out and stars began to accrete across the night sky. A mile to the south, the navigation lights of an outbound container ship slid along kicking up a fuzzy bow wake. The horizon disappeared behind an approaching fog as I checked my watch. It was 9:04. Beyond the pool of yellow light spilling from the boat's cabin, the surface of the sea was now black. Looking down, I could envision the enormous bulk of the sunken liner lying below in the frigid depths and thought of the twisting passages, the churning currents and crushing pressures, and the slow, but inexorable, collapse of the whole structure under its own tremendous weight. Inevitably, I thought of Kate, still beautiful in death, lying next to me on this very deck. I tasted the dry air of memory and, suddenly, the idea of going back down there seemed preposterous—a misguided attempt to make peace with a tragic chapter in my life. I started to question my nerve when I heard Laura's voice behind me.

"Should we be worried about this fog?"

The sight of her helped ease my doubts. Her dark hair spilled over the edges of a white headband. Dressed in a cotton polo shirt with cargo shorts, her pale skin glowed in the dim anchor light.

"Only if you worry about things that you have no control over. Fog is pretty much a given in this part of the ocean, especially this time of the year."

"But what about ship traffic?"

"The radar has an alarm that lets us know if anything gets too close, plus we keep a watch all night just in case. If we have to get out of the way we can do it quicker than you might think."

She nodded and stood quietly for a minute, looking down at the dark water.

"I'm sorry if I've been a little touchy. I've been under a lot of pressure since taking over the responsibility of the foundation. And the sabotage really unnerved me too, I guess."

Her arm brushed against mine and the faint scent of lilac stirred my senses. "My wife used to wear that same perfume," I said, a little stupidly, and immediately felt foolish.

She looked at me and grimaced. "I'm sorry. I didn't know."

"That's OK. The scent of lilac is nice out here. The smell of land in the springtime. It's comforting."

"How did the accident happen?" she asked tentatively. She must have seen me tense, because she added, "You don't have to answer that. I shouldn't ask."

There was an awkward silence for a moment and, at first, I considered not answering.

Finally, I broke the silence. "It was ten-years ago and I'm still not sure just what happened." I looked blankly toward wisps of ghostly fog drifting overhead. "You'll have to excuse me; I haven't talked about it much."

"I understand," she said, simply, and changed the subject. "What do you think caused the *Andrea Doria* and the *Stockholm* to collide?"

I felt the tension fade and I smiled and stretched my arms out at the emptiness that surrounded the boat. "Well, it certainly wasn't for lack of space, was it?"

She laughed. "No. That's what's so amazing to me. How could two ships steam right into each other on a calm summer night out in a big ocean?"

"Amazing, but not so rare. Think of two cars in an empty parking lot crashing, or two people coming towards each other on a deserted sidewalk bumping heads. A system of moves, counter moves, and counter-counter moves can lead to silly accidents—or to tragedy."

"You mean it was as simple as that?"

"No. There were other factors involved. The fog for one. Captain Calamai on the *Doria* testified that fog had been dense that night. But, even so, he hadn't significantly reduced his speed. On the other hand, the *Stockholm* was probably too far north of the eastbound shipping lane. The helmsman that night was a young kid who had a tendency to daydream and wander off the plotted course. You might call it a comedy of errors if fifty-four people hadn't died. Thank God it went down slowly, so there was plenty of time to get the rest of the passengers off."

Laura shivered. The air was not cold, but a penetrating dampness had settled in with the fog. And something else: an eerie stillness. She sat in a deck chair and pulled her legs up so that her chin was resting on her knees. At that moment, she looked very young and vulnerable even though I knew she was pretty tough.

"It's so strange, unearthly, and sad that a ship that was once alive and filled with people, is lying below our feet without any hint or sign that it's there." She paused and her voice sounded quieter. "And somewhere inside that hulk my aunt--who died twenty-five years before I was born--is forever entombed."

"I know what you mean. Being on the water at night can spark the imagination. It also gets people philosophizing about life and death."

We both stood silently looking out over the dark water as I drank the last sip of tea from my mug before turning to her. "Hey, you want to see something? Watch this."

While she looked on I opened a deck storage box and took out a spool of thin, nylon outrigger cord. I tied one end to the handle of the mug, pulled a few yards off the spool, and flung the cup out into the darkness. When it hit the water, a fiery splash burst on the surface like a momentary sparkler, and the twenty-foot length of line glowed underwater as I hauled the mug back in and lifted it aboard dripping a greenish fire.

Laura smiled and clapped at the demonstration. "Bioluminescence, isn't it? I've heard of it but I've never seen it. It's beautiful."

"Yep. Summer nights draw all that plankton life up to the surface. Puts on a nice show when you're fishing at night, and kinda reminds you of how filled with life this ocean is." I paused and peered straight down into the water. "Of course it's also a little eerie when you're anchored out here."

She put her hand on my shoulder. "You mean because of the wreck?"

"Yes. The wreck." I didn't want to start getting morose again but I did wish for a drink to help fight off the thoughts. Then I looked down at her hand, stood up straight, and turned towards the light of the cabin.

"But keep in mind that it's only a rusting relic now and in a few years even that's going to be erased—along with the memories." I smiled at her, and extended a hand. "Come on inside. It's getting too wet out here."

CHAPTER TWELVE

THREE DAYS OF DIVING HAD BROUGHT NOTHING BUT ACHING MUSCLES, POUNDING headaches, and the growing conviction that the cabin Carl Ebner had occupied was buried just beyond reach. Now, to make matters worse, the weather had begun to deteriorate. I stood on the plunging dive platform and looked at the waves building to four feet. Below the platform, bubbles broke the surface from where the two divers who were hanging on to the decompression line ten feet below. This was the last dive of the day. It was almost 7 PM but the tarnished gray sky made it look later.

Laura came out on deck steadying herself against the boat's roll. "Do you think this weather is going to get better?" she asked, shouting over the wind.

The baseball cap was turned around on her head again to keep it from blowing off. With her black hair blowing in her face and a tight, black tee shirt plastered by the wind against her chest, highlighting her firm—and bra-less—figure, she looked a little like a tough biker chick. White duck pants and Topsider boat shoes dispelled the biker image though.

"Oh, it'll get better, but not before it gets worse."

She grimaced and rolled her eyes at that.

Lester was up on the flying bridge listening to the Coast Guard weather report. "Increasing southeast winds and heavy rain by tomorrow afternoon. Seas building to eight feet," he announced.

"We'll try for a couple of dives first thing in the morning and then I think we need to pack it in and re-evaluate our strategy," I said to Laura. "Besides, I think everyone needs a break."

At this news, Laura looked annoyed and frustrated. I could see her transforming again into her CEO persona.

"I hope you don't mean that you're giving up," she snapped.

Just then Book Johnson and Sean Roebling popped to the surface and I turned away to assist the divers. "I didn't say that. Let's wait and see what this latest dive discovered and we'll discuss everything over dinner."

She didn't say anything, but she turned and pretty much stormed off the deck. Mike LeClair was coming out of the kitchen to see how the dive went and she passed him without a word.

"Hoo boy! That lady looks like she could eat dock spikes and spit tacks. What'd you say to her?"

"Just that we might have to take a break back on shore and try to come up with a better plan. She doesn't take to change very well," I said as I helped Johnson pull off his triple tanks and bulky equipment while Mike assisted Roebling. Getting out of a couple of hundred pounds of gear on the deck of a rolling boat is always a group effort.

"I'd vote for some shore time," Book said after he pulled his uni-suit hood down and squinted into the wind driven spray. "I just don't think swinging a pick and a shovel while wearing 200-pounds of equipment under 40-fathoms of water in the dark is a very practical idea. And that's just about the point that we are at here," he added with a grim smile.

Dinner was a simple dish that Hector called *pot au feu*: basically a beef stew, but delicious. The mood was subdued, but everyone was drinking a Beaujolais Village wine, so I let myself have a glass. No one seemed to notice.

Outside, cloud cover smothered the last light of day and the wind whistled through the wire cables on the lifting crane. Once dinner was over, I started in about our progress, or lack of it.

"Let's review what we've done so far and decide whether any of our approaches are worth continuing, or if we have to take a whole new line of attack. Sean, set that laptop over here so that Ms. Morgan can see it."

Laura had said little during the dinner and now had the look of a boss being forced to hear an accounting report that spelled big problems for the company.

"OK, now keep in mind that I said I would take this project on as an exploratory mission. The chance of coming out here and recovering a hoard of diamonds in a few days' time was never even in the cards. The best thing we can hope for is to eliminate the approaches that won't work."

"That sounds like the glass is half empty approach," Laura said sulkily.

"Maybe, but sometimes pessimism can be the right hand of caution. And caution is the name of the game here. No pile of diamonds, and no cause, for that matter—I don't care how worthy it may be—is worth anyone's life. Not on my boat."

I felt my eyes harden as I stared at her, but she held my gaze without looking away.

Book Johnson spoke up to break the tension. "We tried the direct approach, dropping down through Gimbel's Hole. But, that part of the ship is gone, collapsed into a big, black crater leading into the first-class foyer, the kitchen, and a staircase to the A-deck."

As Johnson spoke, Roebling moved the cursor through the computer model like a mouse going through a maze. "It was tough to maneuver the first few times, but we got it down pretty well by the second day and now it takes about five minutes each way. When you get there you're at about 210-feet. So that leaves twenty-minutes, or so, of bottom time to do any work."

Roebling spoke as he "swam" the cursor over the broken debris field. "The problem is the condition of the ship. You get a little idea with this model. It's just a confusing pile of ceiling panels, collapsed bulkheads, furniture, pipes and cables, and general junk covered with a layer of fine sediment. We can only approximate where cabin thirty-five is buried, and it's probably at least ten feet under the junk."

"We found a few lower depressions," Johnson continued. "We lifted and moved a lot of the smaller pieces of debris, but we were always stopped by some large expanse of steel. Stuff that would have to be cut and winched out of the way. Of course you're working almost totally blind down there because of the silt."

LeClair took over now. "Me and Erik found a different way in on the second day of diving. There's an entry from the upper deck of the ship into the starboard elevator shaft."

Roebling put the cursor on the vertical deck of the ship where the superstructure once stood. The upper few decks had long ago fallen into the sand next to the hull uncovering a bee hive of holes that ranged from small airshafts to the gaping cavern where the ship's enormous funnel had once stood. All provided potential entry spots for the adventuresome, but they were all dangerously hidden behind the shroud of fishing nets which festoon that side of the ship.

LeClair continued. "The shaft's a little hairy going, what with cables and wiring and the collapsed remains of the elevator car, but it goes straight in to the A-deck passageway. From there it shouldn't be more than thirty-feet to the cabin," he looked at Laura, who was watching intently as the cursor moved through the deadly obstructions of the 50-foot long tunnel into the guts of the ship. "Of course, thirty-feet ain't much, but when it's mostly blocked by collapsed bulkheads and buckled ceiling and floors it makes a tight fit for an eel. There's just no room for a man to get through."

I saw the frustration on Laura's face.

I waved my hand over the computer model. "We've been working to move some of the loose junk but we haven't made much of a dent in it yet."

"So what you're all telling me is that we have no place to go from here short of a full-blown salvage operation?" Again, the determined set of her jaw said she was not the kind of woman accustomed to giving up.

I started to challenge her but then found myself saying that we would try one more approach tomorrow—a long shot—but one that may lead more directly into the cabin. LeClair started to sputter some protest, but I held up a hand.

"Look, this may sound crazy, but back when Gimbel made that last film he went down through the engine room to inspect a watertight door and found himself outside the ship, on the sand underneath the starboard side of the hull. He had been carried right through the bottom of the crack in the hull by a current, which, he said, was scouring a ditch underneath the ship."

Johnson looked at me skeptically, but I ignored him and continued.

"Suppose we were to follow the curve of the hull down to the bottom, find the trench that leads under the ship—it must be longer and deeper by now—and swim under the hull to the A-deck level? We know the cabin is right on the edge of the crack. Even if it's not exposed, we might be able to uncover it with a suction lift."

"We don't have a suction lift," LeClair muttered.

"I know. But we can get one easily enough. If we get back out here in a few days with some good calm weather it wouldn't take long to clear a lot of sand away."

"At this depth? Sounds like it might be dangerous," Roebling said.

"Probably less dangerous than going through the ship's interior," LeClair answered. "It might be worth a try anyway. But, we would need some calmer weather."

Laura looked relieved by the new prospect.

I felt better that she felt better. "So we'll do this reconnaissance dive in the morning before we head in. The weather's turning bad and we need to take a break anyway."

Before anyone could comment further, Lester's voice rang down from the flying bridge, "Hey, everybody. It looks like we might have company."

Everyone crowded the port rail to look out into the blackness. I climbed the bridge ladder and peered over the port bow. The lights of a boat were clearly visible about a hundred yards off. It looked like a commercial fishing vessel of some type—less than 100-feet in length—but it was hard to identify with just the running lights illuminating it. The sound of its motors was lost in the wind but it was clearly maneuvering to anchor as it powered in reverse.

Then the radio suddenly crackled with the unmistakable growl of Hank Manson. "Boat *Finest Kind*, come in. This is the *White Shark II*."

Damn! I thought. This is exactly what I had been expecting, but hoping wouldn't happen.

"*White Shark II*, this is the *Finest Kind*. What are you doing over there Hank?"

"Is that you Captain Hazen? Hope I'm not crowding you none."

"Well, I was getting used to all the sea room, but, like I said before, it's a big ocean, Hank."

"I got my main anchor in. We'll be tying into the wreck in the morning. How's your filming going?"

I exchanged glances with Lester and cursed under my breath. "Real well, Hank. We might take a little break, though, until the weather clears."

"Too bad. You gonna leave us out here all alone? You know how lonely it can get out on this big ocean."

"Well, I'm sure you're in good company over there, Hank. Just watch your back."

"Ah, you damn Bonackers. Always were a sarcastic bunch. You have a good night now, hey?"

I snapped the radio off and clambered down the ladder. "I think we should all get some sleep so we can make that dive at first light," I announced to the group. "Whatever they're up to over there, I doubt that it's looking for teacups and plates."

CHAPTER THIRTEEN

MORNING NEVER REALLY DAWNED. LIKE A 1940'S FILM NOIR, IT JUST WENT from black to gray with a gradual brightening. The wind, which had moderated somewhat during the night, began to pick up again, heaving the boat in hilly seas as Johnson and Roebling slid cautiously down onto the dive platform. LeClair and I were already in dry suits on deck ready to follow the first team in twenty minutes. Laura leaned against the port rail balancing a mug of hot coffee as she watched the preparations. Over her shoulder, in the distance, I could see the gray and white hull of the *White Shark II* as it rose and fell with the swells. There was no sign of anyone on its deck yet.

The two divers slid off the platform and disappeared under the opaque surface. I stood up and accepted the mug of coffee that Laura held out like a peace offering.

"Whatever you find on this dive, I want you to know that I do appreciate all the effort that you've made so far," she said. "I know I can be a little bitchy sometimes," she added, a trace of irony in her voice. She was wearing a yellow slicker, the only splash of color in a monochromatic scene.

I gulped some coffee. "No hard feelings," I said, trying to lighten the mood. "Take it from a callous bastard, you're not bitchy, just a little impatient. We're playing a high stakes game and it's frustrating knowing that the prize is down there. All we have to do is dig it out. But water has a way of ..." I stopped in mid-sentence as I looked over her shoulder. "Looks like our competition is finally waking up."

Laura turned around and looked at the divers dressed in dry-suits standing out on the rear deck of the *White Shark II*. Suddenly, two figures wearing orange slickers appeared. The smaller of the two was looking directly at the *Finest Kind*. I could see he wasn't a young man, he had a mostly bald head rimmed by gray, almost white, hair. Laura strained her eyes and gasped. "Oh my God! I know that man. That's Kurt Gebhardt! I recognize him from files the Foundation keeps on terrorist organizations active in America. He's one of the worst. He's head of the Aryan Renaissance Movement—ARM—and he has a huge following. "

"You didn't tell me anything about him. What does he know about the diamonds?"

"I didn't think I needed to tell you anything about him. Why would he know something?"

"Good question. Did he know your uncle?"

"Not personally, of course, only by reputation. Certainly he would know the Foundation. We have been actively fighting his organization in courts for years."

I thought for a minute. "The other guy in the slicker, do you recognize him?"

Laura peered through the mist and tried to focus against the heaving deck.

"I'm not sure, but it could be Sten Hajid. He's a much younger guy and rumored to be Gebhardt's protégé."

"Is he tall, muscular, with dark hair and a beard?"

She glanced at me. "Yes, he's a Muslim. But he has that slicker on, how can you tell?"

"Just a hunch. I've seen a guy like that hanging around Montauk."

"He is even more of a problem. He is Palestinian on his father's side and he's linked to a group in New York dedicated to the destruction of Israel. Erik, we can't let those people get to the gems before we do. It would be a disaster for decent people everywhere. I hate to think what they could do with the wealth it might bring."

A lot of thoughts raced through my head, including my grandfather's stories about surviving the landing beach at Normandy and seeing the jubilation on the faces of people in the French countryside as they rolled over Nazi resistance to liberate Paris. "Goddamn it! I thought fighting Nazis ended in 1945. Are these assholes for real?"

"Are you kidding? These 'assholes' are deadly. They make Speer and Nazis of his ilk look like boy scouts. ARM is more than an activist organization, it's an army of armed and trained killers who also happen to be nuts. Now if it's linked up with the Palestinian cause it has the potential to do a lot more harm. Hajid's organization, Free Palestine, is more focused towards wreaking havoc on pro-Israeli groups, particularly those based in New York, and they, too, are fanatics.

"I don't get it. Why would Palestinian terrorists want to work with neo-Nazis? Even better, why would Nazi types want to associate with non-Aryans?"

She had a look of disgust on her face as she answered, "One thing: their hatred of Jews in general and Israel in particular. Hajid's mother is German, his father a Palestinian Muslim. Gebhardt has dual German and American citizenship. It's not the first time that he and Hajid have been linked. Both men are intelligent, if misguided. Gebhardt is a physicist who received his doctorate from Humboldt University in Berlin. He's been a guest lecturer at several prestigious American universities. Hajid is a software developer—a successful one, I should add."

"Software?" I asked. "Why so successful?"

"His main contribution is a video game called 'Terror Threat Red'. It's a sick game that caught on with its appeal to terrorist violence. Hajid has made millions with it."

"Well, that answers my question about why those two would work together. Hajid is the money man and Gebhardt has the connection with salvage divers. I wonder which one is the host and which is the parasite?"

She shook her head in disgust. "Our foundation has collected intelligence on both groups which we have made known to the FBI and to the Attorney General's office in New York State. So far, nothing meaningful has come of any of our efforts."

I could see that she was really worked up about it and I tried to soothe her, even though, in my own mind, I could see we had a real problem. "Look. I don't know how they know what we are looking for, but if they do, they still can't have any better idea of how to find it. And, I'd put the odds on me and my diving crew over them any day."

Laura didn't say anything at first. But, I could see some of her confidence coming back. "I guess that clears up the question of who sabotaged us," I added.

"What's so interesting over there?" Mike LeClair asked from where he sat on the gear bench attaching a regulator to a set of tanks.

I pointed to the other boat. "It appears that we have some bona fide bad guys over there. And I'd bet they're looking for the same thing that we're after."

LeClair gazed across the 100-yard gap of ragged ocean. "Oh yeah. There's the brothers ugly—the same creeps that greeted us at the Scupper Saturday night. They already gave us a demo of how bad they are, didn't they?" he muttered.

"If they get their hands on the diamonds...," Laura said, but didn't finish her thought. "We can't allow that to happen."

"We aren't going to. But, this project is getting more like an enigma wrapped up in a mystery, isn't it?" I said as I turned away and began hauling dive gear out of the locker. "Let's just hope that they don't know something that we should."

As LeClair helped me get suited up I thought about the people on the other boat. I was used to all kinds of divers in my years in the business; everything from cowardly braggarts who shit in their dry suits when they got turned around inside the wrecks, to Gung Ho daredevils who wanted to push the limits of human endurance. But I never saw a more ominous looking group than the ones on board the *White Skark II*.

It was still early when LeClair and I dropped into the water. Book Johnson and Sean Roebling had already been down fifteen minutes when I slid down the new descent line and landed on the huge, curving expanse of the *Doria*'s hull near the keel. I hung above the swaying field of anemones, holding myself in place against the pull of the current. A twilight gloom lit the sloping surface of the great ship that stretched away in all directions except behind me, where the keel ended like the edge of a cliff poised above the bottom, another forty feet down. A pair of 10-foot blue sharks drifted in and out of view. They were regular features on the *Doria* which, like a reef, attracts fish of all types to its protective hulk. Just pests, nothing to worry about.

In a few seconds I was joined by LeClair, who dropped from above like a hulking skydiver. As we paused to get our bearings, LeClair pointed out to where the hull curved towards the deck railing. At first I thought he was pointing to the sharks, but then, just on the edge of the gloom, I made out the silhouettes of two divers as they swam to join a third who seemed to be chipping away at the hull with a hand tool. I wondered what they were doing. Why weren't they entering the hull through the crater near Gimbel's old opening into the promenade deck stairwells?

"What the hell do you think that's all about?" came the helium induced, Donald Duck voice of LeClair.

I still wasn't used to the new Sonicwave communication systems that we were wearing. The digital squelch technology that made it possible to talk underwater was relatively new, and even though it still had a ways to go it was a real luxury to be able to talk to your buddy with the push of a button.

I pushed the yellow PTT button and, remembering that the first word was often cut off before transmission said, "Good question Bub, you've got me?"

Mike made a "crazy" gesture with his finger against his head and we both turned to follow the descent line over the edge of the keel and into the cave-like opening formed by the overhanging starboard side of the hull and the sandy bottom.

Even the twilight was now gone as we snapped on our dive lights and eased under the dark overhang, trying not to kick up to much silt on the sandy bottom as we went. I glanced at my depth gauge: 240-feet. Very deep. Twenty minutes on the bottom if you breathe slowly and don't exert yourself. Ninety minutes of decompression time to get back up.

We were in a trench now, swimming in and under the ship's hull. It was like swimming upstream through a tunnel, except here the tunnel was made of shifting sand and the ragged metal edges of the great V-shaped rent in the underside of the ship.

Up ahead we could see other lights. Johnson and Roebling had dropped down from inside the ship into the trench. Their bottom time was up and they would have to get out to the ascent line quickly. A cloud of silt had now reduced the visibility to zero in the trench as all four of us stopped to confer.

"We went in to the right," Johnson quacked. "No sign of cabin. Dead end at blocked stairwell. Try going left at marker—tighter squeeze, but should be general area."

"Thanks, we'll try it," I responded. Then we all touched hands and passed each other in the darkness.

A minute later I found a phosphorescent green glow-stick jammed into a pile of conduit wire. I rose a few feet and found myself inside a cavern-like space about three feet high. LeClair came in after me and gave a thumbs up before swimming slowly into the blackness ahead. A strong current was flowing out from that direction. It cleared the water up as we shined our halogen beams around. Instead of kicking with our fins, we pulled ourselves along the twisted metal debris that lay underneath. The "floor" here was actually the starboard side of the ship and the "ceiling" was the rusting bulkhead of a half-crushed cabin.

A conger eel, longer than my leg and almost as big around, snaked out from a jungle of debris and kicked up a cloud of oatmeal-colored silt in its wake. I gently fanned away the remaining silt around the crevice it had exited and my light revealed the rusted metal tubing and steel springs of a bed frame. We were definitely in a cabin right on the edge of the gash. Now it was just a matter of figuring out if it was the right cabin.

A tap on the top of my head startled me until I looked up to see LeClair hovering above pointing to something overhead. I rolled over and shined my light towards the ceiling only to see it reflected back in a blinding flash. It took a couple of seconds to realize that I was looking at a mirror, unbroken and still mounted to its wall fastenings. It was framed in an art-deco frame formed by a pair of stylized, jumping dolphins in tarnished green brass. Directly ahead, extending out from the now vertical deck, a porcelain toilet bowl hung like some witty modern art installation.

"I think we hit gold," I sputtered into my mask. "That style mirror was only used in first-class cabins."

"Great! Let's hope we hit diamonds then," LeClair's voice squeaked back. He swam past the toilet, over a crushed partition and was digging at something jammed between the vertical deck and a pile of twisted junk against the far side of the destroyed cabin.

I drifted up and shined my light over LeClair's shoulders. I could just make out the object through swirls of gathering silt. It was a suitcase: 1950's style hard plastic construction with rounded corners. LeClair fumbled with it, bracing himself against the debris pile to wrench it out.

Just then, a dull thump seemed to come from somewhere above, and LeClair disappeared in a cloud of silt and falling debris. Some invisible force shoved me to the floor and knocked my breath out against the sharp bed frame. I saw stars and couldn't figure out at first if they were in my head or just the swirling galaxy of silt particles reflected in the dive light. My face mask was knocked askew and partially filled with water; it took me a few seconds to clear it and suck in a breath. Then something hit me in the face almost knocking the mask off again. I grabbed at it blindly and realized it was LeClair's flailing legs. I pressed my speaker button and called out to him but got nothing in response. My light was useless in the swirl of gray silt as I felt my way to LeClair's hips, which emerged from a solid wall of fallen debris.

"Erik! Erik! What happened?" The disembodied voice of Book Johnson coming from far above vibrated in my ear.

"I don't know," I transmitted back to the two divers hanging on the decompression line 200-feet overhead. The cartoonish sound of my voice didn't match the adrenaline pumping fear I was feeling. "Mike is half buried in a slide. Hold on."

Pulling pieces of metal panels, plumbing, and wall supports off LeClair, I finally came to a large I-beam that had fallen across his scuba backpack just below his shoulders. I reached under the beam and could feel Mike's face where it was pinned to the junk-strewn floor. His mask was still in place but he was drawing heaving breaths. I pulled one of his arms out from where it was pinned under him and squeezed his hand reassuringly. Then I braced myself to get a grip on the beam, planted my feet on the ragged bottom, and strained to lift. The beam moved but my feet slipped on the algae slick ooze and I dropped it.

LeClair's free arm was now flailing to push against the beam and I positioned myself again. Images of Kate were now machine-gunning through my head and I felt the metallic taste of fear rising in my throat. On the second try my footing held and I felt the beam come up a foot while LeClair thrashed out from underneath like a lobster backing out of a trap.

I grabbed the top of his scuba pack and led him out of the ship's maw and back into the sandy trench. LeClair's dive light was still attached to his wrist and the beam twisted randomly on its tether, but in the swirling darkness he was so disoriented that I had to guide him out of the trench and up the line.

By the time we rose to the top of the wreck's hull the water was clear again and the blue-green light allowed me to pause and check on LeClair's condition. I could see that his eyes were signaling pain and disorientation. The sonic system on LeClairs mask wasn't working so I used hand signals to ask "You OK?"

He signaled back with a grimace, holding his side with one hand, his head with the other, but then managed to give a weak thumbs-up.

We rose together towards the growing light. As we passed the silent boat davits, I saw that the divers from Manson's boat were gone. The patch of hull area that they had been working on was curiously outlined now where marine growth had been scraped away into what looked like a barn door-sized rectangle. But, except for the two blue sharks that still prowled along the railing like sleek guard dogs, the water seemed strangely empty of life.

At the 80-foot level we stopped for the first stage of decompression. The anchor line was jerking in the choppy seas above so I snapped in with a tether line, and held onto LeClair to spare him the pain of the violent movement.

Johnson's voice quacked in my ear again. "What's going on down there?"

I looked up and could just see the smudged outline of two divers hanging onto the line fifty feet above. "I think we're OK here. Mike is hurting and he might have some broken ribs, but he's alert and breathing."

"Anything you want me to do up here?" Came the normal sounding voice of Bill Lester speaking from the boat's surface-to diver-system.

"There isn't anything you can do now except get ready to leave as soon as we're out of the water. How's the weather now?"

"Winds are still southeast at thirty knots. Seas are over six feet. Rain clouds are coming in fast," Lester said, and then added in a more cheerful voice, "At least there's no fog."

"Roger that. Thanks for the comforting words," I muttered back.

The initial decompression stops were short—only a few minutes each—before we reached the 30-foot level, where we had to hang on to the snapping anchor line for almost thirty minutes. Johnson and Roebling were at the 10-foot stage waiting another fifteen minutes before they could leave the water. I checked my own pressure gauges as well as LeClair's that showed his spare tank was getting low. I also noticed a thin line of blood coming out from under LeClair's hood. He was breathing faster than normal with the pain, and holding his side with every breath.

I held onto him and thought about the nightmare ascent I had made ten years before holding Kate's lifeless body. I was starting to get the gnawing feeling that the whole expedition was doomed to failure. I already lost a big piece of my life to the cursed wreck, now I came damn close to losing the rest of it. What the hell am I doing here?

Suddenly, something grabbed my arm. I spun around quickly, letting go of LeClair with one hand, ready to fend off an aggressive shark with the other. But, instead, I was faced with the vision of a mermaid. Laura's dark eyes blinked long lashes from behind a facemask. She gripped a snorkel in her mouth--no scuba gear on--and fluttered bright yellow fins like butterfly wings. The whiteness of her body, clad only in a black halter top and nylon shorts, stood out against the dark water like a moth in moonlight.

In one outstretched hand she held an underwater writing slate which said, "Just wanted to make sure you were OK." I looked at it dumbly, then watched as she gave thumbs up, turned, and kicked languidly towards the surface.

Forty-five minutes later I climbed the bucking dive ladder into the boat. The engines were already going and Hector began winching in the anchor line as soon as we pulled LeClair onto the deck where he sprawled like a beached porpoise. We removed his tanks and equipment and peeled away his dive suit. He had a three-inch gash in the back of his head, maybe a concussion, and definitely some broken ribs. Laura wrapped his head with gauze and bandages and Johnson and Roebling carried him into the cabin and got him onto a bunk.

"You're hurting pretty bad, aren't you Bub?" I said to him.

LeClair looked up. "I've got a little headache and some broken ribs," he answered with a forced smile. Then he brightened. "But it only hurts when I laugh."

Johnson rolled his eyes and did a mock sneer. "And you just dumb enough to do that too." he said, adding, "You keep your Cajon ass still and lay there quiet. We got a long trip back."

Then he turned to me. "What the hell happened down there, anyway?"

"I'm not sure, but I've got some suspicions," I answered, rubbing my own chest, which was still sore from hitting the bed frame. "Did you and Sean see Manson's divers on the way up?"

Roebling answered. "Yeah, I saw three guys swimming pretty fast across the center hull headed for a dive line attached to one of the wreck's boat davits. It was weird, but I got the feeling that they were up to no good."

"I know what you're thinking," LeClair said. "Cause I'm thinking the same thing. That shit didn't fall on me naturally. I felt everything shake just before things got dark."

Johnson and I exchanges glances. "Explosives! You mean to tell me those dumb fucks set off a charge?" he said.

"Not so dumb. I think they calculated it," I answered. "A two-pronged attack. Open the ship up and maybe get rid of us at the same time."

"Wait a minute," Roebling said. "How could they expect to blow a hole in the solid plate of the hull?"

I felt the scar on my face begin to redden as I spoke. "Because they weren't on solid plate. They were over the door to the cargo hold. They're probably trying to blow it off its hinges."

"But why do that?" Roebling asked. "I thought you could get into that area from Gimbel's Hole?"

"You can," Johnson answered. "But it's a long swim in the dark. Maybe these dudes want a direct entry. The question is why that spot?"

"I don't have that answer. Even if the diamonds are in there it'd be a heavy handed way of getting to them. But maybe somebody knows something that we don't," I said as I left the cabin and went into the pilothouse.

Laura was there dressed in jeans and yellow slicker, her black hair still wet and brushed back over her ears. She started to question me about LeClair's condition, but I waved her aside as I grabbed the radio.

"*White Shark II*, this is the *Finest Kind* calling. Pick it up Manson!"

A few seconds went by before there was an answer. I looked out the side windows where Manson's boat was riding over the backs of the long rollers. A wind driven rain had begun to fall turning the water to ball peened lead.

"*Finest Kind*, this is *White Shark II*. How goes it, Captain Hazen?" Manson's voice came with its usual raspy bray.

"Cut the bullshit, Manson. I want to know why you've got divers planting explosive charges on the ship. You damned near buried us down there."

"I don't know what you're talking about Captain. I'm just the bus driver. How am I gonna know what goes on under my boat?"

I fumed. "It's your business to know what goes on under your boat. And you know that."

"Hey, I'm sure you're wrong about those explosives. My guys are only interested in archaeology." He laughed sardonically.

"I'll be sure to mention that in my report to the Coast Guard when I get back to Montauk." I slammed the handset into its cradle and headed topside to check on Lester who was turning the boat into a WNW heading and watching the following seas pile up on the stern.

Then I looked over my shoulder at Laura as I gripped the bridge ladder. I was pissed at everybody and I felt my eyes go hard and glassy.

"That was pretty daring of you to make a free-dive just to check up on us. But I have to remind you that you broke one of our agreements."

She gave me a puzzled look.

"Nobody but the professionals was supposed to be in the water," I said, then turned and climbed up to the bridge.

"You brass-assed bastard," she muttered.

CHAPTER FOURTEEN

SUMMER CAME EARLY. IT WAS ONLY A WEEK LATER BUT I WAS TRYING to get back to fishing again and put the *Doria* charter behind me. It was only the middle of June but the Northeast was in the grip of a heat wave. On the weekends, New Yorkers were leaving their air-conditioned apartments and offices to head out to the Hamptons, and beyond—to Long Island's real East End: Montauk Point.

To me, it seemed like the whole damn island of Manhattan. Day trippers in bright tee-shirts crowded the docks and some asked questions about the fishing. I usually answered even the dumb questions politely as I hosed down some fishing tackle on the deck. Bill Lester stood at the filleting table working on a couple of big striped bass for the half-day charter we had just finished. The charter consisted of an elderly lawyer and his brand new forty-something wife. He was a pretty good sport who had been a weekend fisherman most of his life, but she was right out of central casting for Hollywood Boulevard: a big, peroxided blonde with enormous breasts barely tethered by a white bikini top. She had spent most of the five-hour trip giving me as clear a view of her body as she could. Now she and her husband were up on the dock waiting for Lester to finish so they could put the fillets in a cooler before they went to have lunch at Gosman's. The lunchtime crowd that strolled by was about evenly split between husbands who gazed at her cleavage and those that admired the size of the striped bass.

"Captain Erik , I had such a good time. Just think, my first fish ever and you showed me how to reel it in," she called down from the dock. "I hope Herb and me get to go fishing again soon." She smiled showing perfectly shaped, bleached teeth and reached down to shake my soapy hand, nearly spilling out of the straining top as she bent over.

"I'm glad I was able to give you some sport," I said wryly as Lester nearly choked to keep from laughing. Then he handed the plastic bag of fresh fillets up to her and watched as she and the old gentleman strolled off the dock.

"Damn it, Amigo. You've got to stop making those kinda comments when I've got a sharp fillet knife in my hands. Almost lost a thumb this time."

I laughed then lifted my hat and wiped sweat out of my sun-bleached eyebrows with a forearm that had turned to the color of a fine Bordeaux in the last two days.

"Sorry, Bub. But that lady was just pure caricature. At least she'll keep the guys on the dock entertained."

"Hey, watching the two of you kept me entertained this morning. Did you really have to stand that close behind her to show her how to reel?"

"Well, I didn't want her to go and lose a $500 fishing outfit, now did I? Besides, you know you have to keep the clients happy."

"No mystery what would make her happy."

"Never mix business with pleasure, you know that."

"Yeah, well she gave me a $100 tip, so I'm going to cool off at the Nor'easter this afternoon. Want to join me?"

"Not today. I'm going home. Maybe I'll take the skiff out to dig a bunch of littlenecks and then go sit under a tree with the clams, some lemon and a vodka Collins."

"Jesus. You are a damn Bonacker, aren't you? Fishing in the morning, clamming in the afternoon. You do know you can buy clams at the bar? They even open them for you."

"Not the same, Bill. Not the same."

•

By mid-afternoon, the sun hung like a blazing ornament above the still waters of Napeague Bay. I steered my skiff up the tidal creek where my cottage is tucked into a grove of trees. It's probably a foolish and romantic notion, but, for now, I wanted to keep the old way of life alive. Somehow it validates my existence on this island, in this bay, in this corner of the world. Plus, the near disaster of the diving expedition made me yearn, once again, for the simple things.

The skiff bumped up against the dock and I heaved a bag of clams and a long handled rake onto the weathered boards. Shouldering them, I walked into the deep shade of the path that wends through old growth hardwoods and up the hill to the house. A mockingbird's liquid song poured from the cool undergrowth of holly and chokecherry, otherwise all was quiet. I tossed the rake into my pickup and dropped the bag of clams on the porch, then walked through the side door into the cottage that was still cool under the shade of towering plane trees.

I opened the refrigerator and drank from a pitcher of water, took a bottle of Absolut vodka out, noted that it was almost empty, poured the rest into a glass, plopped two ice cubes in, then squeezed half a lime over it. I sat at the table swirling the glass for a minute looking out through the old French doors, past the meadow dusty with heat, to the brilliant bay waters beyond. It wasn't yet 3-P.M. as I took the first drink. The vodka went down smooth and cold. I felt relaxed as I put my feet up on the table and chewed on one of the ice cubes. My big, gray cat jumped up and began rubbing against my arm.

"Bub, you old loafer. You been keeping cool around here?" I said. The cat meowed as though to answer so I went to the refrigerator and slipped scraps of fresh bluefish fillet into a cracked china soup bowl. The cat purred as it ate.

The phone rang and I let it ring until the machine went off. "Hello, Erik?" It was Laura Morgan's voice and she sounded frustrated in spite of the controlled pitch she was trying to maintain. "Please pick up if you're there. I've got some new information that might be important to us. I need to talk to you. Call my cell."

She left the same message twice the night before. Now I sat back and sipped the vodka. Whatever she wanted I wasn't interested.

It had been a god-awful rough trip back from the disastrous charter. Mike LeClair was hurting every time we pounded through another cresting wave. It was 2-AM when we got to the dock and so dark that the ambulance waiting in the parking lot was the only thing visible beyond the yellow flare of dock lights. LeClair had two broken ribs, upper body contusions, a concussion, and a classic pair of black eyes. Book Johnson told him that he looked like the great white dope. Later on, the doctor at East Hampton Hospital concluded that he'd be fine in a couple of weeks.

I filed a complaint with the Coast Guard about Manson's boat using explosives. But the storm had chased Manson back only a few hours later, so that the *White Shark II* was already tied up at Gosman's the next afternoon when a couple of white-uniformed investigators went to check out the story. Of course Manson denied everything and invited them on board to look around. But they didn't even bother, and left after reminding him that federal laws regulated the use of explosives.

I wanted to put the whole dark episode behind me. On the trip back, I had finished off a bottle of scotch and become sullenly drunk. The Morgan woman had confronted me so I blew up at her and called off the whole expedition. I was sick of the jinxed diving on the *Andrea Doria*. I had come too close to losing another life on the wreck. Let the ocean have the ship and the goddamn diamonds too. Hell, if they even exist they're buried under thirty thousand tons of rotting steel and smothering ooze. Nobody'll ever find them.

I swirled the vodka and finished off the drink. My optimism about humanity was sinking faster than the old ship. Alcohol always brought out my cynical side. As a boat designer I had started out with high-minded ideas about form and function and the way boats and people could live in harmony with nature. But that had soured as the bay steadily filled with bigger and more expensive boats, which meant more marinas and docks, followed by golf courses, and monstrous houses with fertilized lawns and swimming pools crowding the shoreline and running their poisons into the bay. I was part of the catch-22: the more boats I designed and built for rich people, the more I felt like part of the problem. I was a traitor to my heritage, contributing to the destruction of the environment that once meant a way of life for my people.

The vodka was cool and refreshing. Condensation from the glass pooled on the table and the cat lapped at it. "You want to drink with me, Bub?" I said as I scratched its neck. The cat's meow sounded enough like a 'yes' that I decided to go into town and buy another bottle of vodka.

Just as I started my truck and put it into reverse a big, black SUV rolled into the driveway and stopped directly behind me blocking the way. At first I thought it was Sheriff Haven's vehicle, but then I recognized it and the guy who got out of the driver's door: the tall, muscular, bearded guy. Then the passenger door opened and a swarthy, acne scarred kid with lightning bolts tattooed on the side of his bald head slid out. What did Laura say the big guy's name was? Hajid?

I opened the pickup's door and stepped out. "What can I do for you gentlemen?

Hajid's smile looked more like a wolf's grin. "We just wanted to straighten out a little misunderstanding," he said.

"Misunderstanding? I didn't know there was one."

Lightning Bolts came around and stood near the pickup's rear fender. His ferrety eyes darted from the bed of the pickup to the house and back to me. Hajid, dressed in a safari shirt over cargo pants, moved a little closer before answering. I kept my left shoulder facing both men.

"Captain Manson isn't too happy about you turning him in to the Coast Guard with those wild stories about explosives."

Lightning Bolts edged his way down the truck bed until he was only five feet away. I still had the truck door open and could see the handle of a baseball bat sticking out from under the seat. I use it to crush clams and crabs for chum or bait.

"I don't care what Captain Manson is unhappy about. There was nothing wild about what I reported. Somebody set off a charge down on the wreck and it damn near buried me and my partner. I think you know damn well who did it."

Hajid sneered. "Maybe you ought to just rethink the kind of places that you and your diving partners mess around in. Haven't you already lost enough in that old wreck?"

Now, he was really pissing me off and I felt my body coil. Even with the control my training has given me I think the scar on my face reddened. "Hold it right there. You may think you know me, but if you think you can intimidate me, you haven't done your homework very well."

Just then I caught the blurred movement out of my peripheral vision of Lightening Bolt's combat-booted left foot moving on a collision course with my left kidney. I flicked my right arm down catching the kid's ankle, then held it as I grabbed the bat and whacked it hard against his shinbone before I yanked him onto his back.

It all happened in seconds. The kid was on the ground scrabbling backward, holding his leg and yelling, "fuck, fuck, fuckin' shit..."

I just braced myself, kept my eye on Hajid, and cocked the bat in one hand.

A look of half surprise half amusement showed on Hajid's face. He lifted both arms in mock surrender as he stepped back, allowing his shirt to partly open. I saw the holstered Glock under his left arm.

"Nice moves, Captain Hazen," he said coolly. "I was hoping that you would be more amenable to reason but I should have known that you're a stubborn man. Heard that all you Bonacker types are stubborn."

I held the bat cocked back. "You don't know anything about me, so just get back in your toy truck and go play badass to somebody that can't fight back."

Hajid looked down at Lightning Bolts in disgust and snapped, "Get back in the car!" Then he turned to me again as he climbed into the vehicle. "I don't know why Rashid went and acted that way. The hot blood of youth maybe? But I think the message is clear, Captain: stay out of our way around the *Doria*. What we're looking for belongs to us. Only to us."

My calmness ebbed and I guess my sunburned face was twisted in rage. "Get off my property now or this bat will be part of your pathetic anatomy."

"No need to get excited. It's far too hot a day for that. Oh, and by the way, don't bother reporting my hardware," he patted the bulge under his arm. "It's fully licensed and legal. Don't you love America for that?" Then he grinned coldly, threw the big vehicle into reverse, and backed out of the driveway in a shower of clamshells and gravel.

I tossed the bat into the truck and went into the house. I splashed some cold water in my face and stood gripping the sides of the sink for a minute. My reflection in the mirror showed my face still pretty flushed and the scar standing out in bold relief. Damn, I said out loud, you may be getting some gray hair up on top but your reflexes are still good.

Then I dialed Laura Morgan's cell phone. She answered on the third ring.

"Erik! I'm very glad you called. We've got to talk," Laura's voice was all business. That breathless New York City cadence that leaves me cold.

"Yeah. I agree that we have to talk. I just had some visitors who you might know."

Her voice sounded wary. "Who?"

"A couple of those Nazi/Arab terrorist mutts that we saw on Manson's boat."

"Gebhardt and Hajid? What did they want?"

"Just Hajid and his flunky. And they were here to tell me what they don't want. They don't want any competition. They say that it's their property we're messing with."

"Oh, God! Erik, I'm sorry you had to deal with that." Her voice sounded concerned even if it hadn't lost its business edge. "I didn't realize this thing was going to turn out this way. Are you OK?"

"I'm fine. But they did succeed in pissing me off. I had to play a little hardball with them and I think I got their attention. The trouble is this Hajid guy isn't going to stop at a little intimidation."

"I was afraid this would happen. Do you think they'll come back?"

"I don't know. But they're not going to scare away. Now that the weather's clear they'll be running out to the *Doria* for sure."

"Erik, listen to me. I'm not trying to change the subject, but, can you possibly come into the city today? I set up a meeting with an *Andrea Doria* survivor in my office around six. I'd like you to be here; this may be important. He may have some light to shed on my Uncle's last hours before the ship sank," she paused and added with a hopeful note, "It might help us."

"Ten minutes ago I would have said I'm not interested. But that courtesy call really put me into a contrarian mood. The only thing I hate worse than being told what to do is being told not to do something."

"Yes, I'm beginning to see that. Maybe you should rename your boat, *Contrarian*."

"Actually, it doesn't sound bad," I said and chuckled.

"Then you'll come?"

"Why not? All of Manhattan seems to be out here now, so I might as well come in and avoid the crowds." I looked at my watch. "It's after three. I might just make it if I leave now, but I better grab a shower first. Don't want to offend."

"Don't worry. I'll keep the meeting on hold until you get here."

CHAPTER FIFTEEN

ON THE WAY INTO THE CITY I THOUGHT ABOUT HAJID. I HAD ALWAYS PICTURED neo-Nazis, and terrorists in general, as misguided morons who got off on beating up little black kids, painting swastikas on synagogues, and blowing up buses. The Shoup brothers and lightning bolts fit that category but Hajid, and probably Gebhardt, were different—educated, efficient, and well equipped. I wondered how far they and their friends would go to get the diamonds. Maybe, LeClair and I had simply been in the way when they used that explosive charge. Then again, the next time it might be a more direct frontal assault. If the value of the diamonds was anywhere near what Laura said it might be these guys were not likely to stop at anything, including murder, to get them.

I relaxed in the air-conditioned truck cab as it rolled past the sweltering streets of Queens and crept into the Midtown Tunnel while I thought about the new challenge. I can't deny I felt a certain excitement as I contemplated the dangers of going against Hajid, Gebhardt, and their team of misfits. It was almost like the thrill I used to get when my SEAL team went on a search and recovery mission that involved the possibility of combat. Something worth staying sober for, I decided.

By the time I found a place to park on the busy streets of TriBeca and took the freight elevator up to the offices of the Voyage Home Foundation, it was already past six. Laura was sitting in a conference room across from a slender, white-haired man in his seventies, who was wearing a moist and ill-fitting summer suit. Feynard was there too. He nodded at me, but stayed seated and didn't look all that happy to see me. But, even in the 100-degree weather, he was dapper and dry in pinstripes. There was a plate of Italian pastry on the table with a large pitcher of iced tea.

Laura stood to greet me, and, once again, I couldn't help noticing how good she looked: this time in a silky white skirt and sleeveless blouse. She pushed a wisp of hair back in place and adjusted some kind of ivory clip.

"Erik, I really appreciate your coming," she said, reaching a hand out for a businesslike shake. The familiar lavender scent was faintly discernible in the air-conditioned room.

I smiled at her polite formality and looked directly into her eyes. "Like I said, that unexpected social call renewed my interest in the project."

She looked a little uncomfortable with the reference. Then she turned to the white-haired man. "I'd like you to meet Gino Bartolli. Mr. Bartolli was a steward in 1st-class on board the *Andrea Doria* when it sank."

The name took me by surprise. "It's an honor to meet you Mr. Bartolli," I said, shaking the old man's hand. "I've read about you in several of the accounts of the sinking."

"And I have read newspaper accounts about your exploration of the ship over the years," the older man said in a gentle voice with just a touch of an Italian accent. "I am deeply sorry for your personal loss, Mr. Hazen."

"Thank you, Mr. Bartolli. I guess you could say my wife was the 60th casualty of the Andrea Doria, fifty years after it sank; and even since then it has continued claiming victims."

There was an awkward silence until Laura spoke. "I contacted Mr. Bartolli through an online announcement for the annual reunion of the *Andrea Doria Survivors Organization*. He knew my uncle and spent the last minutes on board the sinking ship with him."

Feynard, who until now had been quiet, joined in. "Mr. Bartolli was one of the heroes of that night. Now he has been kind enough to come here and relate his story for us."

"Please," Bartolli held up his hand, "call me Gino, and I was never a hero. I think it is a title given out too freely these days. But it was one of the more exciting episodes in the otherwise dull life of a language instructor," he smiled.

I liked Bartolli right away. The man's self-effacing modesty and his quiet warmth of character made him seem like the Old World gentlemen you see in vintage movies.

"Can you tell us your story?" Laura asked.

"I will be glad to, though I'm not sure that it will shed any light on your interests," he said, settling back into the armchair. "I only ask that you hear me out from beginning to end. At my age I can only remember things as they relate in a full story. I'm not good at—how do you say, tweeting? I am more a product of the last century."

We all laughed and he began the tale.

"I was a young man of 21 back then, and sailing the seas on the most luxurious and beautiful ship in the world seemed like a dream come true for a poor boy from the dusty streets of Genoa. But, after the sinking, I never went on another boat again." He looked across the conference table a little misty-eyed. "Forgive me; let me get to the point."

"I was on the ship's bridge when the collision happened. It was 11 PM and the officers were under a lot of strain from maneuvering through the fog. I had brought coffee up to the wheelhouse and was serving it to them. All of the command officers were there: Captain Calamai, Staff Captain Magagnini, and Second Officer Franchini. A young seaman, Julio Visciano, was at the helm. I remember it as clearly as if it were last week.

"There was some disagreement among the officers as to the heading of an eastbound ship that Franchini had been tracking on the radar for some time. He was the youngest officer—not much older than me— and he had a lot of confidence in the new technology. Captain Calamai was from the old school of seamanship. I remember his answer to Franchini's reassurance about having faith in the radar. He said, 'For me, faith must be confined to the church where I worship. Here on the ship I like to see what is ahead of me.'

"No sooner had the captain said this than Franchini pulled back from the green glow of the radarscope and cursed. 'What is he doing? He's turning. He's on a collision course with us.' Then the ship's horn blasted out a warning.

"A minute later, I turned and saw a sight that I can never forget. From out of the bridge window, I saw the fog suddenly part and the bright lights of a ship came into view. It was a large passenger ship and it wasn't more than 200-yards away and turning across our bow. Even in the dark I could see the white navigation light on the ship's bow move to the left of the high mast light over its bridge. I knew enough about seamanship to realize that the red port light was indicating that the ship had angled towards us suddenly.

"I heard Captain Calamai—who was the gentlest and most soft-spoken of captains—spit curses at the other ship as he called out, 'Sound two blasts on the horn!'

"Even the terrible shriek of the horn blasts couldn't get me to tear my eyes away from the scene. It was as though we were caught in some titanic magnetic field which was drawing us together amid thousands of square miles of an empty ocean. At one point I do remember the scene as one might see a tableau: Captain Calamai, his face fire-red, his eyes wide with disbelief, and his large hands gripping the window ledge in front of him as though by sheer will he could turn the other ship away; Magagnini frozen at the chart table; Franchini, in the glow of the radar scope, the green paleness of his bloodless face staring like a man betrayed; and Visciano, gripping the wheel as though he would rip it upwards and sail the ship into the night sky.

"Then, in a strangely hoarse voice, I heard the Captain call out to the helmsman, 'Tutto sinistra! Tutto sinistra!' The helmsman flung the wheel hard to the left and spun it several revolutions. 'Reverse engines,' Captain Calamai shouted into the ship's intercom, and I could feel the ship shudder as the big propellers swung into reverse.

"Of course it was too late. I stood frozen by the chart table and watched as the lights of the other ship filled the starboard window. The bellow of the ship's horn was drowned out by the screech of rending steel plate. Great showers of orange sparks rose from below the window and burst like aerial bombs in the night. The terrible noise and blinding sparks went on for a full minute or more as the other ship was wrenched out of the wound it had made and bounced along the full length of our ship as we continued to make headway.

"Then everything was dark again outside the windows and it was difficult to stand without holding on to the chart table because the ship had tilted over so. And now it was quiet. It seemed like minutes before anyone spoke. My first thoughts were of the lifeboats and I turned to look out of the port side window. The boats that I saw were clearly useless—wedged tightly against the port rail by the 20-degree starboard list. I heard Captain Calamai order the port fuel tanks flooded, and at the same time Franchini cried out for orders, wanting to know if the engines should be shut down. A panicky voice came over the intercom from the generator room saying that it was flooding and some of the generators were already underwater.

"All this happened in minutes. I remember that the captain's face was ashen, his eyes staring dully. I could see that he was in shock. Then he seemed to notice me for the first time.

"'See to the passengers,' he croaked. 'Assemble people on the boat deck and wait for further instructions.'

Bartolli now paused in his narrative and drank from a glass of iced tea. Although I had read many accounts of the accident, his first-hand experience—told as if it had happened a week ago—gripped me. A minute passed. Then he sat back and continued.

"For the next hour everything was confusion. People streamed into the 1st-class lounge. Some were dry and clean and calm; some were wet, half-dressed, and panicky. We tried to make sure that everyone had a life jacket on before sending them out to the deck. No other orders ever came. To this day I cannot blame Captain Calamai. I think that he was just overwhelmed by the enormity of the problem of having only half the lifeboats useable.

"Later I went down to the passenger cabins on A-deck to check rooms and make sure that everyone had gotten out. Most of the corridor was intact, but when I got to the impact area I was shocked. The way was blocked by the burst steel bulkheads folded inward. I opened the door of one cabin where I knew a teenage girl and her eight-year old sister were staying. I had to force it open. The sight was sickening. A small, bloody body, crushed beyond recognition was half concealed and pinned inside a mass of twisted beams and panels. I could see part of a pink nightgown and a small hand curled in death. The next room, where the girls' parents had been, was simply gone. In its place was a gaping hole with a view of the deck lights reflecting off the dark water only a few feet below. I said a simple Hail Mary and shut the door behind me.

"Then I saw the door to Mr. Ebner's room half-open. He had been one of the kindest and most generous of the passengers that I served on that trip and I felt a strong attachment to him and his beautiful wife.

"Voices were coming from inside. When I entered, I saw that the devastation was just as bad as that in the girls' cabin, but here there were no bodies. Instead I found Mr. Ebner and a teenage boy—who I had met earlier in the trip—trying to lift a collapsed section of steel partition. His wife was pinned in her bed underneath. Together we couldn't lift the bent steel. I could hear Mrs. Ebner's muffled groans, but she was shielded from view by the panel.

"A jack! I heard the boy say, and he went running off. I wondered where on the ship he would get a jack, then I realized he was probably going to the garage; I wanted to get him and bring him on deck, but first I handed a mariners tool with wire cutters to Mr. Ebner. The room was starting to flood and he was underneath the panel, half submerged. I knew that his wife would not get out, but I didn't want to say that to him.

"As I left the room I told him that I would come back. But when I did—almost forty minutes later—the ship had settled deeper and most of the cabin was underwater. I called, but there was no answer, then I went back up to the promenade deck to help people into lifeboats. I never saw him again. From what I heard later, he was plucked from the water by the *Isle de France*."

The room was silent when he stopped talking. I looked across at Laura and saw that her eyes were red. Even Feynard appeared moved by the story as he tugged nervously at his tie. Bartolli sat back and drained the rest of his iced tea. He looked visibly older.

"That must have been a terrible ordeal for you, Gino. I can see why you remember everything with such vivid detail," Laura said.

"Oh, the experience is burned into my memory with far more detail than I would want to bore you with," Bartolli said in his gentle voice. "I think that after all the interviews with news people and writers for Life Magazine and Time Magazine and dozens of others, as well as the authors of several books that came later, I have come to remember the stories of many people on that terrible night. But none is more vivid than that of your uncle, Ms. Morgan," he said, turning to Laura.

"Thank you Gino," Laura said, wiping at her eyes with a tissue.

I glanced at Laura and decided to press on with the question that had to be asked. "Tell me, Gino, do you remember seeing any personal items around the room? Did the Ebners have their bags packed?"

"The room looked like it was blasted apart with a bomb," he answered, shrugging his shoulders. "Most of the 1st-class passengers had their luggage already up on deck because we were so close to docking. I don't remember seeing any in their room."

I could see no point in pressing the subject further, so I sat back and looked over at Laura with a look that said, "Now what?"

Feynard's phone beeped with a text message and he apologized as he looked at it. "Gino, thank you for coming in today. You have certainly brought a sixty-year old story vividly up to date for me," he said as he stood up. "Now, I hope everyone can excuse me. I have to tend to some urgent business before I meet my wife for dinner."

"Of course, Marcel," Laura said. I think we are about done here. Say hello to Janice for me."

"I will. Good night, Captain Hazen," he said as he left.

Laura began talking to Bartolli about the course that he teaches in Art of the Italian Renaissance at NYU. I began thinking about the old man's reference to the *Andrea Doria* garage. I had almost forgotten that the ship was carrying a dozen cars when it went to the bottom.

"Gino," I said. "Would you happen to know if Mr. Ebner had a car on board the ship?"

"An automobile? It could be possible. I do know that there were several autos on board, even an experimental sports car designed by Ghia of Italy."

As an afterthought I said, "Then you don't know if the boy went to the garage to get a jack?"

"That I do know. I caught up to him trying to go down the stairwell on C-deck. I knew that the garage was underwater by then and I got him to come with me up onto the outside deck where they got him into a lifeboat."

Laura looked with interest at Bartolli as he spoke. "But, why was this boy so determined to help my uncle?" she asked.

He shrugged. "He said that Mr. Ebner had saved his life. He did not explain how. Years later I asked him about it, but he said it was not something he preferred to talk about."

"Years later!" I blurted. "You mean you know the boy?"

"Oh, yes. Of course, he is no longer a boy. His name is Peter Scott. He often comes to our survivor reunion meetings," he said as he turned to Laura. "Your uncle never did come to one. Too bad. My last memory of him was on that terrible night."

"Would you happen to know how to contact Peter Scott?" I asked.

"Certainly. As I said, he is quite involved in the survivors group. Actually one of the youngest, even though he is over seventy by now. Ahh, life goes too quickly," he said as he took a cell phone out of his pocket. "I have his phone number right here. I know he lives out on Long Island. He is a writer."

"Gino, you have been a wonderful help," Laura said as she walked Bartolli to the door. I am learning a great deal about my uncle that he was always reluctant to talk about when he was alive."

"It is my pleasure, Miss Morgan, as he bowed slightly and brought Laura's hand close to his lips. "He was a wonderful man who did great things in his lifetime. I'm sure he is in heaven now."

"I'm sure he is," Laura said.

"Goodbye, Captain Hazen. It was my honor to meet you."

"And mine to meet you, Gino," I said as we shook hands and the old gentleman left.

Laura turned to me. Her eyes were still a little red from hearing the tale. "Erik. I know you are thinking the same thing I am."

"That a car on board a ship would be the perfect place to hide something?"

"Yes. Do you think it is possible that Uncle Carl had a car on board?"

"Good question. But, it would seem that someone else thinks so."

"What do you mean?"

"Manson's charter. The explosives they placed were at the cargo hold, and the first section of the cargo hold is the *autorimessa*—the ship's garage!"

Laura looked worried. "Oh," she muttered.

I was kicking myself for not thinking of it before. I always knew about the garage on the ship but just didn't make the connection. I looked at my watch. "There's one way to find out. It's seven o'clock now. The New York Public Library is open until nine. They have the best research collection on the *Andrea Doria* in the country. I'm sure they have the cargo manifest on microfilm. That will give us our answer."

CHAPTER SIXTEEN

IT WAS A QUICK CAB RIDE UP TO THE LIBRARY WITH ITS IMPOSING STONE LIONS guarding the steep stairway at the main entrance on Fifth Avenue. One of the research librarians—a heavyset woman named Linda with long, gray, braided hair draped over one shoulder—actually remembered me from when I was researching material for the book I wrote about diving on the ship. I wrote out the request for the microfilm I was looking for and, within minutes, Laura and I were scrolling through lists of cargo that had been on board the ship when it left Genoa.

There were a couple of grand pianos that were being shipped to a dealer in New York, 250-pairs of Italian shoes going to a Fifth Avenue store, a roomful of furniture accompanying a couple moving to Connecticut, two dozen Italian racing bicycles traveling with a group of cyclists competing in an American tour, lots of incidental items such as baby carriages, bedframes, artwork, and several cases of fine French wine.

"Well," I joked, "I hope it wasn't too good a vintage year."

"You would think that," she said, as she jabbed me in the side with her elbow. "I was more concerned about the artwork. I hope there were no Monets or Picassos."

"Probably some velvet Elvis's," I suggested.

Then the list of cars, along with the name of each owner, appeared. "Here we go," I said as I scrolled slowly through the list.

There was a 1953 Cadillac belonging to an Anthony Homer, a new Maserati owned by a Luigi Pagano, a 1950 Rolls Royce owned by W. Farnsworth, a prototype sports car belonging to the Chrysler Corporation. And, then, finally, there it was: a 1954 Mercedes Benz sedan belonging to Carl Ebner; Paris, France.

"Yes!" I said a little too loudly as I pumped my fist in the air. The librarian glanced over at us and pursed her lips.

"Well," Laura said. "That answers that mystery. Do you really think this will do us some good?"

I sat back in the chair and spoke quietly now. "Yes and no. It gives us a whole new area to concentrate the search. On the other hand, the garage is at the impact area pressed into the bottom deeper than any other part of the wreck. The cars, or what's left of them, are probably all stacked on top of each other, and picking through sunken cars is not something a diver can do without heavy equipment."

She looked at me for a minute before she spoke. I knew she wasn't happy with my assessment. "Erik, you're not going to give up on this, are you?"

The woman was like a bulldog. I rolled my eyes and sighed. "Laura, you're a gambler, sometimes you have to know when..." I stopped in mid-sentence. "Shit," again too loud. The librarian lowered her chin and glanced at us over her glasses. I mouthed the word "sorry" and felt like I was in junior high school again.

Laura smiled. "What are you thinking?"

"That it's time to get out of here before she calls security. I'll tell you outside."

I brought the microfilm back to the desk and tried to smile my way back into the good graces of the librarian. Luckily, she did have a sense of humor. She smiled back and said, "I hope that you found the information you were looking for?"

"Yes. Very helpful," I said. "Can I ask one more favor?"

"Of course. Provided you don't shout it."

Laura shook her finger at me and I looked admonished. "Tell me. I know that you keep records of each time these microfilms are requested. When was the last time someone asked for this one?"

She tapped into the computer and said, "Actually it was only a month ago. The first time in, let's see, eight years. Oh, and I see that the request included other documents."

"Really. Which ones?"

"Passenger manifest, schematics of the ship, underwater photos, and records of salvage operations."

I nodded. "Thank you, Linda. You've been a great help."

Back out on the steps of the library we conferred about what we now knew. The likelihood of the diamonds being hidden in Ebner's car was damn good, if not a sure thing. All our efforts so far—which included a near disaster with Mike LeClair—had been for nothing. And, maybe worst of all, Hajid and Gebhardt had beaten us to the punch and already gained access to the ship's garage.

Laura looked stunned. "I can't believe they know," she said.

"They're probably just guessing, like us. The point is, they guessed it before we did."

"What do we do now?"

"Don't worry, I'm not going fold now. I'll think of something. It might get a little hairy out there, but we are going back to the wreck."

She threw her arms around me and kissed me. "That's the kind of talk I like to hear. I can be ready to go anytime."

"I didn't say I was taking you with me," I said, holding her close.

She stepped back and looked at me like I was a lunatic. "There is no way that you are going without me," she said as she reached up and covered my mouth with her hand.

When she dropped her hand all I could say was, "That's what I was afraid of."

"Good. Don't worry about me, I am pretty used to taking care of myself. Oh, I'm going to call Marcel and give him the news."

Now I held out my hand and covered her cell phone. "Wait. I'd rather this stays just between us."

"You don't trust Marcel?" she said, and stepped back from me.

"I don't think it's worth taking any chances. I know you don't want to hear it, but Gebhardt and company heard about this whole business somewhere. So, I'm going to have to insist that we tighten our security. No one needs to know about this except us and my crew."

This time she saw that I meant it and she put the phone in her purse.

"We'll do it your way, Captain. But, how do you expect me to go on an expedition without letting the foundation know about it?"

"You just told me that you know how to take care of yourself, so I'll let you worry about that. I have to figure out a way for us to get out to the *Doria* before anybody knows we are there, and, also, how to sift through tons of rusting cars without using cranes."

By this time, we were in a cab and heading back downtown. "One thing you can do," I said. "You can call that number that Gino Bartolli gave you. Maybe that guy, Peter, can shine a little more light on this mess. It's unlikely, but worth a try."

"OK, let's try." She called the number and got his voice machine. "Hello, Mr. Scott. My name is Laura Morgan. I got your number from Gino Bartolli. I'm working on a project that involves the *Andrea Doria*. I wonder if you could call me back at this number. At your convenience, of course."

We were on the West Side Highway now and I looked out the window and watched a Moran tug lumbering down the river, its enormous props kicking up a frothy head of mocha water, red shards of setting sun crackling in its bow wave. Over near the Jersey side the little triangular sails of a fleet of sailing dinghies tacked back and forth. The water again. I checked my watch, it was after eight. The heat of day was fading and I was feeling restless.

When Laura got off the phone I told her that I was going to get on the road, but she put her hand on my arm and said she had every intention of taking me out to dinner. Against my weathered forearm, her hand looked pale and delicate.

"You don't have to wine and dine me. I promise you that the project is still on. Just as soon as I can figure out a better approach."

Laura looked at me and smiled. "That's not why I want to take you out to dinner. It's Friday night and I think we both need a little time to unwind."

"Unwind? Isn't that an old fashioned expression?"

"What makes you think that I'm not an old fashioned kind of woman? You know, long walks on beaches and sunsets?"

"Sounds like a Match.com date."

She laughed. "I guess it does, but do you know what the Long Island Expressway is going to be like now? You might as well stay in town awhile."

"You're probably right about that. I'll make you an offer. Dinner is at the restaurant of my choice and it's on me."

"Now that's a very old fashioned idea, but I like it."

●

When we pulled up in front of "Accabonne" in the West Village, Laura looked a little skeptical. "I don't want to sound like a cynical New Yorker, but I hope you know that a Friday night in this place has to be booked practically six months in advance, and even then they check your rating on the New York 'beautiful people' scale."

"I don't think there'll be a problem for you then," I said as I came around and held the door open for her. "Maybe they'll ignore my brutish looks."

She smiled at the compliment, but still looked doubtful as we walked through the doors of the busy restaurant. An officious looking maitre d'hotel checked out my boat shoes, khakis, and knit shirt, put on a phony smile and asked about our reservations.

I beamed my best smile back and asked, "Is Jason Ovington here?"

He began to puff himself up and started saying, "I'm sorry sir..." when a baritone voice came from a group of artfully dressed people standing at the crowded bar.

"Erik Hazen! I can't believe I'm actually seeing you here!"

Jason is a very slender guy in his mid-thirties. He looks like a male model, which he once was, and tonight he was dressed in a white linen suit over a black tee-shirt. He grabbed my hand, then threw his arms around me and kissed me on both cheeks while the maitre-d' looked crestfallen. "What on earth brings you into town?"

"Hi Jake. I guess you could say business." I turned to Laura and said, "I'd like you to meet Laura Morgan. Laura, this is Jason Ovington. He owns this chic establishment."

Ovington greeted Laura as if she were an old friend. "Laura, you know that by 'chic' Erik really means overpriced," he laughed, then lowered his voice. "But that is one of the secrets of success in Manhattan; you always have to allow people to spend their money."

"I'm happy to see you're doing so well, Jake."

"I'm doing fabulously well. They can talk all they want about the death of Wall Street, but you wouldn't know it from watching the crowds coming in here every night."

"I was hoping that you might have a table for us," I said.

"Of course I do!" Ovington turned to the sheepish maitre-d'. "Claude, give Mr. Hazen and Ms. Morgan table eighteen, over by the window." Then he turned to us again, "I'm sure you two want to be together. I'll stop over in a little while. I'm so thrilled you came by."

After we were seated at a marble-topped table with a view of the tree-shaded brownstones on Christopher Street, Laura looked at me. "You never cease to amaze me. What was that all about?"

"What? Do you think all of us Bonackers are just yokels with fish scales in our hair?"

She reddened a little but kept smiling. "No. Of course not. It's just that he treated you like a celebrity, or one of the family."

"I guess you could say he's family. Jake tends to be a little flamboyant, but underneath it all he's another clam digging Bonacker—another son of an old fishing family in East Hampton. He worked for a while in my boatyard when he was a kid, but I guess it wasn't' easy growing up gay in that atmosphere, so he went off to culinary school and became one of the real success stories out of Accabonac. Instead of selling his fish at the dock for fifty-cents a pound, he sells it here for sixty-dollars a serving. He and his partner Jerry have a big waterfront house on the stylish side of East Hampton now, and they've invited me to every party that they've ever thrown since moving in a few years ago. Actually, they've become somewhat legendary for their parties on the East End."

"And do you go?

"Not yet."

"Why not?"

"I don't know," I said, looking out the window. "Maybe I don't like going to parties alone." Laura was about to say something when I turned back to her and smiled. "Or, maybe I agree with Oscar Wilde's comment that it's always nice to be expected but not to arrive."

Laura laughed, and the waiter brought a bottle of chilled Perrier Jouet Champagne.

"Compliments of Mr. Ovington," he said, uncorking the bottle and pouring some into two tall flutes.

"Do you like oysters?" I asked.

"Love them. They taste of the sea."

"A woman after my own heart." I ordered a dozen Blue Points.

Then I held up my champagne glass. "This is going to be the last drink I have now that the expedition is back on. So. To our continuing venture."

Laura looked a little disappointed. "How about just, 'To us'? It's too lovely an evening to talk business."

My face felt a little warm as our eyes met. With her compact, delicate features and dark beauty, she didn't look anything like Kate, and I was happy for that. But, this was the first time since her death that I felt a genuine attraction to a woman—something beyond pure sexuality—and I didn't want to think that it was an attempt to recapture the past.

The restaurant was noisy and charged with energy and excitement in the way only a young, New York restaurant can be. The welcome coolness of the Provencal tiled floors combined with the clatter of ice cubes and the aroma of grilled fish and savory sauces made a nice contrast to the dusty twilight settling over the heated city streets outside. Dinner was grilled Montauk sea bass and Chesapeake Bay soft-shell crabs with tender asparagus tips and herb roasted potatoes. Dessert was a dense, flourless chocolate torte and a key lime pie both served with whipped Normandy cream.

Laura talked about her childhood growing up on the Upper West Side, her father a law professor at Columbia, her mother an artist of some local renown whose watercolors of street people juxtaposed over travel posters brought reactions that ranged from smiles to outright anger in the Bleeker Street gallery that represented her.

I talked about my own experiences growing up essentially fatherless; of my mother whose greatest strength was to endure tragedy after the death of my father after he drowned in a fishing accident off the Amagansett beach, and, eight years later, of my older brother who was killed in the first Gulf War. Also, of the profound influence that my grandfather had in teaching me to love the land and the water of the East End.

By the time the meal was finished we were both surprised to see that two hours had gone by. Ovington had stopped by several times and, finally, against all of my protests, insisted that the check had already been taken care of.

"I hope you're both going to be able to come to our 4th of July bash next week. Maybe I can count on Laura to drag you there, Erik." He winked at Laura and laughed.

"That's sweet of you to invite us Jason," Laura said. "I'll see what I can do."

"She might just be able to do that, Bub. But if we can't make it, I'll send my usual."

Ovington shook his head at Laura as if talking to a mother about a disobedient child.

"He doesn't come, but every year he sends a bushel each of little neck clams and blue point oysters. Of course, I'm usually stuck with the job of opening the damn things. But, you know something? I think they're usually the most popular dish at the party." Then he laughed graciously and hugged us both warmly.

We walked the few blocks over to the Hudson River Park, which stretches along the waterfront from Mid-Town to the Battery. The sun had been down for over an hour and a cooling breeze was coming up the harbor from the Atlantic. The promenade was pretty crowded with walkers, skaters, and bicyclists out to cool off and watch the river turn silver under a ¾ moon. Far down the bay, Lady Liberty was bathed in the green aura of spotlights and torch glow.

We walked past ball fields and dog runs and flower beds, while the big river swirled around pilings and lapped against the sea wall. At one point a cruise ship passed—its lights ablaze like an office building—going outbound, probably headed for Bermuda, or maybe just offshore for dinner and an evening of gambling.

"Back in the fifties that might have been the *Andrea Doria* headed out to Europe," I said. "She docked just up the river at the mid-town piers."

"Yes, I've seen the photos of her and the other ships, like the *Queen Mary* and the *United States* leaving the docks with bands playing. It must have been exciting to travel that way. Really part of a different era, wasn't it?"

I nodded. "You know, I can remember when this whole waterfront was nothing but broken down piers and shipping terminals. It may look a lot better now, but it's a shame that all that waterfront history has almost disappeared."

"New York isn't known for its commitment to history," Laura said. "Big money is the only thing that talks in this town. I'm just thankful they put a park here and not a parking lot for the minions of Wall Street."

"Amen to that. I'm no tree-hugger, but seeing the Hudson cleaned up makes me feel good. It's a great thing that New Yorkers are actually getting acquainted with the flow of tides and currents."

Laura laughed. "New Yorkers returning to nature? Is it possible?"

"Look over there." I pointed out to the river where a couple of kayakers were casting with fly rods. "Someday I might be running charters out of here," I said, only half kidding.

Before I knew it, we had walked past the World Financial Center and the Freedom Tower, through Battery Park City and into Battery Park itself at the tip of Manhattan Island. As a joke I suggested taking the ferry to Staten Island. But five-minutes later that's exactly what we did. We rode the outer deck of the lumbering ferry past the Statue of Liberty and through the twinkling array of small boat navigation lights across the dark harbor. Lovers huddled in corners and embraced against the rails as the lights of the city competed with the moon, and the sound of rushing water lent music to the scene.

I took Laura's hand while she looked at me wordlessly. "This is probably a good time to apologize for being an unappreciative bastard when you made that dive to check on us."

"I have to confess, you took me by surprise with that. I told you I've done a little diving. Plus, I was an ocean certified lifeguard for five summers when I was in college. You haven't taken a close look at these shoulders, have you?" she said, flexing.

"Impressive. I hope you don't want to arm wrestle now."

"What kind of girl do you think I am?" she said laughing as she punched me in the chest.

"I know you're not a delicate little thing. But ever since Kate's death I've been jumpy about seeing a woman underwater. I have nightmares about it. I guess when I saw you down there it brought it all back. I don't know if that sounds reasonable or not, but that's the way I felt."

Laura smiled. "You can't protect all the damsels in distress, you know, Sir Erik."

"I know. I just thought . . . Maybe the ones I really care for."

As the ferry slid neatly into the Staten Island slip, I put my arms around her and kissed her deeply. Her mouth was soft and yielding as she pressed herself into my body. We stayed that way for a few minutes.

"It seems that our relationship has gone through some wild changes lately," I said, smiling at her upturned face in the yellow glow of the halogen dock lights.

She smiled back. "It does seem that way, doesn't it? Are you worried about this new direction?"

"I wouldn't call it worried. I am a little nervous about it though."

"With all you've been through in life, you're worried about this?"

"You didn't know I was a worrier, huh?"

"I'm glad you are. It takes the pressure off me, because I like the direction we're headed in now."

The ferry bumped gently into the slip and we watched as a few people boarded from Staten Island. Hardly anyone got off, and in a few minutes we left Staten Island behind for the trip back to Manhattan. The muffled ring of Laura's phone came from her purse and when she answered it, it turned out to be Peter Scott returning her call. It took her a few minutes to explain who she was and that she wanted to talk to someone who had known her uncle on the *Andrea Doria*. He couldn't come into the city anytime soon, but if she were willing to take a ride out to Long Island he would be glad to talk to her at his house. She made an appointment for 10 A.M. the next day and hung up.

"I hope you didn't have any plans for leaving tonight?" she said as we approached the Battery.

"Now that you mention it, I was hoping that you might recommend a quiet little place in town where I can get a good night's rest," I grinned.

"The place I have in mind is quiet enough—at least for Manhattan—but I don't know how much rest you're going to get."

I put my arm around her and held her close as we walked off the ferry and into the terminal. "Look. It's barely past 11 P.M. and we've already had our first dinner date and gone on our first cruise. It must be true about things happening faster in New York."

She laughed as I took her hand and hailed a taxi to go uptown to her apartment on Central Park West.

CHAPTER SEVENTEEN

I WOKE UP TO MY USUAL BODY ALARM CLOCK AT 4:30 A.M. AND LOOKED ACROSS Central Park's shadowy darkness to a faint brightening in the eastern sky. Laura was turned towards me, asleep, with her head propped against my left elbow. She was naked, and in the half-light I admired her body as she breathed softly into the pillow. Her breasts were full and firm, and reflected the soft morning light in their whiteness, except the rosy nipples, which looked hard and erect even as she slept. Her left arm rested across her slender waist which curved upward into slender hips with just a trace of hip bone projecting beneath her silky skin before continuing along smooth thighs, half bent knees, slender ankles, and shapely feet with clear lacquered toenails.

I thought of our lovemaking the night before; of the natural way that I came into her and of how we anticipated each other's moves. The thoughts began to arouse me again as I felt myself stir and brush against her firm buttocks.

"I told you that you wouldn't get much rest," she said sleepily as she rolled over and cupped her body into mine.

●

By the time we had eaten a simple breakfast and taken a cab to pick up my truck it was past 8 AM. Another hot day was well under way. We sped through the Battery Tunnel and onto the Belt Parkway for the drive east to meet with Peter Scott. Past the Verrazano Bridge the gleaming waters of New York's lower bay opened into the shipping approaches from the Atlantic. The walkway along the seawall was lined with sweating joggers and hopeful fishermen waiting for the big one—even if it did come contaminated with PCB's, I thought sarcastically. The Southern State Parkway crossed marsh-dotted bays to Jones Beach, hooked up with the Ocean Parkway out to the Robert Moses Bridge to cross the Great South Bay.

"Beautiful, isn't it? This is one of my favorite drives," I said as Laura squinted into the sun over the bay where a few clam boats were silhouetted in the distance. "Fifty miles of road all in sight of water."

Laura looked at me and smiled. "That makes you happy, doesn't it?"

"Up to a point. But if Robert Moses got his way, back in the 1960's, this road would have continued along Fire Island and Westhampton all the way to Montauk with the ocean on the right," I said as we passed a few bay men wielding long-handled rakes from their clam boats. "Moses was finally defeated by a group of Fire Islanders who felt that sand dunes, bayberry bushes, and marshland were more important than roads and parking lots."

"From what I know of Moses," Laura said, "His favorite scene in nature was a concrete road disappearing across the horizon."

I laughed. "You know, the ironic thing is the 'great road builder' never learned to drive—had to be chauffeured on his own roads. But you're right; the concrete companies lost a big customer when he left office."

When we got to Bellport Village it was still before 10 A.M. The little south shore village looked prosperous and quaint with its lanes of colonial style houses and white picket fences that ended at Great South Bay. The address that Peter Scott had given her was on a low bluff overlooking the sparkling bay towards Fire Island. I saw right away that the house was old, probably late 19th-century, elegantly simple and lovingly cared for. The driveway curved around a big copper beech tree where I parked the truck in the shade.

A very tall, elegantly attractive woman who wore her gray hair in a long braid answered the door. She was wearing a painter's smock, liberally spattered with oil paints, and she was barefoot.

"You must be Laura Morgan," she said, smiling pleasantly.

Laura smiled back. "Yes. And this is my friend, Erik Hazen."

"I'm pleased to meet the both of you—come in. I'm Marie Scott, Peter's wife. Peter is expecting you; he's working in the back room today. It's a little cooler there and the paint fumes from my studio won't knock you out." She led us through the house, which was decorated with good antiques and eclectic artworks that ranged from 19th-century seascapes to postmodern epoxy constructions. "You'll have to excuse my appearance, I'm in the middle of doing a large canvas, trying to finish it before the 4th of July show." As she said this we passed a sky-lighted studio with a canvas the size of a kitchen table resting on it.

I was about to ask about her art when we came to a small, sunlit office and Mrs. Scott was introducing Laura to a robust, bearded man in his sixties sitting behind a laptop.

"And this is her friend, Mr. Hazen. That was Erik, wasn't it dear?"

"Yes, please call me Erik. How do you do Mr. Scott?"

Instead of getting up, the man wheeled out from behind the desk in a wheelchair and extended his hand to both of us. "I'm doing just fine," he answered in a voice that was friendly and jovial. "I'm really pleased to meet the both of you. Call me Peter, and have a seat over there," he said, pointing to a small leather couch near a window that overlooked the bay.

"There's some freshly brewed iced tea on the table there," Marie said as she turned to leave. "If anyone needs anything else, I'll be in the studio. Just give a yell."

"I really appreciate your giving up the time to meet with us," Laura said to Scott after his wife had left.

"It's my pleasure. You must have heard from Gino Bartolli that the *Andrea Doria* is one of my obsessions." He paused seeing me glance at his legs. "No, no! The *Doria* didn't take my legs off. They're attached, as you can see, though they're of damn little use except as something to make a lap for my laptop. Ironically, after surviving a shipwreck, I came down with polio. My doctor still tells me that if I lost weight and spent the better part of every day in physical therapy I might be able to walk with canes. But I like to eat well and I always did prefer a good set of wheels for getting around," he chuckled as he poured some iced tea.

"I admire your upbeat attitude," I said taking a sip of the tea.

"Hell, life is too short as it is to spend much time feeling sorry for yourself," he said and turned to Laura. "But tell me, Ms. Morgan, Carl Ebner was your uncle and he has passed away?"

"Yes. Just last month. Uncle Carl was ninety-six."

"I'm sorry. You know; I haven't seen Mr. Ebner since that night in 1956. Of course I know about his good works with the foundation he created. Over the years I've tried to keep in touch with as many people as possible, but a lot of the survivors are gone now. Our annual reunion once had as many as 150-survivors, but I was never able to get your uncle to attend."

"I think that's because of the way my Aunt Sara died on the ship; he was never able to come to terms with it."

"Yes, I know. But it is a shame I was never able to thank him properly for saving my life."

"Gino told us that you've never said how Uncle Carl saved you."

"I haven't told anyone that part of my story. Not even my parents. It was surrounded by such mystery and danger that I never wanted to say anything without first hearing Mr. Ebner's explanation. But I never was able to ask him."

"This is sounding more and more like a mystery," Laura said.

"Doesn't it? And mystery is my business. Have you ever read one of my books? Max Evans is the detective in all eighteen of my novels."

Laura's eyes brightened and she looked up excitedly. "Of course! Now I know why your name sounded familiar. I love the Max Evans series. He's one of the few really smart detectives in fiction."

"Well thank you. I'd love to put old Max to work on Mr. Ebner's case, but I always felt it was a little too personal to write a novel about it."

I sat back on the couch and crossed my legs. "Maybe, with your help, we'll be able to play his part and solve the mystery."

"Ah, but you don't look like Max," Scott said chuckling. "He's built more like me: more of a Falstaff than a Prince Hal."

We laughed and Scott drank his iced tea in one draught.

"We'd love to hear your story, Peter," Laura said turning serious. "My uncle died with a secret that he never fully revealed. One that—if misunderstood—could ruin the reputation of the Voyage Home Foundation and poison all the good that he did in his lifetime."

Scott looked both of us over. "Well, that does sound like a Max Evans mystery," he said rubbing his hands together. "I guess you should settle back and listen to the tale. I've never actually told this part to anyone, but I'll try to make it short. Of course, you have to remember, I'm a novelist, not a short story writer," he joked.

"I have to start the story the day before the sinking. It was the night of the farewell party and I was feeling bored being around adults for so long. I was out on the 1st-class pool deck, which was almost deserted because it was close to dinner. I hated getting all dressed, and after five days on the ship and three weeks in Italy I was also tired of the continental food. Anyway, what I was really thinking about was how I'd like to have a Coney Island hot dog with yellow mustard, a cup of salty fries, and a cold YooHoo. Also, I was thinking about my friends in Brooklyn Heights and how they would probably be playing handball in the park. All in all, I was feeling pretty homesick and the big propellers kicking up foam out beyond the ship's fantail couldn't push us toward home fast enough.

"That was the summer I turned fifteen. They had had a big birthday party for me on the ship two days before. My parents had surprised me with a cake in the shape of a car. It was supposed to be a brand new '56 Chevy, but whoever made it got the side panel design wrong and it wound up being a '55. Cars were my passion that year. I had more than fifty scale models at home, and I was looking forward to September when the new models were usually released. 1957 would be the year of the tail fins, I knew.

"Anyway, my daydreams were interrupted by Gino Bartolli. He was a young guy then and he had this pretty thick Italian accent. I got a kick out of Gino. I wasn't sure if I should believe everything he told me—he claimed to have driven a Ferrari that belonged to a customer of his brother's auto shop in Genoa at over 200 KPH—but he made me laugh with his stories and he was the only adult I knew that actually listened to Elvis Presley's songs.

Scott stopped talking for a minute to take a drink of iced tea. "I hope I'm not getting carried away with the reminiscence. I just want you to see everything in context."

"No, go ahead," Laura said. "The story is fascinating."

"Well, I guess he saw that he was cheering me up a little, but he wanted to do better, so, the next thing I know, he's telling me that he knows I'm a car lover and he wants to show me something that is very secret, but I have to promise not to tell anybody about it. I couldn't imagine what he was talking about, but I was intrigued.

"We went four flights down the stairwell to B-deck and then walked the length of a city block through the ship where we stopped at a set of double doors. Gino swung open one door and flipped a light switch. Lights flooded a cavernous room where a bunch of automobiles were parked close together.

"I couldn't believe it. I didn't know there was a garage on the ship. I remember most of the cars were European—mostly newer models— but there was a white Cadillac, which was the twin of our own family car, and there was a fancy Mercedes coupe and a huge maroon and black Rolls Royce.

"Gino ignored all of them and walked over to something low slung that was covered with a tarp. He untied the tarp and peeled it back to reveal the swept-back, silver body of a two-seater sports car that looked like something out of Buck Rogers. My eyes must have bugged out at the gleaming chrome and aluminum-bodied car with gull-wing doors, huge tail fins, and wide racing tires.

"The word "cool" had just come into use among teenagers then, and I must have used it a dozen times in the next few minutes walking around the car. I never saw anything like it.

"Gino told me it was an experimental car built for Chrysler in Italy by Ghia. He bragged that Italians understood how a car should look. All I wanted to do was get in a sit behind the wheel, but Gino would have none of that. He claimed that the car cost $150,000.00 and that he would lose his job if we were caught tampering with it. So, after a few minutes we covered it again and I remember telling Gino that this was the car I wanted when I got my license in a couple of years. He winked and told me that I better get a very good job."

Peter paused in the story again. "Help yourself to some of Marie's cookies. She's almost as good a baker as she is an artist." He slipped a large chocolate chip cookie onto a plate and sat munching it a minute before he continued.

"Now I'll skip ahead to the night of the collision. It was somewhere between 9 and 10 P.M. Dinner was over and most of the adults were gathered in the Belvedere Lounge having drinks and listening to the ship's band play Arivederci Roma for about the millionth time. I was sitting over in the corner by myself getting a little drunk from the Canadian whiskey I had snuck into my coke at the bar.

"Then I remembered that one of my birthday gifts had been a portable radio, which I hadn't had a chance to try out yet because we were too far from land. But now that we were getting close to New York, I thought maybe if I took it out on deck I might be able to get some music.

"It wasn't until I got outside that I realized how bad the fog was. The promenade deck was enclosed by big, brass framed windows, but a couple of them were open so you could look down and see dark ocean sliding by, but not much else, except the big lifeboats that hung just outside under the glare of floodlights.

"I got some rock and roll on the radio but it was still mostly static. That's when I got the idea to go to get a better look at that sports car

"There wasn't much security in those days so I was able to make my way to the garage, get in, and pull the tarp off the Chrysler—now I remember—it was called the 'Norseman'. With a name like that it's no wonder that it never made it to production. Anyway, there were no lights on when I came into the garage but the emergency lights had enough of a glow to see by. I got the driver's door up, slipped behind the wheel and closed the door. My word, it was like being in a rocket ship. If you have ever been in a 1950's car, you know how basic they were. This was nothing like that. It even had seat belts!"

Laura and I both laughed. "Advanced technology in those days," I commented.

"Yes. Anyway, I was just admiring everything in the car when the garage lights came on. I really panicked, thinking that it was ship's security, or—even worse—my father!

"I ducked down and listened to footsteps, which echoed on the steel deck as they came closer. I heard the garbled voices of two men and then the opening of a car door. I couldn't tell what was being said, but the voices were definitely angry. Once I realized that it wasn't my father or a security guard, I raised my head to see what was going on.

"Two men—one tall with dark hair and an athletic build, the other shorter, slighter, and blonde—seemed to be arguing over something having to do with the car they were standing next to. It was the Mercedes coupe parked right in front of the Chrysler. Of course, I didn't know it then, but the tall one was Mr. Ebner. But, at that moment, it was the other one who caught my attention. He turned into the light and I could see his face—almost lizard-like—and he was holding a gun.

"Werner Hutt," I blurted out, as Laura grabbed my arm and muttered, "Oh, my God."

"You know him?" Scott asked.

"Only by reputation," I said. "Please continue."

"Well, then I felt the car suddenly swing to the left; it took a few seconds before I realized that the ship had turned, not the car. When I looked back up I saw the movement had thrown the gunman off balance and he was leaning against the Rolls parked next to the Mercedes. Mr. Ebner had been thrown against him and now they were struggling for the gun. Mr. Ebner was holding the gun arm with one hand and punching the blonde guy viciously with the other. I saw the gun knocked loose and the blonde guy break away and chase it to where it had slid across the floor over by the starboard bulkhead.

"And then, the most incredible thing happened. An experience that I'll remember in detail until the day I die. First, there was a thunderous explosion along with an earthquake-like shuddering of the entire garage. Then, I watched the whole side of the garage—the starboard bulkhead—burst open in a floor to ceiling split, and a solid wall of twisted, jagged steel pushed towards me, crushing cars as it came. It must have happened in seconds, but it seemed like slow motion as it came towards us. Arcing flares of gigantic sparks ricocheted off the walls and ceiling like a berserk fireworks display, along with clouds of white smoke.

"I was frozen in place watching a mangled body—it must have been the blonde guy— hanging from the moving steel and spurting blood against the passenger window before smoke blocked my view. I felt the car rock and get heaved sideways as it was pushed against the inner bulkhead and crushed.

"Just when I thought I was about to die, the wall of metal reversed itself. I felt the car released from its grip. The rending screech of metal was deafening and I couldn't hear anything except someone screaming, and it was me."

We looked at each other as Peter stopped and poured more iced tea.

"This is an amazing story," I said, shaking my head. "It's a miracle that you survived it."

"Miracle? Yes, I would say so. But without Carl Ebner, I wouldn't have made it that night."

"Uncle Carl saved you?" Laura asked.

"I couldn't get the driver's door open. Damn gull-wing thing. It was wedged against another car that had butted up against it as the ship heeled over. Where the passenger door had been there was nothing but a void. As the smoke cleared I saw lights outside the ship reflecting off the surface of the ocean. Where the garage wall had been there was now a ragged opening in the ship's side with everything tilted towards it. I tried banging on the door and yelling as loudly as I could. I held onto the wheel because I was afraid that if I let go I'd fall through the passenger door and out into the black water below. I was wishing I had obeyed my parents and gone to bed when they told me, and that got me to thinking about my parents and if they were all right, and if the ship was going to sink. The hole was huge and the whole ocean seemed to be pouring in.

"This went on for a minute that seemed like hours. I was starting to wonder what it would feel like to drown. All the time I was screaming. Then I heard a voice from outside. I turned and saw a face up close to the driver's window. It was your Uncle Carl. There was no way he could open the door. He told me to duck down because he was going to break the windshield. I kept my hands on the steering wheel but curled my body on the seat until I heard the window smash. I sat up and felt arms reaching in and pulling me out.

"The next thing I knew, I was half standing, half crouching in a narrow space between cars, my shoes filled with water, and the gushing sound of the ocean pouring in around the ruined bulkheads. I could barely see Mr. Ebner through the smoke and dim light. I asked him what happened and he told me that we had been hit by another ship. I asked him if we would sink and he said that we probably wouldn't because the ship was built to survive accidents. He said that he was sure the captain had everything under control. Just follow me, he said, and we'll get out of here.

"It took us a while to get out of the garage. The ship was so tilted and the deck was so slick with oil and water that we had to crawl out in the half dark. I was afraid I'd lose my footing and slide right out the hole, but Mr. Ebner held on to me until we got into the passageway where everything was chaotic. Mr. Ebner spoke Italian and tried to tell everyone to stay calm as we made our way up, but, by then, the ship was listing so badly that I don't think he really believed it could stay afloat.

"Anyway it took us about twenty minutes, but we did make it to the staterooms. I guess Gino told you all about the scene there?" Peter said, once more looking up at his small audience.

"Yes, he did," Laura answered. "He told us how you wanted to go back to the garage to get a jack for my uncle. You did a heroic thing."

"I only wanted to help. I owed him my life."

"That's a hell of a story, Peter," I said. "How did you finally get off the ship?"

"Gino helped me climb down a rope ladder from the stern. A lifeboat from the *Ile de France* picked me up. So, I have two people to thank for saving my life. I've already been able to do that with Gino, but I never saw Mr. Ebner again."

"And your parents?" Laura asked.

"Luckily, they were still at the party when the collision happened. They were picked up by a lifeboat from the *Stockholm*—the ship that hit us. We were reunited back in New York."

"This has been quite an education," Laura said. "I think that you just confirmed something that we were just guessing at before."

"That Mr. Ebner's secret had something to do with a car?"

I exchanged glances with Laura before she answered. "Yes, the car must be the key. I wish I could tell you more, Peter, but I guess the *Andrea Doria* will just have to keep its secret now."

Peter gave both of an odd look. "Ah, you're assuming that the car is on the ship," he said, smiling.

Laura said, "I don't quite understand what you mean."

I felt like a jolt of electricity hit me. A sudden wave of comprehension must have crossed my face. "Are you telling us that the car is no longer inside the *Doria*?"

"That's right. At least, I don't think so. The Mercedes was close to the bulkhead that the *Stockholm* pierced. I was staring at the hole for a long time after the accident. It probably didn't dawn on me at the time, but when I thought about it afterwards, I realized that the Mercedes was gone."

Damn! I never thought of that. But, of course, it made sense, the gash in the hull was wider than a barn door. There must have been a load of cargo scattered across miles of ocean as the ship listed deeper into its wound. I couldn't mask the excitement in my voice. "Then it's sitting by itself on the bottom out there, maybe miles from the wreck site."

Scott nodded. "The *Andrea Doria* drifted for over ten hours before it finally sank."

Laura turned to me. "Do you think it would still be there after all these years?"

I smiled. "The way Germans build cars? I don't have any doubt about it. It's just a matter of finding the right bump on the bottom."

I stood and shook Scott's hand. "I want to thank you for clearing up a big part of this mystery, Peter. You just made our quest a lot more likely to succeed."

"Well I wish both of you luck. And if you succeed, I'd love to have you come and speak to our group of survivors before we're all gone. I hope the mystery will be solved by then."

Laura also stood and shook his hand. "I promise you we will. But, until then, please don't say anything about this to anyone."

Peter wheeled himself out of the room and called his wife as we followed. "You have my word on that. No one's known my secret for over fifty years. I'm not about to get chatty about it now."

Marie Scott appeared— even more paint spattered than before—to see us out.

We got into the truck and I drove it down to the village dock to give me time to decide the next step. Laura had to get back to the city for at least a couple of days. I hoped that would give me time to put into action a plan that had been banging around in my head for the last few minutes.

"Erik, please tell me that this is going to be a good thing for us."

"It's going to be a good thing for us," I said, poker faced.

She poked me in the ribs. "How?"

I let the truck idle with the A/C going. "First of all, the best piece of news is that the bad guys don't have a clue."

"Are you sure about that?"

"I am for now. They beat us the first time by going to the records and guessing that the car is the best place for the gems to be hidden. Before the weather chased them back in they were intent on getting into the garage. I'd be willing to bet that the reason they haven't got back out yet is that they are rigging some kind of crane lift so that they can start pulling cars out of the wreck one at a time. Assuming that there are still some cars in there, that's going to give us time to search for the Mercedes that is not where it is supposed to be."

"But, how will you do that?"

"Side scan sonar. I've used it before and now the technology is even better. A good operator can locate something the size of a toaster. A car body should be no problem. Of course, it does raise some new problems," I said and paused and looked out the window as I considered some possibilities.

Laura got impatient and grabbed my arm. "Well? What new problems? Spit it out."

I looked back at her and rubbed my chin. "Well, for one thing, we're going to need a bigger boat."

She started to ask more questions but I put the truck in gear and pulled out of the parking lot. "I've got some work to do and I know you need to get back to the city, so I'm bringing you to the train station to save some time. I'll call you tonight and give you a heads up on what the new plan is. Meanwhile, nothing said to anyone, and that includes the lawyer."

She frowned. "Do you really think that's necessary?" she said.

"You know I do. After all that's happened we can't trust anybody. It's a mystery how Gebhardt and Hajid know what they know. Let's not screw up now."

Laura sighed. "All right, Erik. I'm not saying anything and I'll wait to hear from you later. Please call as soon as you know something."

"I will," I said as I leaned over and kissed her lightly. The train was already sitting at the Patchogue station and she ran to jump on board.

CHAPTER EIGHTEEN

ON THE DRIVE EAST I WAS SOON IN AFTERNOON TRAFFIC HEADED FOR WHAT tourists call "The Hamptons", which is really several old farming and fishing villages on the South Fork of Long Island's east end. Of course, most of the farms and a lot of the fishing access has long been replaced by oversized houses, golf courses and marinas. The villages have gone from "bucolic" to "quaint" to "downtown chic" in two generations. Potato barns have given way to BMW dealer-ships; hardware stores are now coffee bars.

At the Riverhead turnoff I headed north and left most of the traffic behind. I was on the road to the north fork of Long Island's two forked east end instead. Now that Scott's information had changed the goals of the expedition, I needed a whole new game plan. So I headed for the still active fishing village of Greenport. Bob Dylan was playing "Like a Rolling Stone" on the Sirius station, and the coolness of the truck's air conditioning was pleasant while the thermometer registered 97 outside. Some modern changes are good, I have to admit.

As I drove past the vineyards, wineries, and farm stands of the North Fork, my thoughts jumped back and forth between the new relationship with Laura and the strategy I was going to have to use to find the gems now without alerting Hajid and his group. The expedition was the easier one to solve: I knew where to get a side-scan sonar and I had a pretty good idea of whose boat I wanted to use.

The relationship was another matter. As a boat designer and builder I worked for a lot of wealthy, weekend people: the kind that live on twenty-million dollar estates fronting the ocean in any one of the Hamptons. I'm also pretty well traveled, and, I like to think, culturally enlightened. But, I'm still a proud Bonacker at heart. I still have the native East Ender's habit of treating "city people" with suspicion and a degree of disdain. It's a kind of reverse snobbery that a lot of us threatened locals use as a defense against the encroachment of change. So, Laura had at first seemed a typical pampered Manhattanite: high strung and overly controlling, using wads of money to get the local yokels to sit up and perform. But that impression was gone, and, in fact, seemed ludicrous as I thought of the strong willed, intelligent woman who was working for a truly worthy cause—a cause that transcended selfish interests.

She was gutsy, and strong, and beautiful too. I kept seeing that vision of her as she swam down to us through twenty-feet of ocean water to check on me and Mike. I know I was a jerk for chastising her, even though I did it for her safety. But who the hell am I to prevent her from doing anything? The big diving expert who couldn't even save his own wife from drowning?

The idea of falling for her both scared and exhilarated me. I looked out at the wineries whizzing by and wished I could have a drink.

When I got to Greenport's main street I turned right and parked in a lot next to a commercial fishing dock.

The boat I headed for was a squat and powerful ocean trawler with a white superstructure and a steel hull painted kelp green down to a white bootline stripe. It was fifty-five feet long and its name, *Prowler*, was painted in big white letters across the high bow. Smaller letters on its rounded stern said, *Greenport, N.Y.*

I stepped off the dock onto the hot steel deck between the big engine compartment doors, which were propped open. Down below, the raspy voice of Johnny Cash, accompanied by the clank of tools, came echoing out of the depths.

I shaded my eyes and looked into the port compartment. "Hey Bub!" I yelled. "Can you knock off the noise down there? You're scaring the fish for us tourists."

A string of expletives followed by a shaggy blonde head and a round, red face framed by an old time whaler's beard, sans mustache, appeared above the deck. "Goddamn, Erik Hazen!" the head said, breaking into a wide grin and merging with a pair of heavy shoulders and muscular, grease smeared arms. "What brings you slumming over to this side of the Island, Bub?"

"Just checking to see if Mrs. King's son still knows how to fish. How're you doing Fletch?"

"Fishing sure as hell ain't what it used to be," King said as he wiped his hands on a rag and swung his legs up out of the hold. Then he stood up and grabbed me in a bear hug. "But hell, you already know that."

"Yea, I guess we all do. What critters are you after this month?"

"The water's warmed up and we got some decent schools of squid coming inshore, otherwise the pickings have been pretty piss poor.

Damn few fluke and just a bare showing of weakfish. If we ever get the bass quota back up maybe we'd all be able to pay our bills again." He looked at my brown loafers and clean khakis. "What are you this month, Bub, a fisherman or a boating executive?"

I laughed. "Neither one. Can you believe I'm working on a dive project?"

King squinted in the brightness and moved into the shade of the wheelhouse. "Not the *Doria* again?" he said.

"Yes and no. That's what I came to talk to you about, Fletch. I need a boat."

Lester scratched his head and furrowed his brow. "Yes and no and the man needs a boat? You're starting to sound awful mysterious. What's the matter with the *Finest Kind*? You're not in some kind of trouble, are you?"

"Not in trouble yet. That's why I need your boat. I'm trying to stay out of trouble," I said. That just added to King's confusion. "Look, Fletch, I'm sorry to have to be so spooky, but I can't let anybody see the *Finest Kind* out near the Doria wreck. Trust me. I need a commercial boat that's going to look like it's hauling net for squid or fluke or whatever. But I need it rigged for diving and hauling salvage. And I need it by this weekend. The project might take a week or two. Might take less or it might take more. The money will be good: double what you can make hauling squid, a lot less work, and a big bonus if we come up with the prize. What do you think?"

King wiped sweat out of his eyes with the back of his hand. "I think we ought to get a cold beer or an iced tea up at Claudio's and figure out what I've got to do to this tub to get it ready."

"Iced tea sounds good," I said. Even I couldn't make that lie sound very convincing.

CHAPTER NINETEEN

It was only 5-P.M. when we walked into the bar at Claudio's. A few couples were eating at the tables, but the bar was already humming with commercial fishermen types, sun seared and dressed in faded dungarees with fish stained tee shirts. King and I went into the back and sat in a quiet booth to discuss the modifications he would have to make on his boat to set it up for dragging a sonar "fish" instead of heavy nets. I ordered a couple of dozen cherrystone clams for us and then sat topping them off with fresh horseradish and black pepper as I watched little beads of sweat drip down the sides of King's frozen mug of pilsner beer. The iced tea was bitter.

We were done with the plans and just talking about the latest miserable state of the commercial fishing business when King's phone rang and he rolled his eyes as he listened to the grocery list his wife was apparently giving him.

"Gotta go, Bub," he said after he finished listening. "A week or two at sea sounds like a pretty good deal right now," he joked.

I laughed, and thought, how easy it is for a woman to bring a big boat captain back to earth with a phone call. "You go ahead. I'm going to take care of this tab and I'll give you a call tomorrow."

"Don't worry, we'll be good to go in two days," he said as he slid out of the booth and walked out past the bar.

I sat for a few more minutes after paying the check, enjoying the cool air and wishing that iced tea had a little more of a kick, when I saw a familiar figure sit down at the bar. Zeke Tredia is hard to miss. He was wearing a camouflage jump suit and a safari hat. His flying business mainly focuses on bringing weekend people from South Street Seaport to the Hamptons. But, he affects the bush pilot image. He also likes clients to think he flew in Vietnam, but I know that he was an airplane mechanic there, not a pilot. A hero in his own mind. Still, I like the guy.

On my way out I tapped him on the shoulder. He turned on the barstool and did a double take. "Captain Erik! What brings you over to this side of the island?"

"I could ask you the same thing, Zeke," I said as I reached over for a fist bump. "I just had to pick up a couple of spare props for my boat."

"Yeah, I heard that you had some kind of a problem a couple of weeks ago when you left for that charter. What happened?"

I don't know how much Tredia knew but I wasn't about to give away any information about it. "A goddamn steel cable got caught up in my props. Probably fell off the deck of one of the draggers. Sticking up just enough for me to snag it. Just bad luck."

Tredia looked thoughtful. "Too bad," he said. "I just brought this Southampton couple over here to meet their friends on that big-assed yacht out there," He pointed to the outer dock where the gleaming hull of a 120-foot yacht was tied. Crewmen in white shirts stood by its boarding ramp. Its tender boat mounted on davits was bigger than some of the fishing boats in the marina.

"These rich people are something else," he continued. "That couple could have taken the ferry over from Shelter Island, but they'd rather pay me five hundred bucks to fly them over. Hell, I'm not complaining. Buy you a drink?" he added.

"Thanks, Zeke. Another time. I've got to get back to Montauk now," I said. "I'm glad business is good for you, though."

"It is. By the way. I brought a couple of guys from the city out to Montauk yesterday. They're chartering the *White Shark II*. What's going on with that?"

I played dumb. "Going on with what?"

"Manson's boat. There's a big tarp over the stern and there was some welding going on under it."

I wasn't really surprised so my face didn't register any reaction. "Damned if I know. What did your clients say they were doing?"

Tredia sneered. "Those guys? Hell, they don't say anything. Not even to each other. The older one is a thin-lipped scary looking bastard with a smile that looks like Hannibal Lecter, and the big guy looks military—and I don't mean our military," he said, then added, "And he's packing. Can't hide that in this weather."

"Well, in our kind of business' you can't always choose your clients, can you?" I said as I started to walk away.

"Hey, Erik. How did it go with that woman that I brought out to you a couple of weeks ago? Is she still working on that documentary?"

"Not on location." I said. "I think she got all the footage she needed. And I'm finally finished with *Andrea Doria* business."

"Too bad. I was hoping she would get a few shots of me flying her around. I always wanted to be in the pictures."

I laughed as I left. I'm sure you do, I thought.

CHAPTER TWENTY

I WAS SITTING IN MY TRUCK ON THE SHELTER ISLAND FERRY AS IT MADE THE 10-minute crossing to Sag Harbor when my phone rang. It was Laura. Her voice sounded scared and shaky.

"Erik. Something terrible has happened," I could hear her voice tremble and heard some commotion in the background.

"Take a couple of deep breaths first. Then tell me what happened," I said, then added, "Are you okay?"

I heard her breathe before she answered. "I'm okay. My secretary, Nora, isn't. Erik, someone sent me a package—actually a padded envelop. It was a bomb! It blew up in the office!" I heard her break off and sob.

I tried to calm her down but there was no answer. "Laura. Are you still there," I repeated a few times.

Finally she came back on the phone. "Erik, I'm talking to the police now. I'll call you back."

"Is your secretary hurt badly?"

"Yes. They think she will live, but her hands. . ." she sobbed again.

"Okay. Do what you have to do there and I'll drive in to the city."

"No. Don't do that Erik. I'd rather be there. I have to get out of this city. Today, I'll have to close down the office after the police finish—it may take weeks to clean up and remodel. Tomorrow I'll be at the hospital until I'm sure Nora is going to recover. I'll stay at my mother's apartment tonight. Sometime tomorrow I'll take the train out to East Hampton." She paused. "That is, if you don't mind having a guest."

"Only if you don't mind staying on the rough side of town," I said, and heard her laugh a little. "Call me from the train and I'll pick you up at the station."

"I will. And Erik, please be careful. These people are out to win at any cost."

By the time we hung up the ferry had docked. It is about a twenty minute drive up through Sag Harbor and the back road to my house. I thought about the salvage operation as I drove. Since we hadn't called it off, the crew was still on the payroll. Mike LeClair was back in

Brooklyn nursing his wounds, but Johnson, Roebling, and Gonzales were still staying in a motel near the dock in Montauk. Now this latest incident in Manhattan had to be factored into our plans. I decided to call and have them meet me at my house in the Springs. People that talk on phones while they're driving piss me off so I didn't get into the story of what had happened in the city yet. I just wanted a meeting of the minds.

It was near dusk when I pulled into my driveway. Everything was quiet. Just the fluid trill of a pair of cardinals in the big swamp maple. Just the way I like it.

Before driving up to the house, I stopped and checked my mailbox. I can't say I was really surprised when I saw the padded, brown envelop tucked in with the junk mail. I stepped back and looked around, trying to use all my senses to make sure no one was hiding somewhere with a cell phone or some other type of triggering device. Then I thought, hell, why bother? They could just as easily have a sniper in the woods to take me out cleanly.

Still, I wasn't about to take the chance. It's never a sure thing to try to outguess fanatics. You just have to stay one move ahead. So, I left the mail in the box and went up to the house.

The cat greeted me with purring as he rubbed up against my leg. "Hang on, Bub. As soon as I take care of business you'll get some fresh bluefish. I don't want you eating any mockingbirds."

I'm not a big gun guy. When I was in the Navy I shot just about every weapon that they make, but, as a civilian, I never had the need to fool with them much. But, my grandfather, Captain Jack, used a double barreled Parker, twelve gauge, for duck hunting and I still keep it above the fireplace as a memento. I hauled it down, found an old box of shells in the kitchen cabinet, dropped two into the chambers, and walked back outside.

I was coming down the driveway with the shotgun over one shoulder when Roebling's Outback pulled in. Book Johnson emerged and confronted me holding his big mitts up, palms out.

"Whoa, brother! I know you ain't happy about all the shit that's gone down, but you ain't going to go and do a Hemingway, are you?"

Roebling and Gonzales stood behind him looking puzzled.

"I thought you knew me better than that by now, Book. Just stand aside and watch." Then I added, "In fact, everybody get back by the truck."

Before anybody could protest, I snapped the barrels of the shotgun closed and turned to aim it at the mailbox. I pulled the trigger twice and discharged both barrels almost simultaneously. The mailbox ripped open and mail flew out of both ends like confetti. But, there was no explosion.

"Holy shit!" Roebling said. "You shot your mailbox!"

I snapped the gun open and ejected the smoking shells. I was grinning a little sheepishly.

"Yeah," I said, as I walked over to the ruined box and picked up the remains of the padded envelop. "I thought there was a bomb in it." The shredded envelop was wet. It contained a free sample of a new mouthwash.

Johnson burst out laughing and that got Gonzales and Roebling going too. "Hey," Johnson said, as he reached one arm out to me in glee, "I know people don't like junk mail, but you got to focus your anger better, brother."

"I think the season on mailboxes is closed now, isn't it?" Roebling said smiling, and then added when he looked at me holding the dripping mess, "That's got to be one powerful mouthwash."

"Maybe the man's just loco," Gonzales said, half seriously.

"Okay, wiseasses." I said. "I'm glad I could amuse you, but let me put a serious note on this party. Come on into the house."

After I told them about the letter bomb that Laura's secretary had opened they lost their sense of humor about my cautious escapade.

"You don't think it could be related to something else?" Roebling asked.

"I haven't had a chance to talk to Laura yet in any detail. So, I'm not positive. But it would be too much of a coincidence for it not to be a job done by our competition."

Johnson spoke up. "So that posse tried to scuttle our boat, bury us in the wreck, and now try to blow up our lady. I don't know about you guys, but I'm about ready for some pay-back time."

"I am too, Book," I said. "That will come in time. But, we aren't going to do anything stupid. In spite of their political bent, these people are smart, organized, and well trained. I doubt that the cops will be any use in this, so we proceed, but we do it with caution and, when the time comes, with extreme prejudice." I paused and looked at Roebling and Gonzales before I added, "Of course, I wouldn't blame anyone for dropping out. Our competition has pretty much decided the rules of engagement from here on out. It doesn't look like a fun in the sun diving trip anymore."

Roebling, who had bent down to scratch the cat's ears, stood up and spoke first. "If the project is on, I'm in. I can't stand skinheads and fanatics; and I hate cowards who send bombs in the mail. Those creeps need to be stopped one way or another."

"That goes for me, too," Gonzales said. "We Mexicans know enough about hate—we don't need people like that to spread more."

I looked at the three of them with the same kind of pride I used to feel for my SEAL team before we went into harm's way. "Good. Then it's decided. We will be going back out to finish what we started. But, we are going to go about it in a different way now."

They looked puzzled and Book spoke up. "What does that mean, brother?"

"That means that Laura and I found out some information this morning that changes the whole game plan."

It took me a few minutes to explain the story that Peter Scott had told us. I also explained the arrangements I had made with Fletch King. When I finished talking I asked if anybody had any input.

"What about weapons?" Book asked. "We know what to expect from this bunch now. If we meet them again, we need to be armed." Then he added, "Just call LeClair. That fucker's got more guns than Nicaragua."

Roebling and Gonzalez shook their heads in agreement.

I hated to admit it, but I couldn't argue the point. "Okay. I'll get in touch with LeClair. I hope he's feeling good enough in a few days to join us. He won't have to do any diving anyway."

We were all standing around in the kitchen and through the French doors the sun was setting on the marsh. The hoarse squawks of a great blue heron drifted up from the creek.

"There's some beer in the fridge. Help yourselves," I said.

"You drinking with us, brother?" Johnson asked.

"Only if you call seltzer-water drinking." I said. "I'm not drinking anything stronger until this job is done."

We spent the next half hour going over some of the plans. Part of the plan was for all three men to stay on the *Finest Kind* for now. I'm sure the boat was being watched and I didn't want to telegraph any change in plans yet. Let them think we were getting ready to go back out. I also told them to keep an eye on the activity on Manson's boat, but to do it quietly because I didn't want any unnecessary confrontation. I suggested that Roebling would be the best man for the job as he was least known around Montauk and wouldn't stand out as much.

"You telling us that I might stand out?" Johnson said, putting on his widest black man grin.

"Get the hell out of here now before I have to get that shotgun down again." I said.

CHAPTER TWENTY-ONE

LAURA CALLED THE NEXT MORNING. HER SECRETARY WAS RECOVERING AFTER surgery to re-attach three fingers; she was still deaf from the explosion and she had some bad burns on her upper body, but the doctors assured Laura that Nora should have a full recovery.

Her voice sounded steadier, but still a little shaky. "Erik, I feel guilty about this. That envelop was addressed to me personally. It came by bike messenger and it was marked 'confidential'. It looked like it came from the Simon Weisenthal Organization. I thought it must be the dossiers on both the Palestinian and neo-Nazi groups that I had requested. I was just about to open it when Marcel called me into his office for a conference call with a congressman from Florida who has been monitoring a piece of property in the swamps that looks like a terrorist training camp. Anyway, I dropped it at Nora's desk on the way out and told her to open it. Dear God!"

I heard her sob a little and felt the blood rise in my face as I pictured the creeps that were responsible. "Laura, it's not your fault. You know that. We are going to win this war and they are going to get what they deserve. I promise," I said, and thought to myself, payback will feel good.

"I hope you are right, Erik," she said. Then she added, "I really want to see you. I need to get out of town. Can I take the train out tonight and take you up on that sleepover?"

"I'd love it. I have to go over to Connecticut today to pick up some of the electronics we need for our new search. I'll take the New London ferry out of Orient Point at noon. Should be back by around five. See if you can get a train that gets in around then."

"Okay," she said, her voice sounding a lot more upbeat. "I'll be travelling light."

"Just bring your toothbrush if you want. We'll have dinner at a quiet little place I know on Three Mile Harbor."

"Sounds delightful. See you then."

After we hung up I made a couple of calls, one to Ballan Electronics in Mystic Connecticut where I could lease a side-scan sonar and a sub-bottom profiler, the other to Cross Sound Ferry to reserve a spot on the 10-am ferry to New London. Then I drove into town to get some coffee.

Just as I walked in my cell rang. It was Roebling. "Erik, I'm just on my way over to your place, I think I have something interesting."

"Good. There's a coffee shop, The Sweet Spot, on the highway right after the windmill. I'm there now."

"See you in ten minutes," he said.

I sat in a rear booth and sipped my coffee. Then I made another call to Laura. When she answered her cell I could tell she was in the middle of a meeting with the police. "Laura, I'll make this short. Did you mention the new information to anybody? Just say yes or no."

"No."

"Good. Does anybody know that you are coming out here tonight?"

When she answered I could tell that she had walked off to the side. Her voice was soft. "Only Marcel," she said. "He is going to be here to deflect the media. Why? Is anything wrong?"

"I don't know. Just a gut feeling. I'll tell you about it later. Meanwhile, say nothing."

I hung up and a few minutes later Roebling came in and slid into the booth. After the waitress poured his coffee, he leaned in close and spoke quietly."

"I did a little recon work this morning. I noticed that the dock where the *White Shark II* is berthed is closed off, so I couldn't wander down there looking like a curious fisherman. But, I remembered that there was a kayak in your boat storage shed so I figured an early morning paddle would feel good—all this waiting around is tedious—and maybe let me do a little spying. I was just getting into the kayak when this little, yellow float plane landed and taxied over towards Manson's boat."

"Zeke Tredia," I said. "He runs a flying service out of Manhattan."

"Yeah, that's what I figured because by the time I paddled to within a hundred yards of the boat he was at the dock there and his passengers were getting out. One was the big, bearded guy and the other one was the skinhead with the lightning bolt tattoos."

"Hajid and his inept sidekick."

"Right. Of course I haven't had the pleasure of their acquaintance, yet."

"Did you get any closer?"

"Oh, yeah. Kayaks are wonderful things. Nobody notices you much, low to the water, and you can go anywhere. The two men walked down the dock as the plane taxied back out on the bay. The *White Shark II* has a big canvas over the working deck so I kept that between me and the two guys as they boarded the boat. At first I couldn't hear anything because the plane was making such a racket, but after it took off I heard voices raised. Somebody wasn't happy with Hajid and lightning bolt."

"Did you see who it was?"

"No, but it was the voice of an older man. I don't think it was Manson because I heard his voice when we were out at the *Doria*."

"Gebhardt," I said. "Sounds like the old Nazi is trying to stay in charge. Could you tell what he was ranting about?"

"He was pissed that they botched the job in the city. I kinda figured it must have to do with. . ."

"The bombing," I interrupted. "Well, well. I guess that confirms what we already suspected."

"But, there was one more thing," Roebling continued. "They all seemed pissed at somebody else that might have gotten in the way. I heard the name, 'Feynard' mentioned. I don't know who he is, do you?"

I felt the blood drain out of my face. Of course! I had the feeling all along and it kept getting knocked down by Laura's trust of the lawyer. Now it was all clear. "Yes, I know who he is, all right," I said, looking across the booth at Roebling who was waiting for an answer. "If things weren't interesting enough before, they're going to get even better now," I said as I left money on the table and stood to go.

"I'm heading over to Connecticut to pick up the electronics we'll need. Just sit tight in Montauk for now. I'll call you later and let you know how we are going to proceed."

Roebling looked disappointed that he was going to have to sit around longer. He reminded me of myself when I was his age, always looking for the next piece of action. "Don't worry, we're getting back into the game real soon. I promise you that."

●

I was at the East Hampton train station at 6:15 that evening when Laura's train pulled in. As soon as she stepped off, I was glad to see her. She looked great in white, canvas pants with a plain, button down, short-sleeved shirt, and leather boat shoes. Her hair was pulled back with one of those big pincher kind of clips holding it in place. She carried a little overnight bag and she smiled and waved, but all I could think was 'oh shit' I have to tell her something that she is not going to like, and may not even want to accept.

"Oh, thank God, Erik. I'm out of that city. I couldn't take any more questioning from people," she said as we hugged in the parking lot and kissed a little shyly.

"I know just how you feel. I'm taking you to Lindy's on the Harbor for dinner. We can sit out on the deck if you want and watch the sunset."

"That's just what I need right now—a sunset, a glass of wine, and good food. The food is good, isn't it?"

"The finest kind," I said, and added smiling, "But you didn't say anything about the company."

She squeezed my arm and smiled back. "You crazy Bonacker," she said.

Two hours later, the sunset had been great, the grilled weakfish superb, her first and second glass of wine—in her words—'distinctive', and my sparkling water merely 'healthy'. I told her about Fletch King's boat, *Prowler*, and of the electronics I had brought to it today, and that the new operation would be ready to go very soon, but that it would be out of Greenport, on the North Fork instead of Montauk. She was in good spirits and seemed to be in agreement with everything, so I couldn't delay anymore and had to tell her what Roebling had heard.

It hit her hard. Disbelief, denial, anger. The whole range of emotions that go with hearing that a person you trusted has betrayed you. When she finally calmed down I held her hand across the table and spoke quietly. "Do you have any idea why Marcel had any connection with these people?"

She looked vulnerable and sad as she answered. "Marcel has been with the foundation for two years as our in-house attorney. In that capacity, he has represented us in legal actions taken against several suspected terrorist and/or anti-Semitic groups in the United States. Gebhardt's Aryan Renaissance Movement and Hajid's Victory for Palestine group are among those that we pursued most fervently. I'm sure that at times he might have come in contact with either one or both of them."

She stopped and looked around. Except for candle light, the deck was dark and most of the restaurant's patrons had drifted off. We were alone in our corner as she turned back to speak softly, but still with disbelief in her voice. "But, that doesn't explain why he would have told them about the diamonds."

"Not unless he's one of them," I said, and then added, "Or, he is being blackmailed by them."

"Blackmailed?" she responded. "What could they possibly have against him?"

"I don't have any idea. What do you know about his personal life?"

"Not much. He seems happily married. No children. He is a dedicated son to his elderly father, who I once met." She stopped and looked like she had remembered something important but couldn't put her finger on it.

"Is there something about his father?" I asked.

"Yes. I'm not sure if it is important. Marcel was born in France in the 1950's, but his father is distinctly German, he has a heavy German accent. I remember when I met him last year in the rehab center where he happened to be at the same time as Uncle Carl. It was near the end and Uncle Carl was slipping in and out of dementia, but I couldn't help thinking that he somehow knew Marcel's father. I also remember that Marcel seemed very uncomfortable that I was speaking to his father. He seemed to be anxious for me to leave."

"That sounds important to me."

"Yes. I think you are right," she said. "If his father is a former Nazi, and he has been trying to protect him all these years, that would make him very vulnerable to anyone who had the information, wouldn't it?" she asked academically.

"You're the Nazi expert," I said. "What do you think?"

"That there's a good chance we are right." Her voice sounded weary now as she continued. "This wouldn't be the first time that the foundation was faced with the protective family of old war criminals. It's just the first time the 'family' is practically my own."

I nodded and squeezed her hand. "I'm sorry it had to happen this way. I think we have to talk about the direction we go in now."

"Can it wait till tomorrow? This has me so strung out I just need to sleep."

"Of course," I said as I called for the check. "Hope you don't mind sleeping with the windows open; I don't have central air, but the breeze off Gardiner's Bay is usually better."

"Wonderful," she said.

That night I had one of my recurring Kate dreams. I was suspended in water, but could see nothing in the pressurized blackness. I could hear my own breath, tinny and wheezy, from inside my head, and I could taste the metallic dryness of air, but when I reached behind there was no tank, and there was no regulator in my mouth. Suddenly, a spotlight lit an underwater stage. In the center—which now appeared to be more like the altar of a great cathedral—someone was struggling under the weight of a massive stone column pressing down from the darkness. I tried to swim towards the person but couldn't kick my feet or move my arms.

Then Kate's struggle ended; her legs floated weightlessly and unmoving in the glowing water. She began rising towards the surface. I looked up and saw the face behind the diver's mask: but it was Laura, and her eyes were open in death, staring upward.

"Erik, Erik! Wake up. You're dreaming," I heard Laura shout as she held my shoulders and tried to silence the animal grunts that were coming from my mouth.

It took a few seconds to come out of it and absorb the reality of the bed, the darkened room, and the faint lilac scent of the woman holding me in the pale glow of moonlight.

"I'm sorry. I'm sorry," I said, letting her hold me as I lay on my back looking up at her silhouette against the ceiling. "It's a dream that I have sometimes. I didn't mean to scare you."

"Does it have to do with Kate?" she asked.

I was quiet for a minute, assuring myself that the dream was really gone. "Yes. It's the moment when I . . . found her."

She didn't say anything, only held me tighter and brushed her lips across my forehead. I didn't tell her the new variation on the dream, though. I couldn't even allow myself to think about it.

"Go back to sleep," I said, pulling her down next to me and wrapping my arm around her bare shoulders. "I promise to be quiet the rest of the night."

"If I weren't so exhausted right now, I might take that as rejection."

I lay there for a while listening to her breathe. The window was open and a whiff of breeze drifted in to cool the room. A whip-poor-will called from somewhere back in the woods, and the occasional hooing of a saw whet owl perched up in the white cedars helped break the monotony of the cricket static.

I'm not sure how much later I awoke, but the moon wasn't throwing shadows on the floor anymore. It was the quiet that woke me. No bird or insect sounds. I turned towards the window and caught a faint odor of cedar and a subtle hint of mildew in the night air. Laura still had her head over my left arm and was breathing deeply. Then I heard a slight scratching coming from somewhere in back of the house. I thought of the cat, but Bub was sleeping at the foot of the bed on Laura's side. I eased myself up on one elbow and strained to listen over the constant hissing in my ears caused by too many years of diving.

When I heard it again, I gently put a hand over Laura's mouth and nudged her awake.

"There might be somebody outside," I whispered, and she looked up at me and nodded without speaking.

I got out of bed and took the Parker shotgun from where I had left it leaning in the corner. Laura was sitting up in the bed now and I handed the heavy gun to her and eased the safety off. "Take it and use it if anyone comes in here."

From my desk I picked up a dive knife with a serrated blade and a weighted handle. Then I slipped silently out of the room, moved carefully across the dining room and past the kitchen.

The sound came again from the French doors in the study that led out onto the rear porch; I crouched low to move up behind a leather club chair. The moon was low over the bay, but just bright enough to make a nice silhouette of someone kneeling and working a set of picks in the door lock. A slight click as the lock turned and the figure stood up.

He was thick bodied and wide as the doorway as he stood there listening before he turned the handle and eased the door open. My muscles tensed as I began calculating the move I would have to make to bring the knife butt against the gorilla's temple. He was dressed in black and, in spite of his bulk, moved with surprising grace and silence across the planked floor.

I gripped the knife and readied myself, but just then Laura screamed my name from the bedroom, instantly followed by the deafening roar of the shotgun. The guy in black stopped and jerked backwards through the door like he was tied to a bungee. I ignored him now as I jumped up and ran to the bedroom.

Laura was braced against the wall with the gun still in her hands. She was shaking all over and her eyes were wide open and unblinking. There was a big hole blown through the window screen.

"I saw him come right up to the window and put a knife into the screen. I don't know if I hit him. Oh God, I hope not!"

Now I could hear someone running across the soft ground. "It doesn't sound like you did," I said as I took the gun out of her shaking hands. "Get behind me and stay low."

We moved quickly out to the kitchen and saw two figures crossing the meadow and heading down to the wooded trail that led to my dock. One was the gorilla that had been at the back door; the other was tall and moving like an athlete. I told Laura to stay in the kitchen and call 911. Then I slapped another shell into the shotgun and ran after them.

By the time I got to the trail I knew it was too late. I heard the roar of a powerful outboard engine kick to life, and came out of the woods just in time to see a Boston Whaler surge up onto a plane and rocket out towards the mouth of the bay. In the moonlight, I could just make out that the tall guy at the helm was definitely Hajid.

When I got back up to the house, Laura was waiting for me on the porch, looking a little forlorn, but still sexy, in the oversized Annapolis tee shirt that I had lent her to sleep in.

"Did you call the cops?"

"I did from my cell. There's no dial tone on the house phone. Do you think they could have cut the phone lines?"

"You can bet on it. That was our friend Hajid and one of his ape-man helpers. This time they didn't come to give us a lecture on playing fair. Are you okay?

Laura rubbed her right shoulder, which was bruised from the kick of the shotgun. "I don't know which end of that thing is more dangerous," she said.

PART THREE

SEA CHANGE

CHAPTER TWENTY-TWO

THE NIGHT SKY PULSED WITH BURSTS OF COLOR AND THE SEISMIC THUMP OF distant explosions. A big summer crowd was gathered on Greenport's town dock to see the Grucci fireworks raining down over the harbor. Just west of the main action, where it lay tied at the commercial dock, *Prowler* sat in shadow, lit only by the strobes of the flickering light-show overhead.

Three days had gone by since the break-in and now we were ready to put our new plan into action. Of course, the police report was duly taken and some officers had paid a visit to Manson's boat, but no Boston Whaler was discovered and the men on board professed total ignorance of the event. That same day Laura and I discussed how to proceed with the new expedition. I wanted her to take a trip somewhere and lay low while we went after the diamonds without her. She wouldn't agree to that so we worked out a compromise. It turns out that there is a yoga retreat center on Martha's Vineyard that she goes to every summer. It is isolated on a neck of land surrounded on three sides by water. Every day for two weeks, participants do yoga and meditation, eat vegetarian meals, drink no alcohol, and must go without phones and TV. It sounds like pure hell to me, but she claims it strengthens a person's spirit.

Whatever.

Anyway, she said she could leave quietly after a day or two and have someone cover for her. That way we could pick her up from the Vineyard dock on the *Prowler* as it headed out for its "fishing trip".

As for the *Finest Kind*, Roebling, and Gonzales left separately and then met up at a hotel near Greenport to hole up for a few days. Johnson went back to the city so that he and LeClair could take care of their business. My cousin, Jack Hazen, also runs a charter boat out of Montauk. We are the same age, height, and build. From a distance, we look pretty much alike—especially with the long billed fishing cap and wrap-around sunglasses. Over the years, I've thrown a lot of business Jack's way; like a lot of fishing captains, he just manages to stay alive in this boom and bust business. So, since he had charters booked for the next week, it was pretty easy for me to convince him to use my boat instead of his old tub. Bill Lester would stay on as mate.

Of course, I had to tell him a little bit about what I was up to, without going into any details. He would always be leaving the dock in the darkness of early morning, as usual, and when they got back in for the day he wouldn't hang around. He would be using my truck to go home, and he and his wife live in the Springs not far from my place.

It would work—for a while, at least. In any case, it would give us cover long enough to disappear.

So here we were, on the deck of the Prowler watching Fourth of July fireworks lighting the sky. Book Johnson and Mike LeClair had arrived by train just an hour ago from the city. Sean Roebling and Hector Gonzales stepped aboard only minutes before. Big Fletch King shot a stream of chewing tobacco over the stern and announced he was ready to shove off anytime.

We were all holding a bottle of cold beer in our hands as I made the toast: "Here's to success." Everyone drank and I swirled the beer in my mouth and then spat it over the side. "Damn waste of good beer," I said a little sadly before I turned back to the group. "Let's go."

The fireworks were over and the night sky dark as we slipped out past Orient Point and, with Plum Island on our portside, headed for Martha's Vineyard—a few hours away.

●

It was 3-am by the time we pulled up close to the beach where Laura would be. We used cell phones to coordinate with her and then picked her up with the Zodiac. She stepped on board with wet feet and a canvas duffel bag—smiling and as beautiful as ever.

"Just like a James Bond movie," she said.

Johnson winked as everyone gave her a quick embrace. "I don't know about Erik as Agent 007, he ain't never wore a tuxedo in his life."

"At least I could fit into one if I had to," I said, eyeing his hulking form.

Then I opened a waterproof deck box. "But, speaking of James Bond, we are a little better armed than he was." The box contained weapons: a pair of AK-47 rifles, a Browning automatic shotgun, and several semi-automatic pistols. "I don't have to tell any of you guys that we're not playing games here." I'm sure my voice was tempered by a controlled anger because everyone got serious.

"We should be okay for now, they're clueless as to where we are and I'm hoping it stays that way until we find what we're looking for. But if we do meet up offshore again, I'm sure there'll be a confrontation that could get ugly. So we have a few weapons on board in case we have to defend ourselves. Everyone here except Laura has had experience with these things," I said as I looked at Laura and added, "I hope it doesn't come to that." Her face was lit by the reflection of the cabin lights; she looked composed and unsurprised.

"You forgot so soon? I'm the only one here who has actually taken a shot at those misfits. And I've got a sore shoulder to prove it."

Book Johnson smiled and asked, "Where are these clowns now, Erik?"

"The *White Shark II* pulled out of Montauk sometime early Sunday morning. They're probably anchored over the *Doria* right now. Maybe they even got in a couple of dives. I don't know how long it'll take them to realize that the car isn't there, but eventually they will. We have to make sure we can find it and recover the gems before that happens."

LeClair rubbed his side where the broken ribs were still healing. "My grandfather fought the real Nazis in the French underground during the war. Now these neo-freaks and their Middle Eastern buddies owe me a little debt. Funny how these things come full circle."

"Plus ça change, plus c'est la même chose," Laura said, and her face reddened a little. I guess because she realized she had spoken aloud what she had only been thinking.

I nodded. "The more things change, the more they stay the same,"

"Yes. It was Uncle Carl's favorite expression," she said with some sadness in her voice.

A few minutes later, Hector had stowed the Zodiac and Captain King was steering the boat to sea. Out on the horizon, off the starboard bow, lay the dark smudge that was Nantucket Island, stretched like a starfish on the open water. Soon we would pass the northern point of that island and head for open sea, and the final resting-place of the *Andrea Doria*.

CHAPTER TWENTY-THREE

THE NEXT DAY THE FOG WAS BACK. IT EFFUSED AIR INTO WATER, BLANCHED the sea's summer colors to a lifeless gray, and gave some relief from the blistering heat of the sun. Sure enough, Manson's boat was already anchored over the wreck, probably with a three point anchoring system to hold it just over the hole they had blasted into the ship. We passed within half a mile, but a blip on the radar screen was the only indication that anyone was there. I was happy about that. The more cover we had, the better it would be for our search. Of course, Manson would have no reason to suspect anything—deep water trawling was common enough out here—but it still felt better to be able to move around on deck in the anonymous fog.

Laura looked over my shoulder at the radar screen. She was wearing a yellow headband, yellow windbreaker, faded jeans and canvas boat shoes. "Is that spot of light Captain Manson's boat?"

"Yes. They're anchored over the wreck. Probably knocking themselves out right now trying to locate the Mercedes before we get there."

Laura's grimace conveyed some of the worry that she was feeling. "They can see us on their radar screen too, can't they?"

"Sure. But we're just another commercial fishing boat out here to trawl for bottom fish, as far as they're concerned."

"I hope you're right. What's that bigger flash on the edge of the screen?"

"A good-sized ship. Inbound. Most likely an oil tanker or cargo carrier. This is still a pretty busy highway out here, isn't it Fletch?"

Captain King, who was sitting at the helm and watching the radar screen and the GPS as he held the wheel steady, just grunted. We were making good time at about 14-knots. He picked up a chipped mug that sat by his elbow and spat a stream of tobacco juice into it before answering. "Sorry Ma'am," he said. "Bad habit. But, oh yea, this place gets hopping sometimes, especially when the Russian and Japanese fish-factory ships come around."

"Are we in international waters?"

"No. We're still inside the 200-mile limit. The foreign fishermen aren't allowed to trawl these waters so they send their factory ships here to buy the fish from local catch boats like this one. I'm not sure what the law says about underwater salvage rights though."

"This isn't salvage," I said half seriously. "It's recovery of stolen property."

Laura nodded. "Whatever we find—if we're lucky—can change the lives of people who were victims of the Holocaust. Even if it is a couple of generations late."

"You've got that right," King grunted amiably and went on chewing. A brass plaque mounted on the instrument panel seemed to reflect both his taciturnity and his personal habits: it stated simply, "Bless this Mess".

The digital depth recorder was flashing depths that ranged between 235-245 feet—barely within diving limits, even using advanced gas mixtures and state of the art equipment. I could picture the smooth undulating bottom below; mostly flat and uninteresting sand stretching outward towards the continental shelf and underwater canyons of the oceanic abyss, with only an occasional erratic hump rising from the plain to break the monotony. I only hoped that the one erratic we were looking for would still be detectable.

The cabin door opened and Mike LeClair came out carrying a six-pack of cold Coke. "Thought somebody might want a late morning cocktail. We must be getting close to the deployment area, no?"

I popped open a can and handed it to Laura. "We're already over the western edge. Another 30-minutes should put us at the starting point."

"How do we know where to start looking?" Laura asked.

"Ahh! Don't you believe in the Hazen legend?" LeClair said, grinning and grabbing onto my arm to hold it up for scrutiny. "The seawater blood of eight generations of fishermen runs through this man's veins. He can find a school of cod under forty fathoms of ocean just like a mortal man would spot a beach ball floating in a swimming pool."

Like a long-suffering older brother, I patted LeClair's smooth head. "Speaking of beach balls," I said. "Even if that were true, I don't think it would translate into finding a Mercedes Benz that's become part of the bottom after half a century."

"Then how will you do it," Laura persisted.

"Technology mainly. Roebling here is our man for that," I said nodding at the geek who was making some adjustments on the sonar tow. "Advanced search equipment combined with patience, guesswork, and a lot of luck. We know where the collision took place, but we have to take into account the inaccuracies of 1950's technology as well as normal human error—God knows there was plenty of that then. So, we start the search five miles east of the reported accident coordinates and add in the possibility that the ship drifted in a northwesterly direction as much as five miles after the collision. Remember, it took ten hours for it to sink. So that makes ten miles of bottom along a corridor five miles wide. Fifty square miles of ocean! It could take us two weeks to cover that much water—unless we get lucky."

"And how do we know when we've found it?"

"Well, we don't know for sure until we actually make a dive. We'll be towing two pieces of sensitive equipment: side-scan sonar and a sub-bottom profiler. One or both will pick up any large object on the bottom, but only a diver will be able to make positive identification."

LeClair drained his can of Coke and burped discreetly into his hand. "These new generation sonars can really print out a pretty accurate image of the shape of objects, so I hope I won't have to make too many 250-foot bounce dives just to find a glacial boulder or a pile of old lobster pots."

Captain King passed the spittoon cup under his mouth again and chimed in trying to impress Laura. "There's all kinds of stuff on the bottom out here. I remember when I was a kid back in the 60's and Erik's grandpa was deep trawling out here on the forty fathom curve and he snagged a WWII bomb in the net."

"That was a dark period in Hazen history," I said, shaking my head at the reference. "Grandpa told me about it years later when I was first thinking of following the family trade. Said he radioed the Coast Guard and told them they had a 500-lb aerial bomb on deck and asked them what to do about it. They made him stay ten miles at sea and sent a cutter to take him and the crew off. I think they had to handcuff Grandpa to get him off his boat. The next day they scuttled it, along with $12000.00 worth of cod. Navy divers set charges to detonate the bomb. The government paid Grandpa the value of the boat—their value. No consideration that he had built that boat with his own hands and had fished on it for over thirty years. Grandpa bought another boat, but it was never the same for him. I don't think he ever trusted the government after that. Of course, that would put him in the company of quite a few million people," I added.

Laura ignored my sarcasm and looked incredulous. "My God! That's a terrible story. It seems so unfair."

"That's an extreme example, maybe, but professional fishermen never do get much of a break any way you look at it," I said in disgust.

"I wonder how that would have gone if it was some congressman's yacht instead?" LeClair commented.

King eased back on the throttles and slowed the boat to about eight knots. "We're coming up on the deployment site now. You want to get the tows ready?"

We all looked out at the featureless wedge of ocean that we were cutting through. The boat parted the soft fog, which seemed to slide along beside it momentarily before closing behind in the wake.

"Maybe we'll get lucky and find this rusty antique in the first few passes," someone said hopefully.

•

Time was dragging—literally—for all of us aboard the *Prowler*. We towed the two sonar "fish" at a conservative four knots-per-hour, twenty-four hours a day. Now, into the third day, we had racked up three false targets. They all looked like good possibilities on the monitor, but each one proved false when we dove on them. The first one was a humpbacked glacial erratic the size and general shape of a Chevy Suburban; next, came what appeared to be the mostly buried boiler from an old wooden wreck, whose hull had long ago rotted away; finally, we found the twisted remains of an empty shipping container that might have been washed overboard in a storm, floated briefly, and then been run down by another ship. Sending two divers down on a "bounce dive" to check out the object is time consuming; the boat has to be accurately positioned and anchored before it is possible to find a small object in deep water. The whole process is tedious and repetitive. I was reminded of my grandfather's term for deep water trawling: he called it "plowing the field". The only thing that kept it interesting to him was the possibility that the next pass would fill the net with fish. In my case it was that the "fish" would point to the remains of Carl Ebner's car and the fortune that was stolen from a million dead people.

I was relieving Fletch King in the wheelhouse of the *Prowler*. The sun was down, but there were no stars to be seen again this night.

Since leaving Montauk Point, we had been in fog which erased the sky and horizon and draped the sea in billowing clouds that sometimes thinned but never cleared. At best, there was a half-mile of visibility; at worst, the bow of the boat was a ghostly image. We had covered almost half of the ten-mile long swath of ocean we had mapped out and were now a little over two miles from the sunken *Doria*—and the anchored *White Shark II*. If the fog were to lift, we would be clearly visible to Gebhardt, Hajid and their crew of murderous fanatics.

And I had a feeling it would lift soon. Marine weather reports were calling for a break in the heat wave as a cold front pushed down from Canada. That also could mean some nasty weather was on the way. I hoped we could locate the car and retrieve the diamonds before that happened. Then we could all go home.

Laura came up from the galley carrying a cup of coffee in one of my old Annapolis mugs. As usual, she looked damn good. The denim shorts she wore with a faded blue cotton polo showed off her tanned dancer's legs. Her dark hair was burnished by the red glow of the sonar monitors mounted overhead, and she smelled faintly of lavender soap and something minty.

"I thought you might need a caffeine fix by now to keep you from running off the road."

I smiled and accepted the coffee. "Yeah, thanks. There aren't any white lines out here to keep you in your lane." I sipped the coffee and quickly looked back at the monitors, which were unrolling a wavy electronic view of the bottom as we passed slowly over it. I really wanted to look at her. In fact, I wanted to do more than look at her, but a target image could come at any second and to miss it would be disastrous. Of course, Mike was watching another set of monitors down in the cramped chart room, but it was always prudent to double monitor, especially when the target was as small as this one.

"Anything interesting on your TV tonight?" she joked.

"Pretty boring show right now. But if we ever get to the part where the vintage car rolls into view it's going to get real exciting."

She was standing behind me now massaging the back of my head. Her fingers were cool and she was flexing them along the ridged muscles of my neck in a slow motion that was sensual as well as relaxing. So far, we had kept the intimacy of our relationship a secret from the rest of the crew. We both agreed that it would be better that way; no need to complicate the expedition more than we had to. So Laura was sleeping in a guest cabin forward of the captain's quarters while I was jammed into a lower bunk in the crew's quarters where Book Johnson's snoring easily drowned out the rumble of the big diesels.

"Do you really think that we'll be able to spot something as small as a car?"

"I think so. They used the same equipment to find the fuselage of John/John Kennedy's little plane years ago: that wasn't much bigger than a car, and it was in pieces. The technology's even better now."

"Yes, but this has been on the bottom for more than fifty years. Suppose it's completely buried?"

"I don't think it will be. The bottom out here is mostly hard sand and gravel, not mud or silt. But if it is, the sub-bottom profiler there," I pointed to the screen on the right, "will show the rough outline of anything buried down to ten feet. It's sort of like a sonar version of a metal detector."

She stopped massaging and stepped to my side again. I couldn't help feeling aroused and wished I could just stop the boat and take her below to make love. Instead, I kept my eyes on the monitor and occasionally checked our course with the GPS.

"What happens if we don't find it until we're right next to the *Andrea Doria*?"

I shook my head. "That would be a problem," I admitted. "But let's not think about that unless it happens. We've got enough odds against us as it is. I thought you were the optimistic one?"

She smiled and shrugged. "Optimistic? Yes. But I'm no Pollyanna. If this turns out to be a knock down fight, I just want you to know so that I'm ready for it." Then she added: "The slogan 'Never Again!' comes to mind."

"I have to admit, I misjudged you in the beginning. I thought you were a spoiled princess with a big city attitude and an overblown ego."

"Well, I'm glad to see I make such stereotyped first impressions. Actually, now that you mention it, I thought you were an anti-social bastard with a real-life dropout mentality."

I smiled. "Well, you pretty much nailed me down, but I was mistaken about you."

She laughed and put her hand on my shoulder. "I'd like to think we were both wrong and that maybe we are more alike than not."

I put my hand over hers but didn't say anything for a minute; just enjoyed the intimate connection. She kissed me on the side of my head.

"You never told me about that scar on your cheek," she said. "Is it from your warrior days, or just from wrestling big sharks underwater?"

I kept my eyes on the screen and answered in a monotone. "Neither. I ripped it open on some jagged metal trying to lift the partition that pinned Kate inside the wreck the day she died."

Her face flushed and she began to sputter apologies. I looked away from the screen and put my other hand on top of hers. "No apologies necessary. You didn't know. I should have told you before. I'll tell you the whole story sometime."

She nodded, kissed me again, then turned and went below.

After she left I continued staring at the monotonous screen and thinking the thought that had plagued me for the last few hours. What if Peter Scott was wrong? What if—in all the confusion—he had been mistaken about the Mercedes being gone? What if it was still down in the ship's garage, or tangled in the wreckage? Then this whole exercise would be a waste and the terrorists would win. I shook the thought back into a dark corner of my brain and went back to concentrating on the monitors.

•

That night we dropped anchor and shut the diesels down. It was my decision to do it because everybody was getting punchy from watching monitors and from the sheer tedium of the search. We all needed a good night's rest without the rumbling vibration of motors. So when I awoke at four in the morning, I thought it was the silence that got me up in the pre-dawn darkness. Instead it was the smell—the dank, fetid smell of death. I pulled on a pair of shorts and went barefoot up on deck.

Book Johnson was up on the bridge doing the early watch. He too had noticed the smell, faint at first, but growing more powerful as dawn came on. He came down the ladder when he saw me out on deck.

"Erik, what the hell you think that smell is?" Johnson asked.

The ocean was starting to breathe again and the boat was rolling lightly in a growing swell out of the northeast as I peered into the thick black air and took a whiff. "I'd know that smell anywhere. That's whale meat—rotting whale blubber. There's a floating carcass out there, and judging by the wind, it's floating right down to us."

"Shit. That's going to ruin my breakfast," Johnson said.

"That's going to ruin more than breakfast if we happen to find a target around here and have to go into the water."

"What're you talking about, brother?"

"I'm talking about sharks. Not just any sharks—great white sharks. They almost always find their way to a whale carcass in these waters."

Johnson flicked a nervous look over the side and then back at me. "Damn! Now you got me going. You think we have anything to worry about in the water? I mean, I swam with sharks before."

I shook my head. "Depends. Right now we don't have any reason to go into the water. I'm just hoping that when we do, that carcass isn't too close by," then I looked at Johnson and smiled. "If it is, you remember the old Navy rule of thumb: you'll just have to hope that you can swim faster than your diving buddy."

"Yeah. Well, I hope them great whites don't have a taste for us great blacks."

●

By 8:00 am we were underway again. Everyone felt revived after Hector laid out a huge breakfast of omelets, sausage, warm French bread, and mugs of black Colombian coffee. Fog still stitched the sea and air into a monochromatic quilt, but it was beginning to thin. Visibility increased to half a mile. There was a bracing feel to the breeze and the sea was now running in long, three-foot swells. Sometime around dawn the whale carcass must have drifted downwind, so that only Book and I knew it was out there. Which was fine with me—no sense in getting anybody else nervous now.

What happened next happened quickly. We were all on deck when Captain King yelled from up in the wheelhouse. "There's a plane heading straight towards us and flying low."

I knew right away that it had to be Zeke Tredia and that he was snooping for the *White Shark II.* "Laura, get inside! You too, Book." I turned to the other guys and yelled, "Quick! Get all this diving gear in a pile on the deck and let's get a tarp over it."

By the time we scrambled everything out of the way and squatted down next to the big net reel for cover, Tredia's yellow plane came over at under a 100-feet. I peered out from my hiding place and could clearly see Tredia's face looking down. In the seat behind him I could also see the unmistakable white-haired head of the lawyer, Feynard!

The plane melted into the fog beyond *Prowler*'s stern but I could hear the change in pitch of the engine as Tredia made a turn and came back in for a better look. I also noticed a pair of orange and black dive fins that we had overlooked sitting on top of a deck box, but it was too late to do anything about them now. He passed low over the starboard and I saw Captain King outside on the bridge shaking a big fist that held a shotgun. The plane shot past the port bow and waggled its wings just before disappearing again.

"Sonovabitch," King yelled. "He comes over again I'll blow his little fucking pinwheel out of the sky."

"Relax, Fletch. I don't think he's coming back, at least not right away. Where's the *White Shark II* now?" I asked.

King glanced over at his radar screen. "About four miles off our port bow. Still anchored over the *Doria*."

"That's where he's headed," I said. "I have a feeling that he's delivering a passenger."

"What are you talking about?" Laura said.

"Feynard. I saw his face. He wasn't looking too happy, either."

"Oh, no," is all she said. Her expression was that of a woman who has been betrayed.

CHAPTER TWENTY-FOUR

At a little past noon, the second big event of the day happened. We were trolling the two sonar units on the fourth northeasterly course of the day, when we got a reading at the far northern end of the grid. The side-scan sonar showed something sticking up almost four feet off the bottom and close to twenty feet in length. It even had the rough outline of a car.

"Bingo!" yelled LeClair when he saw the image come into view. I was up on the bridge with Captain King and we both let out a shout of excitement. King marked the exact spot on the GPS and brought the boat into a wide turn while Johnson and Roebling released a marker buoy and began reeling in the two sonar fish.

Laura ran out on deck and looked up at the bridge smiling. "Do you think this is it?" she asked excitedly as I came swinging down the bridge ladder and ran into the chart room to plot the target on a NOAA chart.

"Don't get your hopes up too high yet," I shouted over the whine of the winch gear and the beat of diesels. "But it looks to be the most promising thing I've seen so far. It looks good." I showed her the position on the chart. "Hard bottom, just under forty fathoms, a little less than three miles from the Doria, which is right here," I moved a pair of antique brass dividers a few inches to the west. "We're still safe from prying eyes, for now. As far as the *White Shark II* crew can tell by their radar screen, we just look like a fishing vessel towing an otter trawl for ground fish and we have to stop to haul our nets in." I looked out at the wisps of fog rolling past the stern. "Now, if this fog will just hold a while longer," and knocked on the wooden chart table for luck.

"Still the superstitious fishermen, I see," Laura said smiling.

"Why not? Good luck is a fisherman's best friend, and we need all the friends and all the luck we can get right now."

Fletch King circled the *Prowler* around into its own wake and came up close to the marker buoy before he released the bow anchor. Then he backed the boat down and Johnson lowered a stern anchor to keep the boat from swinging and hold it almost directly over the underwater target. LeClair began hauling diving gear back out on deck while Roebling started to suit up. Twenty minutes later they were both ready to make the dive.

I kneeled down next to them on the dive platform. "You ought to know that early this morning we were near a whale carcass. Couldn't see it, just smelled it. There might be more shark activity than usual in the water if it's still around, but I don't think it is."

LeClair looked up at me with an amused look on his chiseled face. "You're talking white sharks, aren't you?"

"Could be," I said looking at Roebling, who was scanning the tops of the gray swells that slid quietly in from the mist-shrouded horizon.

"Hey Sean," LeClair said. "When you signed on for this gig did you know you'd be live bait for an overgrown cuisineart with fins?"

"Shut up Mike. I'm already hearing that goddamn movie sound track in my brain."

"Yeah. I don't think your mother would want you to go swimming today. I know mine wouldn't," LeClair said.

I laughed but tried to sound reassuring. "I'm just telling you this to caution you. I haven't seen anything. Just watch your asses. Remember, you're just going down to identify this target—nothing else. You should be back on deck in twenty minutes."

"Roger that." LeClair said. "Hopefully with arms and legs still attached. If we don't come back call my mother and tell her I gave up booze and fast women," Then both men pulled their masks on, dropped into the water, gave the thumbs up and disappeared.

I turned to Johnson, who was wearing a set of headphones that were attached to a small console. "Book. Have you got good contact with them?"

"Loud and clear. They're going down the line now. No sea monsters in sight yet."

Laura put her hand on my shoulder and I turned to look at her. She was wearing her faded Yankees cap with a strand of her dark hair spilling out from under the peak where it fluttered in the breeze over one eye. She wore little or no makeup, but her lips glistened with the moisturizer she used against the wind and salt air. As usual, I liked the way she looked and was hoping that the project was almost over so that I could concentrate more on what I wanted to do about how much I liked her.

"Try some. It'll help soothe your nerves," she said as she handed me a cup of mint tea she had been drinking from a blue mug.

"I look like I need some soothing, huh?" I took the mug and sipped, thinking how much more a good double shot of bourbon would soothe me now.

"You do look tense. Is everything all right with Mike and Sean?"

"So far. I just hate the suspense. If this turns out to be another rock or pile of old junk I'm going to need something stronger than this tea."

"I have a good feeling about this one. Even a lucky fisherman can use a woman's intuition, can't he?"

"Like I said before, even a lucky fisherman can use all the help he can get." I grinned, looked at my watch, and turned back to Johnson. "Are they there yet?"

"They're just coming close to it now. Visiblity's not so good with this cloud cover. It's pretty dark down there. Wait a minute." Johnson cupped a huge hand over his ear as he listened to the squeaky voices below. Then his broad face broke into a grin. "It's definitely a car. It's on its side and covered in anemone, but they can see wheels and undercarriage. They're making their way around to the other side now."

Laura spilled most of her tea when I threw my arms around her and picked her up like a rag doll and started dancing her around. She must have felt such a sense of elation that she shouted, "Yes! We did it!" so loud that Captain King came out from the pilothouse and Hector Gonzales stepped up from the galley to see what all the commotion was about. Everybody was feeling heady.

But it was short-lived. A minute later, Book's face became serious as he listened to the divers talking 235-feet below. "It's not a Mercedes," he said and paused while the bad news sank in. "Sean scraped some growth off what's left of the front grill: it's got a Rolls Royce insignia."

"Tell them to come up now," I said as I let go of Laura and felt my own body go limp. It was similar to the way I felt the time I hooked and played a blue marlin for over six hours only to have the hook pull out when the big fish was ten feet from the boat.

"I don't know why, but I never even thought about the possibility that there might be another car on the bottom," I said to no one in particular.

"I don't think any of us did," Laura said. "But isn't this a good sign? If we found this one we'll surely find the one we're looking for. It's got to be around here. Close by."

"You're probably right. It's just that I thought we had it," the frustration in my voice was clear and I didn't want to sound pessimistic, so I added, "But, you're right, we have to be getting close now."

Johnson spoke up. "There's a good chance that if you draw a straight line from here to the Doria our target should be right on it somewhere."

"I think you're right Book, but I don't want to chance missing it. So we'll make this the mid-point of the track and make our sweeps a mile on each side along the north/south axis. That'll cut our search time down," I looked grimly out at the thinning fog and up at the brightening sky and thought of Manson's boat out there somewhere. "We don't have much more time to operate in privacy."

CHAPTER TWENTY-FIVE

THAT NIGHT THE SONAR PICKED UP ANOTHER TARGET. IT WASN'T MORE THAN two hundred yards away from the last one, but we had run several miles back and forth on the grid before we spotted it. Once again, we anchored up, but this time we had to wait until morning to check it out.

By five in the morning the seas were starting to get dangerous. Captain King was looking at the latest weather fax from NOAA and shaking his head when I came into the pilothouse. I muttered something like good morning, even though it really wasn't, then stood by the starboard window and scratched my week-old beard as I peered out at the plum-colored bruise that was the sunrise beginning to spread across the eastern horizon. With all the cloud cover I knew there wouldn't be any discernible sun coming up today. It was still too dark to see much, but the main anchor line creaked like an old stairway as it stretched in the bow chocks with ten-foot swells rolling under the boat, and the wind was playing an atonal solo on the wire cable stays that supported the outrigger booms.

King handed me the weather fax. "According to this report, we've got a low pressure system laying right over the George's Bank and winds building to gale force by the afternoon. Highly unusual this early in the summer."

I glanced at the paper. My eyes were red-rimmed from lack of sleep. "Unusual, but I'm not surprised. Not with that three-week heat spell. The surface water's as warm now as it would be in mid-August. Hurricane conditions."

King tucked a fresh chew into his cheek. "Even if the system stalls, we'll get twenty-foot swells pretty soon. If it moves this way, we're gonna have a helluva ride getting back in with a following sea and maybe cresting waves."

"Then we've got to get divers in the water at first light."

"You think it's a good idea to dive in this kind of weather?"

I slapped the weather report down on the chart table and laughed. "It's a goddamn piss-poor idea and you know it, Bub. But what choice do we have? I think we're over the right target. I suspect we already gave away the position to the storm troopers on Manson's boat. If we don't go for it now we might lose the prize forever—and I'm not about to let that happen."

"Maybe we don't have to worry so much about Manson," King said, pointing back over the stern. "He left sometime during the night. They must've been spooked by the storm."

I turned and looked back at the gray gloom to the west. There was no anchor light in the distance as there had been a few hours ago. Just an empty void of shadowy darkness into which the ominous rollers disappeared. The size of the rollers made it almost impossible for the radar to pick out a small boat a few miles away.

I furrowed my brow as I scanned the circle of ocean. "I don't believe that they left. Those sharks are circling. They want this prize too bad to be spooked, so we're going to have to watch our backs."

King picked up his chipped mug and released a brown stream of tobacco juice into it before he spoke. "I intend to keep this boat floating, Erik, so just do me a favor and let's get this job done pronto."

I left the pilothouse and went down into the galley. I was surprised to see Laura already there brewing a pot of coffee. The white cotton fisherman's sweater contrasted with her black hair, still damp from the shower and brushed back over her ears. Her lips were still pale, but most of her color had returned. She held on to the counter top with one hand while she poured the dark coffee into a skid proof mug.

"I don't even want to look outside right now," she said holding the mug out to me. "Don't tell me how big the waves are, I don't want to know because I think my stomach already does. Just reassure me that we're not leaving until we accomplish what we came for."

"How're you feeling?" I asked, trying to sip the hot coffee without spilling it as the boat rode down the back of a big sea and wallowed a moment in the trough.

"I'll live, but ocean cruises are off my 'to do' list."

I smiled and put one arm around her, drawing her close so that her head rested against my shoulder and neck. Her damp hair smelled of citrus. She wrapped her arms around my waist, her fingers going up under my shirt, warm against my skin. For a moment I felt myself getting aroused. Then I thought of the storm bearing down from the North Atlantic, and of the deep water beneath our feet that might hold the prize we would have to get before any one of a number of things went wrong. Mainly, before my luck ran out again.

I kissed her on the side of her head and stepped back balancing the coffee again. "I know that your seasickness is probably throwing off your intuition, but I have a fisherman's instinct that we're over the target this time. If I'm right, we'll have the diamonds on board this morning. It'll be light enough to dive in an hour." I hoped that my voice wasn't giving away any of the apprehension that I was feeling about the approaching storm or about what to make of the disappearance of Manson's boat. "If the target we marked is the car—the right car—we should be able to finish the job in a few hours. Then it's home, and dry land, and a celebration dinner—with no seafood."

Laura smiled, then hung on to the counter as the boat dropped into a deep trough. "It's not too dangerous to dive, is it?" she asked.

"These aren't the conditions I'd pick, but all the guys are ex-Navy divers. They've seen worse." I rubbed the white scar and ran my hand through wind-blown hair as I thought to myself, 'but not much worse'."

Just then the door leading into the crew quarters opened and LeClair stepped into the galley. "Seen worse than what? This weather or your scruffy face early in the morning before I have breakfast?" he said, and turned to Laura. "Good morning, Ms. Morgan. Don't you think Erik should at least drag a razor across that ugly landscape?"

Laura smiled. "Good morning, Mike. "I think he's just superstitious. He figures if he shaves it might break our luck."

"I didn't know we were having good luck yet," LeClair answered.

I clapped him on the back and headed for the steps to the upper deck. "We're not going to have any luck if you don't get up on deck in about five minutes and suit up for this dive," I said. "Save breakfast for the trip home."

●

The deck of the *Prowler* was heaving like a carnival ride. Each time it reached the bottom of a ten-foot swell, its rounded stern plunged into the trough and sent a halo of white spray into the base of the next wave. A blood-red sun hung behind gray clouds over the broken horizon, but towering, black clouds, like distant mountains, threatened to swallow it in a few minutes. The whale carcass was now about a hundred yards away, but it was downwind so the air smelled only of green water brine and fragments of blown sky. There was an ominous absence of seabirds. The gregarious little storm petrels along with the swooping gannets and noisy gulls had disappeared overnight.

I squinted into the wind as I helped Mike LeClair adjust the heavy tank pack on his back. Sean Roebling was already sitting on the dive platform, ready to go. Once LeClair moved onto the platform, I had to shout above the wind.

"There's not much light up here, so it's going to be almost night down there. Use your lights as soon as you get near the bottom. I don't want to waste any time looking for the target."

Both men gave me the thumbs up, waited for the stern to drop into a trough, and slid under the next roller. They disappeared in the murk almost immediately. I put on a pair of Divelink headphones and sat at a portable communications console on the gear bench. Across from me, Hector was helping Book Johnson get suited up.

"As soon as I hear that we're on the right target, I'll hand these phones over to you, Hector. I'm going to get ready to dive with Book."

The slender Mexican nodded, his black ponytail standing straight out in the stiff wind. "Okay, Captain Erik," he said, grimacing. "I just hope this El Niño doesn't blow me overboard."

Johnson grabbed a thirty-pound weight belt and held it out to him. "Put this on. It'll put you over the hundred pound mark at least," he joked.

"Yeah, and it'll also put me on the bottom before you get there if I do go over. I think I'll just tie myself to the rail."

Laura came out from the cabin hanging on to the rail as she stepped gingerly along the wet deck to the stern. She was wearing a runner's headband to hold her hair down and her cotton sweater was wet from spray coming over the side.

"Is this what they call Nantucket weather?" she asked.

"I can think of some words that rhyme with that to describe this weather," I answered. "I'm not sure that you ought to be on deck in this. It's going to get worse. Rain's on the way."

"I want to help out. I know all about your 'no amateurs in the water' rule, but I can do something on deck, can't I?"

"You can listen in on these headphones while I start getting ready to dive."

She put the phones in place and huddled down on the bench while I started pulling on the uni-suit. A few seconds later she announced that there was a transmission.

"It's Mike. He says they're on the bottom right on top of the target. Doesn't know what it is yet. Visibility is only about five feet," she said, and added, "It's so funny to hear a big he-man type with a squeaky little voice."

"That's caused by the helium in the air mixture. You get used to it after a while. Ask him how the bottom current is."

Laura transmitted and listened to the answer. "He says it's bad. It's running in a southwesterly direction at about two and a half knots."

"Looks like we don't get a break from the weather even underwater," Johnson said.

I nodded my head in agreement. "Yeah, I see that. The current's going to cut down our bottom time. If this turns out to be the car, we've got to work fast. We're not going to get another chance anytime soon—maybe never."

Laura held her hand up as she received another transmission. "It's a car, and it's drifted over with sand. The top is gone but the windshield is sticking up out of the growth. They're looking now to see if they can uncover an insignia. The inside's filled with sand."

Johnson clapped his big hands together like a pair of catcher's mitts. "Shit, how many old cars are sitting on the bottom out here? That's got to be it."

But I wasn't smiling because I wasn't convinced yet. "If it is we'll know in a few minutes. Meanwhile, we're going to have to move that sand away to get at the trunk and under the floorboards and the seats. If the diamonds were in the car they must have been concealed. What do we have for that, Hector?"

"There's a couple of flat shovels in the deck locker."

"Perfect. Cut the handles off short and we'll just take the scoops down with us."

Laura held up her hand again. "They scraped away the front end and found a Mercedes insignia," she said, the excitement building in her voice so that she had trouble getting the words out fast enough. Then her face opened into a beaming smile. "We found it! I can't believe we found it!"

Her excitement was contagious and we all did a quick fist bump. I would have hugged her and Book and Hector too if I hadn't been struggling with my bulky backpack. Johnson was already walking bent over with gear on to the dive platform and just held his right fist in the air in a victory sign. Laura grabbed Hector and danced him around on the slippery deck, and when Captain King stuck his head out of the pilothouse door up on the bridge she flashed the thumbs up to him.

"Okay, it looks like we got the hardest part done," I said as I stood up under the weight. "Now, let's see if we can get the prize. Tell those guys to clear away as much sand as they can until we get down there."

I didn't have to tell her that this was our one and only shot. If we failed to uncover the diamonds on this dive, there would be no time for another. With the decompression requirements for diving at this depth, we wouldn't be able to dive again until the afternoon. By then, the storm would make that impossible. We were going to have to run for cover within the next couple of hours. So, it was now or never.

I shuffled over to the dive platform where Book was waiting. The fog had cleared enough so that visibility was up to a half-mile. Clouds were scudding by and in the distance a great albatross slid along stiff-winged. Odd, I thought, not only was an albatross a fairly rare sight in these waters, but all the other birds had cleared out a while ago as the storm intensified. Then Johnson tapped me on the leg and I slid down to the deck and looked behind me one more time at Laura. She was soaked now with wind driven spray where she huddled behind the big net reel watching me and Book drop off the dive platform and disappear almost instantly under the next gray swell that lifted the stern of the boat like a leaf. There was nothing left to do now but wait and pray.

●

I had gone only about twenty feet down the anchor line when I saw something move on the limit of my peripheral vision. I turned to my right and looked into the gray-green cross section of water, but nothing was there. Below me, Johnson was going out of focus as he dropped rapidly towards the bottom. I followed him, kicking downwards, away from the feeble light that came from the darkening sky.

Then something heavy brushed against the tanks on my back. This time when I turned I saw the massive bulk of a large shark fading back into the water column. I pressed my communicator button and warned Johnson.

"Book. There's a big shark playing hide and seek with me. Watch your back."

"I hear you. I'm watching."

This time, as I dove deeper, I did it with a spiraling motion so that I could see anything coming. Sharks are just a part of the scenery in a lot of dives and, ordinarily, I wouldn't have been concerned. But the animal that had just brushed past was a great white: uncommon, unpredictable, and, most of all, very big. Big enough to cut a full-grown man in half, judging by the set of jaws hanging in a Montauk bar that came from a two and a half-ton white that Manson had harpooned many years ago in these same waters. This one was every bit as big, and it had been feeding on whale—mammal meat—for the last few days. Who could say what it might do?

Of course, even great whites weren't as bad as their press. As a veteran diver, I knew that being underwater and staying vigilant gave me an advantage that a swimmer wouldn't have. But it was still nerve racking, and that used up oxygen, which I couldn't afford to squander now. I glanced at my depth gauge: 123-feet—ambient light fading fast, it was now like being in a darkened cathedral with the only light coming from stained glass windows high above.

A sudden movement in the shadows again caught me by surprise as the shark came straight towards me at a ramming speed. I acted reflexively and held the big shovel scoop out in front of me like a shield. The blunt snout of the shark hit it hard enough to spin me sideways. Then the shark's immense gray side passed like a commuter train and vanished into the gloom again.

I resumed my dive, dropping quickly now, but breathing faster than I wanted to breathe. I forced myself to slow down, measuring my exhalations. A minute later I saw the bottom and the lights of the other divers. They were gathered around a raised section of the bottom, which was impossible to distinguish in the cloud of sand and silt coming from the digging operation. This billowed out into a plume, caught in a strong bottom current, which flowed like an underwater river off to the right.

One of the divers—it was LeClair—swam out of the cloud and we communicated for a minute. I told him about the close encounter with the shark and handed him the shovel.

"When you and Sean go up, stick together and use this to fend him off. It works well."

"Damned ingenious. Probably work better than hitting him with my pocketbook," LeClair quipped in a comical, underwater voice.

I was almost startled by Laura's clear voice that sounded like it came from behind me. "What's going on down there? Are you okay?"

"We're good. I'll let you know as soon as we find something. Still have to dig more," I transmitted back to the surface.

Roebling swam out of the cloud and gave the thumbs up sign to LeClair. Both men held the anchor line and rose together towards the surface. I swam into the cloud, felt the anemone-covered side of the car sticking a few feet up from the bottom and leaned down inside the sandy depression where Johnson was busy scooping sand like a man on a beach racing the tide as he dug for buried treasure. And that's exactly what we were digging for, I thought. We're too close now to stop. If the diamonds are here, only a couple of feet of sand stand between us and them.

I checked my pressure gauge and my watch. Fifteen minutes of bottom time left. Maybe less because of the effort required to move the sand and fight the current. I tapped Johnson's arm and relieved him on the shovel while the big man rested a minute before resuming the dig using just his gloved hands to fling sand aside.

After five-minutes the effort was becoming exhausting. Then the shovel hit something solid. The seat springs! The seat covering had rotted away decades ago, but some of the rusted springs were still intact. We both stopped digging until the current cleared the water. Then Johnson shined his light down into the hole while I used a pair of cutters to snip the wire mesh. Next, I slipped a heavy duty salvage knife from the sheath on my leg and probed under the thin layer of sand that now covered what seemed to be a flat, rusted steel shelf that spanned the width of the car. I plunged the knife into it and began using it like a can opener to cut through the thin barrier.

Between the two of us, we pulled up on the shelf and folded it back like a trapdoor. Underneath, after the silt had swirled away in the current, we saw the cases! They looked like hard plastic attaché cases. They were corroded but still intact and fairly clean after two generations buried underwater.

Neither of us talked. There was no time for celebrating yet. We were both breathing hard and there was only about two more minutes of bottom time left. Johnson fumbled with a big net bag while I eased each of the three cases out and placed them inside. I probed around to make sure there weren't any more, then I pulled the net shut, snapped it onto a big, orange lift bag, which, in turn, was tethered to the anchor line, and inflated the bag until it began to lift off the bottom.

It rose almost languidly at first, then it began to pick up speed as it slipped upwards towards the light. Johnson and I followed, rising slowly under our silvery dome of bubbles.

"Watch out up there," I transmitted to the divers hanging on the anchor line high above while we decompressed. "There's a payload coming up the line." Then I switched over to surface communication and spoke to Laura. "We got it! It's on its way up now."

She didn't even try to mask her excitement. "Oh my God! I can hardly believe it!"

I smiled to myself, but I was too tired to get excited. "Tell Hector and Captain King to get a line tied onto it when it breaks the surface. But don't lift it into the boat yet. I don't want it out of the water until Book and I are both out. Then I want to cut the anchor and get home quick. We've got about an hour of decompression. How's the weather?"

"I understand. The sky is dark up here and the waves are immense. The Captain's worried that we're going to start dragging anchor."

"Tell him to hang on. We don't want to miss our ride."

I didn't say why I wanted the cases to stay in the water. It was just a feeling. My gut told me that somewhere up there somebody had to be watching this operation.

CHAPTER TWENTY-SIX

HALF AN HOUR LATER, MY BRAIN CAUGHT UP TO MY GUT. WE WERE HANGING on to the line at the 20-foot decompression stop with another 25-minutes to go when I looked up at the cases suspended in the water overhead attached to the big orange buoy. And then it hit me: the albatross I saw at the beginning of the dive. It seemed out of place at the time for good reason because it was no albatross. It was a drone! A surveillance drone made to look like a bird. I remembered seeing one just like it on a nature program where somebody in Australia was studying oceanic birds: a big, birdlike drone mounted with cameras. By now, its camera must have seen the big orange bag bobbing on the waves.

All this flashed through my head before two things happened at once. First, I heard the unmistakable thrum of diesel motors overhead approaching at high speed. Second, Laura's voice came through my headphones sounding panicky.

"Erik! Manson's boat is coming right at us. It doesn't look like it's going to slow down. Oh, my god!"

"Laura!" I shouted into my speaker. "Get down and take cover. Let Mike and Sean ..." but, before I could finish my sentence I could hear gunfire erupt through the headphone. Just below me Johnson cursed, and seconds later the big hull of a boat sliced overhead and slammed into the *Prowler's* stern ramp with such force that Johnson and I were jerked like puppets on the dive line.

From 20-feet below I could plainly see the hulls of both boats briefly locked bow to stern and hear the screech of steel on steel. Then Manson's boat slid back as the engines kicked into reverse, leaving a fifty-foot gap of ocean between the two. The aft section of the *Prowler* looked damaged, but I couldn't tell how badly.

My first reaction was to let go of the decompression line and start for the surface. But, a big hand grabbed my leg and I turned to look at Johnson who ran an index finger across his throat and pointed at his dive watch. He was right. We had just worked 20+ minutes on the bottom and rushing to the surface now would be deadly. Besides, there were people up there with automatic weapons. We would be sitting ducks.

I tried the Divelink phone again. "Laura! Are you okay? What's happening up there?"

Her voice came back muffled and shaky. "Erik, Hajid is on our boat. I think Sean is dead. He's lying on the deck bleeding. Oh, my god!"

"Where's Mike?"

"I'm not sure. I think he is up near the bow. There was a lot of shooting. I'm crouched behind a storage box on deck."

"Can you get down below and lock yourself in . . ." I was cut off by Laura's screaming.

"Get your hands off me, you stinking bastard!" is all I heard before another blast of gunfire. Then the line went dead.

I looked at my watch. Another twenty minutes of decompression. I let myself slide up the line a few feet to get a better look of the surface. There was still a fifty-foot gap between the boats and they were heaving in a swirl of foam each time they came down from the crest of massive seas. Then, I saw something else. The bottom of a rubber life raft appeared behind the *Prowler's* stern. It slowly moved away from the boat and headed across the gap towards Manson's boat. Somebody was half rowing, half paddling and having a tough time in the heaving seas. It had to be Hajid. I looked back up at the bottom of *Prowler* and realized that the cases and the buoy were gone. I tried the surface phone again but it was dead. It didn't take much reasoning to realize what was happening. All I worried about was Laura.

A minute later I knew where Laura was. There was a splash next to the life raft and someone was swimming back towards the *Prowler.* I could see it was her, but it only lasted a few seconds. The life raft turned and Laura was plucked out of the sea and pulled back inside the raft. Shit! I felt helpless as I watched the raft finally get to the side of the other boat. It was difficult to make it out through the distance and the rough surface, but nothing seemed to happen for a few minutes, though I guessed they were struggling to get the cases and Laura out of the raft and into the boat.

A couple of minutes went by before the raft lurched away from the side of the boat as if it was being pushed. This was immediately followed by the trails of high velocity bullets being fired through the fabric and penetrating the water to a depth of five or six feet. Then I realized that the raft had not been empty; as it sank, the body of a man—it was Hajid for sure—sank with it, both in a billowing cloud of blood. So, the game has changed, I thought, Hajid had outlived his usefulness and Gebhardt was going for the full value of the prize. And, now he had Laura.

Things happened quickly. The big shark that had been harassing us earlier now materialized from below and seized Hajid's body shaking its head from side to side as it took him down. I made my decision quickly and let go of the decompression line and began swimming out and up towards the bottom of Manson's boat. Johnson was still on the decompression line flailing his arms at me to come back.

When I was ten feet from the boat's stern an object the size of a football hit the water overhead and sank. I ditched my tanks and weight belt and lunged for the plunging dive platform on the *White Shark II's* transom. Just as my head broke the surface and I grabbed onto the platform's support strut a deep, muffled rumble came from under the keel as a powerful detonation shook the platform and vibrated through the entire steel hull. Then, a white mushrooming boil rose six feet out of the water behind me and burst outward into the thrashing, rain beaten surface of the ocean like a giant pot boiling over. The shock wave that followed shoved me under the dive platform and whacked my head against the bronze stanchion, knocking my dive mask off and, momentarily, stunning me.

It probably took about a minute for me to shake off the dazed condition and remember Book. I let go of the stanchion and dove as deeply as I could in the direction of the *Prowlers's* dive line. Without a mask all I could see was shadows, and without a weight belt I was too buoyant to get much deeper than ten feet. Johnson wasn't there. I made a few more desperate dives but there was no sign of my friend and diving partner.

Back on the surface, I heard loud voices followed by a few gunshots from the deck overhead. By holding on to the underside of the dive platform, I could push my head under and turn a 360-degree search looking downward. In the direction of the port bow a shadow materialized from the depths and my heart leaped thinking that Book had, somehow, made it. Then the shadow turned and revealed itself to be the profile of another big shark, a line of cruel teeth stitching its partly open jaws as it headed for something on the surface and out of my view.

I came back up in the shallow space under the dive platform and peered out at another horror unwinding not more than thirty feet away.

The kid with the lightning bolt tattoos was screaming and flailing on the surface while a cloud of blood spread out from what was probably an arterial wound in his leg. The white shark made one pass and made a big circle before coming straight in and taking the kid by the bloody leg. Once it had him it shook its head violently and the leg came off neatly. The rest of him folded into a ball and sank out of sight while the fish struggled to swallow its prize.

Grieving for Book Johnson would have to wait; it was time to get out of the water. I didn't feel any prickling sensation on my skin, no pain in my joints. Maybe having the bends ten years ago gave me some kind of immunity; at any rate, I didn't feel bent now. However, cold and exhaustion were beginning to drain my body, and the constant plunging of the boat as I tried to keep my grip on it was bruising every part of me. Nevertheless, I managed to roll myself up onto the dive platform and flatten myself against the high transom. Even after twenty years, my Navy SEAL diver training was helping to save my ass.

The gap between the two boats was now a couple of hundred feet. There were still bursts of gunfire coming from the *Prowler's* deck and these were answered by similar bursts from Gebhardt's crew. I figured that when Hajid had boarded the boat to get to the diamonds he had somehow disabled the engines. Either that, or when the *White Shark II* had rear-ended *Prowler* it damaged the prop and the rudder, or even bent the shaft. At any rate, *Prowler* appeared dead in the water.

The voices I heard up on *White Shark II's* deck were coming from mid-ships where whoever was talking had the protection of the boat's superstructure against the gunfire. Then I heard the engines kick into gear and we were heading, slowly, away and into the still building seas. I didn't anticipate anyone walking back to the stern to look over the dive platform, but, just in case, I reached down to my right calf for the only weapon I had: a 6", heavy-bladed dive knife. In underwater military operations it could be a deadly weapon in close combat. Still, it was used more for cutting enemy air-lines and disabling divers rather than cutting throats or slaying sharks as the movies always seemed to show. Up on deck it might not be much against the automatic weapons, but it was something.

Then I just held on and tried to access the situation. The platform I was struggling to stay on was like a bronze and teak catwalk. It extended the full width of the boat's beam—about 16-feet and out from the transom about 4-feet. A door on the starboard side gave divers access to it, and—in the old days—had served as a means of hauling big sharks out of the water. Manson still held the western hemisphere record for the largest white shark landed on rod and reel— 2,130 pounds—considerably smaller than the one that was somewhere in our wake now finishing off the skinhead.

Anyway, right now, the boat was wallowing in the huge seas because whoever was piloting it—I knew it couldn't have been Manson—was inexperienced in extreme conditions. He wasn't using enough power to maintain a head-on course and, as a result, the boat was yawing as it climbed each wave, and taking on too much water over its port rail. The stern scuppers were blasting torrents of water overboard like church gargoyles in a hurricane. At this rate the boat was in danger of turning turtle in the huge seas.

A single shot followed by Laura's voice gasping, "Oh, my God," got me to my knees. A hawse pipe opening in the transom allowed me to see into the boat's deck. Laura was being held by a big goon with a huge, black beard. He had one muscular forearm wedged under her chin while she kicked and shouted at a lean, chisel-faced older man, who I took to be Gebhardt. His other arm locked Hank Manson in a choke hold. A few feet away, against the port rail, one of the Shoup brothers held the limp body of Feynard, the lawyer, in one hand and a Beretta in the other.

"And now it is time to bid adieu to your faithful servant, Ms. Morgan," Gebhardt said. "His information was of great value. Not so much his life."

With one shove the body was gone over the side.

Laura continued to struggle and scream. "You stinking, cowardly bastards! Let me go. You've taken everything else from me. What more do you want?"

Gebhardt smiled and wiped streaks of rain from a cruel face.

"Only some additional insurance, my dear Ms. Morgan. But, don't worry. I'm sure we will allow you to swim the final few miles to shore."

"You and your fucking goons will never make it to shore," Manson choked out.

"Yes, that was a foolish thing you did, destroying the electronics in your own boat, Captain. What did you expect to accomplish by doing that?"

Manson glared and spit. "It's going to put you at the bottom of this ocean, you Nazi bastard."

As the boat slid down the crest of a wave, Gebhardt steadied his feet on the deck and faced Manson. "Not before you get there, my gypsy fisherman," he said as he pulled a commando style, gravity knife out of his pocket, plunged it into Manson's solar plexus, and jerked downward with both hands.

"I don't need a gun to kill scum like you. Much better to filet you like a fish."

Manson dropped to his knees, wide eyed, as he held his guts in and stared at his own blood running into the boat's scuppers.

"Feed the fish, Sikes," Gebhardt said as he grabbed Laura's arm while the bearded goon and Shoup hoisted the dying man over the rail and let him drop into the sea.

"You inhuman monster!" Laura spat out as she struggled against the arm lock grip that he held her in.

"To the contrary, Ms. Morgan. Monsters are an aberration of nature. I and my more serious followers are interested only in purity— the purity of the white race—even if desperate measures must be taken to achieve it. Unfortunately, your tribe does not fit into the category either."

He signaled to the wheelhouse to go ahead and the boat picked up speed. Then he turned Laura back over to the bearded one he called Sikes. He looked around and edged his way across the sloping deck to a fiberglass life preserver chest that was bolted to the deck just outside the main cabin. Stenciled in black on its side was the image of a white shark, mouth open as if attacking something. Opening the chest, he tossed out most of the orange jackets inside. Shoup dragged the cargo net containing the cases of diamonds up to it. Gebhardt took two of the three cases and placed them inside the chest, then he slammed the lid, dogged it down, and reached into his pocket to retrieve a small, brass lock. He looked at each man as he slipped the lock into the hasp and snapped it shut. He picked up one of the life jackets and put it on. Then he hefted the other case and opened the cabin door.

"That should keep our precious cargo secure for now," he said. "Put this tiresome bitch in the forward rope compartment and lock it up. I'm going to go check on Burris. He's not doing a great job of running this boat."

As Sikes dragged Laura through the hatch, she turned and looked out over the stern. I guess she must have been looking for the *Prowler* but the rain had cut visibility to a few hundred yards and there was nothing but a wild ocean to gaze at. But, in that two-second pause I could see her eyes clearly: they didn't reflect fear, only anger.

Good girl, I thought to myself. Don't fight them, I'm coming to get you.

CHAPTER TWENTY-SEVEN

Now, as I knelt on the platform, I could feel my strength returning. I looked at my hands, which were white-knuckled and raw from gripping the bronze step. For a second, I was reminded of my grandfather's hands, deformed by arthritis in his later years, but still powerful in grip from a lifetime of hauling nets and pots, and doing all the heavy lifting of a life at sea. Then I thought of Hemingway's old man feeling betrayed by his clawed hand. I flexed the hand until feeling returned. Not that old yet.

The boat bottomed out in a deep trough, shuddering and bucking like a rodeo bull as it threatened to shake me off the platform before it began climbing up the back of the next wave. If I didn't get off the platform and into the boat soon, I knew I wouldn't be able to hold on much longer.

I took a chance and raised my head up over the transom. The backs of three people showed clearly up in the wheelhouse. One of them was Gebhardt, the other two appeared to be the Shoup brothers. The rest must be somewhere below, along with Laura.

As the boat paused at the crest of the wave, I rolled smoothly over the transom and dropped down onto the teak deck. Luckily, I never liked orange dry suits. The one I was wearing when I slipped over the transom and moved behind the big crane hoist on deck was black. Pretty good camouflage in a raging storm. I wasn't really worried that anybody'd be looking back towards the stern anyway. The boat was wallowing into the plunging seas ahead and I'm sure that would keep everybody's attention for now.

I took a mental inventory of the *White Shark II*. I had been on it years ago when Manson and I had been on friendlier terms. It's a big boat with an enclosed salon area on the main deck containing diving gear racks, two long dining tables on each side, and upholstered banquets for large parties of divers and fishermen. Forward of that is a door leading down to the galley, the heads, and a couple of staterooms. The engine room can also be accessed from down there. To the right, or starboard side of the door, a stairway leads up to the bridge which contains the wheelhouse and main control room.

I ducked low and crossed the open space between the transom and the superstructure that housed the passenger salon area. I crouched and steadied myself, holding on to a fixed bench seat under the window, and flexed the stiffness out of my fingers again. Then I raised my head and looked inside. Some of the portside windows had been shattered by the impact of boarding seas, and one of them was knocked out completely. Diving gear littered the floor. But no one was there. So, the ones that aren't in the wheelhouse are below deck. So far, so good, I thought.

I stayed low and made it over to the galley door on the other side of the dining tables. I tried listening at the door first, but the constant pitching of the boat and the clanging of the hull in the full fury of the storm made it impossible to hear anything. Heat was building up inside my dry suit, so I took a minute to pull it off. Underneath I wore sweatpants and a sweatshirt. I kept the neoprene boots on and took the dive knife out of its scabbard. I eased the door open and slipped inside.

Just as I started down the stairs a wave rolled the boat thirty degrees to port and a column of white spray came surging through the blown out window, and lashed against the bulkheads with the force of a fire hose. A burst of thunder added to the shrieking wind and clatter of loose gear skidding across the deck.

It didn't take a rocket scientist to know that the boat was top-heavy; her fuel tanks were low, making her light in the hull, and there was a lot of heavy salvage equipment lashed on deck, including the extra weight of an oversized lifting crane which probably caused the boat to lean a few degrees out of balance even in calm seas. If the helmsman didn't use more power there was a good chance we'd get caught in a beam sea. Then, any rogue wave could easily roll the boat over. I was surprised that, with all the rolling, the fuel tank sediment hadn't already fouled the engines. If they lost power in this storm we would all be fish bait.

I crouched again and went down the stairs. The passageway I descended into was dimly lit and led forward past the captain's quarters, amidships, and the crew's quarters on the starboard side farther forward. On the port side, a door was slamming open and shut each time the boat rolled and I could hear coughing and retching noises coming from inside, even above the muffled roar of the storm and the groaning of the boat's frame. I eased up to the door and flattened my body against the bulkhead, gripping the knife in my right hand. As the door flew open on the next roll, I saw the back of an enormously muscular young guy who was kneeling in front of a toilet bowl dry heaving almost in rhythm to the boat's rolling motion.

Now I moved quickly. I held the door open as the boat rocked back in an impossibly wide arc, and brought the heavy hilt of the knife down on the side of the man's skull. The muscleman collapsed like a hammered steer and lay face down on the steel deck. I removed the man's heavy garrison belt, looped it around his ankles, split the free end down the middle with my dive knife, and used the two heavy leather strands to hog-tie his hands to his ankles. Poor bastard, I muttered, no more seasickness for now.

Then I stepped back out into the passageway and latched the door behind me.

The passageway ended at a steel door up where the bow narrowed down to about eight-feet. As I flattened my body against the bulkhead to the left of the door, I could hear a man's voice on the other side speaking in a loud, but mostly garbled stream of words. The crashing seas outside the hull made it difficult to hear anything clearly—or even to keep standing—but I managed to press my ear against a louvered ventilator in the bulkhead and listened. The words, spoken in a deep, guttural voice, sounded like disconnected, made up, or just nonsense biblical phrases:

"And behold, there met him a woman with the attire of a harlot and a subtle heart.

Jezibel! Jew Bitch! The Sodom of New York is in thy veins. For by means of a whorish woman man is brought to destruction..."

I burst through the door and nearly fell over Sikes, who was kneeling in the dimly lit storage room facing a chest-high door, which led into the rope locker at the nose of the bow. He leaned with his hands straddling the door and his thick body swaying in a trance-like state. His pants were pulled down to his knees.

I got one arm around his neck while I held the dive knife up under his chin. "What does the Bible say about cutting the throats of your enemy, you perverted freak?"

Sikes froze in position without struggling. "Who are you?" he rasped.

"I'm a messenger from God, come to tell you that you've got the Bible all wrong. Now open that door in front of you. And if you move wrong you'll die."

The burly Nazi did what he was told. Laura, barefoot, soaked and shivering, dressed in a thin tee-shirt and shorts emerged from the darkness rubbing her eyes before opening them wide in disbelief. "Oh my God Erik! I thought you were dead."

"So did these throwbacks. I'm happy to disappoint them." I gave her a little smile as I added pressure to the chokehold while Sikes gasped for air.

She took a step towards me but I jerked his head downwards. "Get the gun out of his shoulder holster first."

She reached under Sikes' arm and pulled out a WWII-vintage German Luger, the original 9mm sidearm of Hitler's SS officers.

"Well, what's this? A little nostalgia for your hero?" I said as I snapped off the safety and checked that a round was already chambered before pressing the antique weapon against the back of Sikes' head.

He sucked a breath and tried to curse, but coughed instead, spraying bloody phlegm over the front of his yellow storm jacket. Laura looked down at him, and for the first time noticed that the burly Nazi was naked below the waist. She jumped back and cursed.

"Gruesome sight, isn't it?" I said. "Shocking attire for a man on his knees reciting his Bible."

"I'll kill you," Sikes wheezed. But before he could say more, I shoved the pistol hard into the back of his neck forcing him forward, face down, onto the deck.

"You already had your best shot at that. I don't give second chances."

I put my knee between the man's shoulder blades and turned to Laura. "There's a piece of rope on the floor there. Tie his hands behind his back while I hold him down."

Once his hands were tied, we both pulled and shoved him into the rope locker and I hog-tied his ankles to his hands. The bow continued making stomach-dropping plunges into the seas sending fountains of water through the hawse pipe hole overhead. Sikes now pleaded with us not to leave him there, but when the door slammed shut his pleas were drowned out in the din of groaning hull and booming waves. It was probably like being trapped inside a kettle drum.

Laura turned and put her arms around my waist. I hugged her back but my body was tense and coiled. When she looked up into my face she ran her finger along the white scar that must have been standing out like a ghostly pressure ridge.

"Did Book get back to the..." she began to say, but saw the answer in my face before I said it.

"He didn't make it. I never saw him after the explosion. I tried to find him but I . . ." My mouth stopped talking, my eyes burned as I closed them, and I pressed Laura to my chest.

"Erik. I'm sorry. So, so sorry. Oh my God, this is a nightmare. You did everything you could. These people are not human; there's nothing that anyone could have done."

We embraced tightly for a few more seconds as the boat pitched beneath our feet.

"There's something that I can do now, though. I'm going to stop them. They're not going to win. But I won't risk your life to do it. Let's go up on deck now, before somebody comes down here looking for you."

Then, I pretty much lied to her. "I've got a plan."

"Erik, I want you alive. Nothing else really matters."

I looked down at her and forced a smile. "I feel the same way about you. But we're not going to survive unless I can take over this boat. If we play this smart, and have a little luck on our side, we may both get our wishes."

Shoving the Luger into the back of my waistband, I took Laura by the hand and led her aft to the stairway. As we passed by the head where I had left the muscular skinhead tied up, there was no sound coming from behind the locked door. Then we were up the stairs and inside the deckhouse.

It wasn't a pretty sight.

Every time the boat rolled to port a column of sea water streamed through the blasted out window and raked the lounge area with knee deep water that flung loose dive equipment around like a flash flood. We staggered across to the door and exited onto the starboard deck underneath the cabin overhang. Laura's face was already pale, but she blanched further when she looked out at the maelstrom before her. An enormous thunderhead blotted out the sky and reflected a deathly yellow pall on the foaming tops of the waves. The wind continued to rage, wailing like a church organ as it blew out of the northeast, ripping the tops off seas that rose well above the wheelhouse. The air was so filled with water that it threatened to drown anyone out in the open.

I estimated that the boat was running a west by southwest course. Even without a compass, I knew that the course was all wrong. If they kept on it, we'd wind up on the Jersey Shore. Of course, that's if we didn't sink first.

The wind made it difficult to stand. I pushed Laura down to the deck where she could hold on to a cleat. Then I eased my head carefully out from under the overhang and peered up at the wheelhouse. All I could see were two figures inside. There had been three people before. I didn't know where the other one had gone, but knew I had to work fast.

At the far aft end of the cabin top I spotted an eight-man, rigid plastic life raft that was lashed down with thick bungee cords. It had about a foot's clearance underneath. It would have to do.

Grabbing Laura under one arm I stood her up and signaled her to move towards the stern with her back to the cabin bulkhead. When we got under the spot where the raft was lashed overhead I stopped her and handed her my dive knife.

"I'm going to boost you up onto the cabin top. There's a life raft up there. Slide underneath and tie yourself to it. Don't come out for any reason. If anything happens to the boat, cut the lashings and hang on to the raft."

She looked a little puzzled and started to protest, but I just smiled and told her, "Trust me, we're going to make it."

Then she nodded, and when the boat dropped into the next trough I pushed her up and over the lip of the roof. "There you go, Bub," I said. She turned, looked grimly at me, and mouthed "Be careful, Erik" before she slithered quickly under the raft.

Now all I had to do was figure out how I was going to get up into the wheelhouse, overpower three armed fanatics, and bring the boat to a safe refuge in a near hurricane. Piece of cake, I mumbled to myself sarcastically.

I peered inside the lounge area again just as the boat took another big sea on the port sending white water surging through the shattered window like a log flume. I ducked down and began crawling forward on the slanted deck, keeping my body pressed up against the cabin bulkhead so that the overhang would shield me from anyone looking down from the bridge. Once I got underneath the outside starboard ladder, I'd be able to get up to the bridge. I was counting on the people up there keeping their backs to me as they focused on the seas coming from straight ahead. By taking advantage of the blind spot and the element of surprise, I hoped I'd be able to rush Gebhardt and the others before they could react. I checked the ancient luger that I had taken from Gebhardt's gorilla and wondered if German craftsmanship could still be counted on after more than seventy years. I didn't want to have to kill anybody, but I knew they wouldn't have the same scruples towards me, so I was ready to do whatever I had to do in order to overpower them.

Suddenly, I felt the bow slip to port and a mountainous wave rose up above the starboard rail. It continued to rise beyond the height of the bridge, expanding and swelling until it blocked out the dark sky with its granite-hued face laced with streamers of white foam. Time seemed compressed into a super slow motion as I watched the wave poised overhead and felt the boat begin to roll over onto its port beam. At the same moment, the cabin door, five-feet in front of me, burst open and Burris Shoup appeared, stumbling and shouting something that was drowned out in the roar of wind and water.

Before I could react from my prone position, I felt the sharp jab of a gun barrel thrust against the side of my neck.

"Get up and keep your hands clear," Shoup shouted in my face.

I wanted to say that now was not a great time to be standing up as I watched him struggle to keep balanced. The boat continued rising up the face of the monster wave, at the same time tilting onto its beam ends like a carnival ride. Then it was like a delayed reaction as the whole situation registered in Shoup's primitive brain. He turned partly around and muttered, "Oh shit!" as he looked up at a wall of water crashing down on us.

I felt the gun slip away from my neck. I braced myself with one hand against the cabin bulkhead, which was now canted over at a 45-degree angle, and lunged at Shoup, who was knocked off balance and clawing for a handhold. I grabbed his gun hand and twisted it up behind his back until the shoulder tore. Shoup screamed, the gun fell away, and then everything disappeared in chaos as we were buried under the giant wave.

I barely had time to take a breath as we were both swept under. I let go of Shoup's arm and grabbed onto the door handle. My lungs were bursting for air as I strained to hold on under the weight of green water dragging the boat into a steeper angle. I wondered if it had the spirit to rise again. A steel-hulled boat of this size might turn turtle at a thirty or forty degree angle. If that happened, I doubted that there would be enough air in my lungs to reach the surface from under the overturned hull. I thought of Laura hidden under the life raft. If she was underwater now she'd soon break free along with the raft. She was a survivor. Also a hell of a good swimmer. And she had already demonstrated her breath-holding abilities when she made the free-dive when LeClair was hurt. Remembering that now made me feel another twinge of shame at the way that I had reacted: chastising her for her thoughtfulness and good intentions. What an idiot I had been for not appreciating her. It would serve me right to drown like a rat along with the Nazi bastards on board. There would be a certain justice in that.

My lungs were screaming to breathe, and a knot of pain radiated out from my chest threatening to close down my brain. But, just before that happened I felt the boat slowly roll back to an upright position, and my head broke out into the shrieking storm again. Shoup was gone, along with the gun, as well as the Luger that I had shoved into my waistband. The boat was turning more to starboard now to take the waves on its quarter, but I could feel the big diesel engines running rough and hesitating. I pulled myself upright and looked back towards the lifeboat. It was still lashed in place. I hoped that Laura was all right but never had a chance to go check.

Still on my knees, I turned to go forward just as the bridge door opened. This time Gebhardt's cadaverous face looked down at me. Clad in the bulky, orange life jacket, he was pale and shaken by the near disaster, but he pointed a 9mm pistol at my chest with a steady enough hand.

"Welcome aboard, Captain Hazen!" he shouted. "I don't know how in the hell you got here, but we might be in need of your skills. So don't make me shoot you. Just climb up the ladder."

CHAPTER TWENTY-EIGHT

THE VIEW FROM THE BRIDGE WAS HAIR-RAISING. SHEETING CURTAINS OF RAIN that slanted down from acid-hued clouds erased all trace of a horizon. A confused turmoil of vertical water—humped and spiked without predictable pattern—assaulted the boat from every angle, and turned the ocean into a lunar landscape set in liquid motion. The main set of mountainous, rolling seas swept in from the aft, port quarter, sometimes burying the stern in breaking white water and shoving the 75-foot boat sideways across the face of a wave like a surfboard. Other times, a lateral set of spiky waves came from mid-ships and broke dangerously across the port bow. Some of these latter waves I estimated at over twenty feet.

Russell Shoup was at the wheel. His face was as tense and as drained of color as the veined marble of a Greek sculpture. He was muttering under his breath with a running commentary of profanity as he struggled to keep the boat angled into the waves. I could see that he had given up any attempt to run a course and was just trying to keep the boat upright now.

Gebhardt pressed the gun into my side and shoved me towards Shoup. "Take over the wheel, Captain Hazen. If you want to see Ms. Morgan alive again, you'll get us back to land."

I grabbed the wheel and Shoup stood back shaking. "Fucking waves are trying to sink us," he mumbled, his face set in fearful disbelief.

I looked up at the ruined Loran and the chart plotter monitor and realized that neither was working. Hank Manson had smashed out the screens of both instruments along with the binnacle compass. The radio wires had been ripped out as well. Nice going, Hank, I thought, at least you did one good deed in your life.

"Have you been trying to keep any course at all?" I asked the grim-faced Shoup.

"Course? Shit, even if I knew where we were I couldn't hold any course in this storm. We're lucky we're still afloat."

Gebhardt spoke up. "This is your home water, Hazen. You should be able to navigate your way back home."

I looked over my left shoulder where a steep, gray wave with a crown of breaking water rushed towards us laterally. At the same time, I saw the stern begin to be overtaken by a huge Atlantic swell. I leaned the wheel hard over to face the lateral wave, goosed the throttles ahead at the same time and the boat angled along the leading edge of the roller as it turned to climb the face of the steeper wave. The boat shuddered and rocked but stayed relatively even-keeled as it slid through the yellow foam on the wave's crest. Then I throttled back to slow its descent.

I turned to Gebhardt, who was standing near the port side window that had been shattered by Mike LeClair's shotgun blasts. "Just as important as steering a course is to keep the engines running. All this pounding and rocking is stirring up sediment in the fuel tanks. I need somebody to get down into the engine room and start changing fuel filters nonstop. If we foul a filter or an air intake we could lose both engines. In this sea we'd be done for real quick."

Gebhardt looked over at Shoup. "Where's Nolte and Sikes?"

"Nolte went below an hour ago. He was too sick to be good for anything. I haven't seen Sikes since he took the woman to the rope locker. What happened to my brother?"

I glanced at him and grinned. "He went for a swim on the last wave that you almost sank the boat in."

Shoup cursed and lunged at me, but Gebhardt held him back with the pistol.

"There's no time for that now. Our fearless captain will get his rewards soon enough," His normally expressionless blue eyes flared with anger. "Now find Sikes and get him to do the job in the engine room."

The port engine sputtered and hesitated as I gave it more throttle to ride up the back of the next wave. "We don't have time for that! I need somebody in the engine room right now."

"Get below and do what the captain says," Gebhardt ordered as he nudged Shoup, who didn't look very happy as he opened the bridge door and disappeared down the ladder in an enveloping swirl of rain and spray.

I could see Gebhardt in my peripheral vision as the old Nazi propped himself against the port windows and kept the gun leveled in my direction.

"So, Captain Hazen, I see the fortunes of fate have sent you to guide us back to land."

I felt my jaws tighten as I gripped the wheel. "That's a big leap in faith. How do you know I can? And if I don't, what are you going to do, shoot me?"

"That would be foolish and unnecessary. Are you forgetting that we have your lady friend? Such a pretty little thing—for a Jew. Sikes admires her greatly. Of course he is a crude fellow—not the type to respect such delicate beauty."

I didn't react to his threat but was thankful for the storm-driven seas bearing down on the boat. They forced me to concentrate and keep my hands on the wheel. If the weather were calmer, I probably wouldn't have been able to keep myself from lunging at the despicable maniac standing behind me—and probably get shot in the attempt. Instead, I focused on keeping the boat upright. I could also take some satisfaction in the fact that, at least, Laura was out of Gebhardt's reach—for now.

"If we do get to land I suppose you're going to just drop us off with a handshake at the nearest dock before you go on to catch a plane back to Germany?"

"One should never look too far into the future, my friend. Just steer the boat."

With no navigational instruments and an enforced radio silence, I tried to keep the bow pointed to what I figured was a north/north/east direction. I reached overhead and flipped a switch. Gebhardt tensed and snapped the gun up.

"What're you doing? What's that switch for?"

I pointed at the screen overhead. The only one that Manson hadn't damaged. "Just the depth recorder. It's the only electronics aboard still working. At least with a bottom contour I can get some idea of where we are."

The recorder showed an evenly sloped bottom 120-feet below. I was a little surprised. We had already come quite a ways. The following seas had pushed the boat closer to shore than I thought. If the weather would just clear enough for me to get an approximate position, I could probably run into the lee of Block Island. But then I reminded myself that that probably wouldn't happen. Once he saw land, Gebhardt wouldn't need me anymore. He wouldn't waste any more time before executing me—and Laura if he found her—and dumping our bodies at sea, where they were not likely to ever turn up—unless they wound up just like my father, tangled in the net of some fishing boat.

"You impress me Captain. Any man that can navigate by looking at the bottom of the ocean must be a magician."

"No magic involved. And I can't really navigate this way, but I've looked at this bottom long enough to get a little hint of where we are."

As I said this another rogue wave appeared in the starboard window, barreling in fast from out of the blowing curtains of rain. I throttled back on the starboard engine, gunned the port, and leaned the wheel over. My own body leaned, too, as I willed the boat to make the turn towards the approaching cliff of water.

For a minute it looked like the boat would climb the near vertical face of water. Then the wave broke across the bow pushing the starboard rail under and dipping the wheelhouse down into the raging surface. Gebhardt slid across the wheelhouse from the port to the starboard window, where he sat pinned against the bulkhead trying to orient himself and hold on to the gun at the same time. I held tight to the wheel with my right leg jammed against the helmsman's seat stanchion. I thought the boat might keep going over as the wave buried us in green water, but after what seemed like several minutes it began to right itself and shake the ocean out of its scuppers. When it broke out into the trough, I gave it more throttle, and *White Shark II* shot forward to meet the next hill of water head on.

Amazingly, the windows had held for the few seconds that the wheelhouse had become a submarine. Below decks everything not bolted down would have been flung about like an earthquake temblor. It gave some small satisfaction to think about the two skinheads locked below being shaken like a pair of dice. But I hoped that the bilge pumps would keep up with the water that washed through the hatches, and that Shoup would still be able to change the fuel filters. Both engines had to keep running. That was our only ticket to survival.

I heard Gebhardt cursing and struggling to get back onto his feet behind me. Then I turned and looked out to where the raft was lashed to the cabin top. It was still there. Laura was still safe; I was sure she was.

"Is that the best that you can do, Captain?" Gebhardt sputtered. "I thought you were used to navigating in rough weather?"

"In case you haven't noticed, those waves out there are three stories high. This isn't 'rough weather.' This is a killer storm. And it doesn't discriminate. It'll drown your Aryan ass as well as my Bonacker behind. So maybe you ought to start praying to your Teutonic gods; I'm sure as hell praying to my God."

For the next two hours the boat was pounded, tossed, shaken, and nearly capsized a dozen times but still managed to stay afloat and maintain some semblance of a course. My legs were aching from trying to maintain my balance behind the helm. My hands were cramped from gripping the wheel and my neck muscles were tight from tension. Except for an occasional curse, Gebhardt was quiet. I had to admit that the old man was one tough son of a bitch.

I looked at my dive watch; it was 3:20 PM. I knew that we must be getting close to Block Island—that would be the first landfall before Montauk Point—but I couldn't be sure how close without using electronics or getting a visual sighting. Time was running out. Pretty soon I would have to do something drastic if I expected to save myself and Laura. What that would be I still didn't know.

And then it suddenly stopped raining. Within a few minutes the wind shifted more to the north and the clouds began to blow south. Soon, the sky brightened and patches of blue showed through the bullet-scarred windows of the pilot house. Wind still howled through the cables and the seas were as mountainous as ever, but the storm was on its way out.

Still, there was no land in sight. In a way the scene before me was even more ominous as the view became clearer. It seemed that the boat rode a vortex along a swirling circle of leaping, curling seas. Now, the sparkling glare of sun impinging on the fractured surface was almost blinding after the dark sepias and gray monotones of the last several hours.

Gebhardt looked out across the broken ocean, shading his eyes with one hand. A satisfied grin spread across his lean face.

"It seems that the gods were looking down on us after all, Captain Hazen."

I didn't answer right away. I was focused on searching the horizon for something familiar, something that would give me a position and, maybe, buy more time. I still held out hope that Fletch King was able to radio the Coast Guard after the attack on the Prowler—assuming that King and LeClair and the rest were still alive—a risky assumption given the type of people we are dealing with, I thought.

Then I half-turned to Gebhardt. "We're not out of it yet," I said, pointing to the depth recorder, which was indicating a jagged bottom profile in about 90-feet of water. "This shallow water is more dangerous. More breaking waves coming at closer intervals. Don't start celebrating until you're tied up at the dock."

Gebhardt sneered. "You are a cautious man for someone in such a risky business, Captain."

"If you're talking about diving and salvaging, it's only risky when you fail to respect the elements of nature. Or, when you just plain fuck up."

"Ah! Good homespun advice. I almost forgot that you are descended from generations of simple fishermen. Perhaps it will make a good epitaph."

"I wouldn't be the first Hazen to die at sea, if that's what you mean."

I couldn't see it, but I knew that Gebhardt was smiling his wolfish smile. There wasn't much time left now. At any time Shoup might leave the engine room and discover the other two locked up below. There would be a search for Laura. Land would heave into sight and my own usefulness would come to an end.

Images of the dream from a couple of days ago flickered in my mind: Laura's face, white and lifeless, staring up at me from shadowy depths. It's just not going to happen, I thought as I pushed it from his brain and tried to stay focused on navigating the boat.

It was then that I saw something bobbing in the water ahead. It was a lobster buoy with a short staff and a red flag attached. As we passed it, I could see the narrow bands of green and white above a broad band of orange. Every lobsterman has a coded color for his buoys just like a rancher has a brand. This one was the property of Calvin Hedges in East Hampton. Calvin is one of my neighbors and I knew he was running a string of lobster pots just south of the Southwest Ledge, not far from Block Island. This was one of them, which meant we should be just coming in sight of the island.

The ledge area is a treacherous piece of water where the bottom suddenly rises from 80-feet to 17-feet. It's marked on navigational charts with a warning to mariners that there can be breaking water in storm surges. It's actually part of an underwater moraine left over from the last ice age. I knew it intimately from years of fishing and diving for the abundant schools of stripers and big cod that frequent the protective pile of glacial boulders that lie hidden there.

Sure enough, as the boat rode up the back of the next wave, I could just make out a tiny sliver of land appearing and disappearing against a ragged northern horizon. That would be the dark, boulder-strewn cliffs of Block Island. Between here and the island lay the ledge. Finally, a desperate plan began to form in my mind as I eased the boat in that direction.

I stole a glance at Gebhardt and saw that he wasn't feeling great. He had been fighting off nausea for the last couple of hours, but it kept coming back. He was sitting on a narrow bench built into the bulkhead and every time the boat bottomed out in a trough he grunted with the pain that must have shot up through his ass. I guess he figured it was better than standing and having to look at the nightmarish conditions on the water. That was a good thing for me, maybe he wouldn't notice that land was beginning to come into view.

He still held the gun in his right hand. Meanwhile, he looked like he was concentrating on something in his left hand, and I realized it was a rubber ball that he was squeezing. Every so often he switched hands.

"Keeping yourself in shape for the next revolution?" I said.

"Very funny, Captain Hazen. Even a man of your limited intelligence should know that any weakness can be conquered by intense concentration. Seasickness is just a weakness and I'm beginning to feel better already."

He shoved the ball into his pocket and reached down and hauled the single attaché case up from under the chart table where he had put it hours ago. I thought he might become distracted enough to give me a chance to go for his gun, but he was eight feet away and I knew his reflexes were still good. I watched out of the corner of my eyes as he swung the case up onto the table. I knew the other two were locked away in the equipment box on deck. This case was amazingly intact. It had a thin coating of brown algae over its surface and the locking mechanisms were probably rusted shut, but it looked like it might have been in the water a couple of years, rather than half a century.

Gebhardt rummaged around in the chart drawers and found a big screwdriver which he used to jimmy the rusted locks on the case. They snapped easily. Now, as the boat still pitched, he carefully forced the case open. I could see a gooey, black silt covered everything, but as he scraped some away I saw that the case was crammed with small, black bags, possibly made of some silky material. He lifted one out and the material fell apart in his hands revealing five diamonds the size of small marbles. When he lifted his hand to the sunlight, they sparkled as only perfect stones can. Jesus! I thought. They really do exist.

Gebhardt seemed mesmerized as he gazed at the glittering handful. Then he saw me stealing glances, grinned, and seemed to read my mind.

"Yes, Captain Hazen, the Fuhrer Gems are no legend. Thanks to your diligent work here they are, or, at least, a small sample of them."

I continued to grip the wheel and felt the blood rise in my face. "Yes. I see that they exist. The trouble is they don't belong to you, they're stolen loot that have the blood of a million people on them."

"A million people? Acch! There you go with your ignorant holocaust theory. These gems," he held the diamonds out towards me, "always belonged to the German people. They just had to be liberated from some sub-human scum who claimed to own them. And now they are liberated from the sea and shall, once again, be used by the faithful to bring about changes in the world. Changes that are long overdue."

The man was so obviously over the edge that I don't know why I bothered to say anything. Maybe it's because I remembered from my grandfather's stories that the Hazen family had, long ago, merged with some people of color: my maternal great, great grandfather was reputed to be a freed slave. Also, a Shinnecock Indian had married another relative early in the 20th-century.

"How can a man of your supposed intelligence believe that swill? It's not 1940 anymore. Most of the world doesn't match the color scheme that your great mentor envisioned."

He slipped the handful of diamonds into his pocket and looked up at me as I stood ramrod straight behind the helm.

"Ah, Captain Hazen. There you go again with your made-up statistics that come from the media, which is dominated and controlled by the Jews. But, what can I expect from a man with such strong, Aryan features, and, yet, works for the Jews? And, is so obviously a Jew lover?"

I said nothing. I could see his nausea was beginning to pass. He was still sitting down but he craned his neck around looking at the waves and out towards the horizon. I'm sure he could see that, very soon now, Shoup could take over the helm; the weather was improving by the minute. Then I could easily imagine what he planned to do with me—and Laura, if he found her.

"I see that the weather is looking much better. Soon we should make landfall—that is if your navigational skills are as good as they are reputed to be. These little beauties," he tapped the open briefcase, "will be on their way to a secure bank vault by morning."

He began busying himself with some fishing line to tie the case closed. It was good that he was preoccupied as I kept my eyes straight ahead and eased off the northerly course as we came to within a few miles of Block Island. The Southwest Ledge lay just to the west and I began turning the boat in that direction. While the old Nazi stayed mesmerized by his loot, I had time to get the boat in position for the plan that I only hoped would work.

Suddenly, Gebhardt was standing close behind my left shoulder. "What land is that over there?" he asked.

I nudged the throttle ahead to pick up speed before I answered. "The southern end of Block Island."

"Why aren't you headed in that direction?"

"There's no harbor there. Lots of shoal water and rocks. We have to pass around the ocean buoy up ahead before we can turn into Block Island Sound. From there we can head in to Montauk or Orient Point or Block Island or any number of deep water docks in New York, Connecticut, or Rhode Island. Whatever suits you."

"Very good. You make a good tour guide, Captain Hazen."

I was surprised when I looked at Gebhardt's pale face, ringed by a border of perspiration. Up close, the old man suddenly looked his age. Even his movements were sluggish now as he fumbled with the intercom button on the console before speaking.

"Shoup! We're coming around Block Island now, so finish what you're doing and get up here. See if you can find Sikes, too. He must still be up in the rope locker with the woman." Gebhardt winked and smiled at me as he made the comment, but if he was expecting a reaction he was disappointed. I knew Laura was safely tucked away, so my face remained expressionless and locked in concentration.

What I was concentrating on was an acre-sized area in the ocean just ahead that looked like an erupting geyser in the dark center of the steep hills of water. Only once before had I ever seen the Southwest Ledge breaking like this. That had been after Hurricane Gloria back in 1985. I had been young and stupid enough back then to go out the day after the hurricane looking for a 30-foot sailboat that had radioed a distress call the night before. The sailboat had later turned up— dismasted but safe—in the Mystic River, but I had had a harrowing ride skirting the ledge's thundering seas.

I wasn't that young anymore, but maybe I was even more stupid. As I looked at the ruptured water ahead, I thought, hell, maybe this is worse than stupid; maybe this is just plain suicide, but I was out of options now, and Laura was huddled under the life raft depending on me. So I said a quick, silent prayer, and pointed the *White Shark II* directly at the maelstrom.

Gebhardt's voice broke my concentration. "Captain Hazen, I would hate to keep you in suspense about the salvage job you so expertly did for us. He held out a single diamond that flashed like white flame at the tips of his fingers. "Look at this up close. I want you to see the great deed that you have done for us. The future Aryan race thanks you."

The flash of the stone strobed into my memory and I saw black and white images of concentration camps, and I saw Book Johnson's body rolling with the current over a twilit landscape. "Shove it up your ass," I said.

Gebhardt just smiled.

The seas were still so rough and the western glare so intense, that Gebhardt didn't notice anything at first. He continued to be mesmerized by the glinting facets of the diamond as he turned it in the light. Shoup still hadn't come up from below and Gebhardt must have been wondering what happened to him when he looked up. In an instant, he saw the suicide course we were running, and screamed at me.

"What are you doing? Turn the boat! Turn the boat!"

I held the wheel in an iron grip maintaining the collision course. Then the cold, hard barrel of Gebhardt's pistol was shoved violently against the back of my neck.

"Turn the boat now, or you're dead!"

So I did turn the boat. I spun the wheel hard to the starboard— not away from the thundering explosion of a near vertical ocean, but directly into it. At the same time I shoved forward on the port engine throttle and dropped to my knees, with my hands still holding tight to the wheel.

Gebhardt—fumbling with the diamond and the gun—was knocked backwards by the violent lurch of the boat, which pinned him against the rear bulkhead. His gun clattered across the wheelhouse floor, but I made no effort to grab for it. I was too busy holding on and watching the huge wave that held the boat heeled over on its port rail before dropping it into a seething trough that had opened up around the ledge like the gates of Hell.

The boat slid down the face of the wave sideways and hit the ridge of black glacial boulders at the bottom with such force that I knew the half-inch steel plate bottom had split open like a dropped melon. I saw the next wave rise well above the wheelhouse, but this time the boat didn't ride up to meet it. There was a deafening roar of ocean joined by the high pitched shriek of rending steel as a dark wall of water collided with the starboard side of the mortally wounded *White Shark II*.

The big wave hit the side of the wheelhouse like a locomotive, ripping the wheel out of my hands and catapulting me across the wheelhouse floor. The force of the wave blew the side window out, flooding the cabin as the boat continued to topple over onto its port side. In the seconds before the boat continued its roll, I sucked air into my lungs.

Then I was underwater. Everything turned to dark shadows, and I could feel the sandpapery surface of the no-skid decking pressing down on my head. There was no up or down. Quickly clearing the pressure on my ears, I reached out to grab onto something and felt the helmsman's seat pedestal. I hung on as the ocean swept through and the deck ceiling plunged deeper into the water. I knew the steel hull, over-weighted as it was with a lifting crane, would go straight down within seconds. If it slid past the glacial ledge it would plunge into water eighty feet deep and I might never make it to the surface.

A full minute went by with the boat seesawing on the edge of the rocks. Every time another wave crashed down on the overturned hull the scream of stressed metal reverberated through the water. The wheelhouse was ten feet under being slammed against the ledge with every surge.

I thought about drowning. Of the irresistible urge to take a breath. To fill my lungs with seawater because there was nothing else to do. From deep in the past an image flashed through my brain: my father's body lying on the beach after Uncle Harry snagged it in his net. White, bloated, grotesquely comical in the way it sagged on the warm sand like a half-inflated balloon. A man stripped of his dignity, as well as his life. As his body lay in the hot sun a little crowd of beach strollers gathered to gawk.

I thought of Kate, still beautiful in death, but with the pale look of a marble sculpture, as though the ocean had sucked all the blood from her body along with her life. She was rising above me like a pale angel, ascending through green water, blue sky and into the whiteness of summer clouds where she would wait for me to follow. Just one deep breath and I'd be there.

Then I remembered Laura—her dark eyes peering out from under a lifeboat. I had left her out there with nothing but a knife and a piece of advice. She must be somewhere up there now, I thought, on the surface, in the air, up where a deep breath brings life, not death. Gradually, I realized that the lack of oxygen was anesthetizing my brain. If I didn't act now I'd be dead in less than a minute.

Pushing away from the ceiling, I dove down in the dark and felt around for the shattered side window. Shards of glass cut my hands as I pulled my body through while the boat continued to shudder and groan against the underwater cliff. There was no pain. Only a growing urgency to live again. Steel rigging cables hung from the deck above my head coiling and swinging in slow motion like water snakes. I pushed through them, my head pounding and chest searing with pain, willing myself to fight the primal instinct to breathe. Finally, angling my ascent out from under the swaying deck above, I drove hard for clear water and the distant surge on the blurred surface above.

CHAPTER TWENTY-NINE

A DISK OF FLASHING LIGHT BURST IN MY BRAIN. AT FIRST, I THOUGHT THAT I must have suffered a stroke from the strain of holding my breath for several minutes. Instead, I gasped air into my lungs and squinted into the blinding sunlight. Miraculously, I was on the surface treading water at the edge of the shoal. For a moment I reveled in my newly granted life.

Plastic cups, bags, and assorted flotsam from the sunken boat skittered across the oil-slicked surface of the waves. Close behind me, the roaring surge of breaking water thundered over the submerged ledge obliterating the air bubbles that rose from the drowning boat. I began to kick away from the sound to keep from being sucked into the pounding breakers, swimming down the curving face of the big rollers like a surfer, heading into the western sun. There was no horizon, only vertical water left in the aftermath of the storm. Block Island was only a few miles to the north; I might be able to swim it, I thought.

Then I remembered Gebhardt. Could he have somehow gotten out of the pilothouse? It was doubtful. The others must be dead too, certainly the two I had tied up were, and probably Russell Shoup as well. But Laura had to have made it. The raft would float free, all she had to do was hang on.

I struck out towards the west to find her.

I began to shout her name once every minute as I swam. There was no echo. Except for the now muffled sound of the waves and the chuff of wind over water, the ocean was quiet. No sea birds broke the silence. I felt small. Held in the grip of a great force of nature where my own life was of no consequence, I knew I might live or I might die. Nature was indifferent to my survival.

I licked my lips. The salt water tasted as much like home as the scent of lilac and the cut grass of the meadow behind my house. It tasted of schools of cold, sleek mackerel, of hard-shelled crab and ribbed mussel, of spiny sea stars and floating rockweed, and sea lettuce, and sunken ledges. It must have tasted the same to my father, to his grandfather, and to all the men of my family who went to sea to find life—and death. Even in the sunlight, I thought, death still loomed. I supposed that if I died out here I'd simply be completing the long tradition of drowning at sea begun many generations ago in the Hazen family. At least I had no children to continue the tradition, I thought. The Hazen line would stop here. There probably would be no body to bury. Only a marker in the family plot, and a new owner of the house who might think it quaint to have a fisherman's graveyard on the property.

Jesus! I'm hallucinating, I thought. I snapped out of the morbid spell and re-concentrated my efforts to the job at hand—find Laura and survive.

Gradually, I became aware of another sound above my own, raspy breathing. It came from off to the right and out of sight beyond the backs of the green wave hills. A faint voice in the distance? Or just the hissing of wave crests or mewling of a distant gull? I wasn't sure, but I began swimming towards the sound.

I called again but no answer came back. I was swimming on the surface now, up and over the backs of the big waves, practically bodysurfing down their speeding faces. The sun was sinking fast and I swam in the wave shadows when I dropped into a trough. Something was wrong. I could sense it. The water tasted of fear.

At the top of the next wave, I saw the raft. It looked like a smudge of orange in my sight for a few seconds before I slid down the back down into the trough. It's hard to judge distance when you're at water level surrounded by huge seas, but I estimated that it was 100-yards away.

I struck out in the general direction and waited for the next wave to raise me up again. This time I saw Laura's back as she knelt in the boat and seemed to be waving her arms in the opposite direction. I tried shouting, but in the few seconds I had sight of her she made no move to turn around. A couple more waves failed to bring me in sight of the raft and, when one did, I only caught it out of the corner of my eye, so I had to alter my course.

The next time I saw it, the raft was, maybe, 200-feet away and I instinctively shouted her name. Just as I did, I realized that she wasn't waving to signal somebody, she was slashing at something next to the raft with the dive knife. Just as she disappeared from sight again, I saw her turn towards the sound of my voice, and at the same time an arm reached up from the water and grabbed her knife hand. In seconds she was out of sight again, but I knew that the arm must belong to Gebhardt.

I swam with all the strength I had, but the next time I saw the raft Laura was gone. In her place sat Gebhardt in his orange life vest, clutching the knife and waving it in my direction, his face twisted in anger.

"Stay away from the raft," he shouted as he rose on the next wave and I dropped into the trough below it.

Now no more than thirty-feet separated us. I could see that he was holding his shoulder and that there was blood on his life jacket. But, Laura was nowhere to be seen.

"Where's Laura?" I shouted. But at the same moment I saw a dark form suspended in the water just out from and below the raft. I dove and jackknifed down towards it. My heart pounded in my ears against the rising fear. It was almost like the dream. Laura suspended face down slowly sinking into the darkening shafts of green water. I reached down to her and grabbed onto one white arm, then turned and kicked for the surface, at the same time drawing her body close to me and gently cradling her head with my other arm.

As soon as I broke the surface I sucked a couple of deep breaths of air and began giving her mouth to mouth while I struggled to keep her head out of the water. Her black hair framed the lifeless pallor of her face. Only the blueness of her lips added color to her face.

As I struggled with Laura in the water, the raft began to slip away, borne on the crest of waves and driven by the gusting wind. Gebhardt laughed and taunted me as the distance between us widened.

"You soft hearted fool, Captain!" I heard him yell like a victorious bettor. "This is just the reason that I will survive and come back to claim my treasure. You are a sentimentalist. A lover. You are willing to sacrifice success for the sake of a woman—and a Jew at that!"

But I was way too busy to pay much attention. I was tiring in my efforts to keep both myself and Laura afloat. Seawater gagged me between desperate breaths to revive her. I felt the twisting worm of fear stirring in my guts and beginning to rise to my chest.

For a moment, everything seemed frozen in a tableau. The waves continued to roll in from the deep ocean, sunlight slanted in from the land where people were probably barbecuing under rain washed skies and breathing the sweet air of a summer evening. But here, the high drama of life and death would play out to no observers save a few white birds that were now wheeling high above. Them and a demented castaway drifting to his own questionable fate.

CHAPTER THIRTY

Then, two small miracles happened. First, something slammed hard against my back.

I spun in the water and faced the image of an attacking white shark, mouth wide open, huge jaws thrust forward in the final instant before snapping shut. It took a split second before I realized that it was only a stenciled image on the side of a large, fiberglass storage box, but in that time a surge of adrenaline brought me back to life.

I recognized the box from Manson's boat. It was six feet long, neatly locked with a little brass padlock, and watertight enough for it to ride a few inches above the surface. I immediately grabbed on to the hasp and held Laura's body tightly against the box as I blew yet another breath past her blue lips. This time she choked, took a shallow breath, and groaned in pain from the pressure against her broken ribs. Her eyes fluttered and finally opened. She moved her mouth to speak, but she took in a mouthful of water and choked again.

"Don't try to say anything," I told her. I looked into her eyes and smiled. She smiled back weakly, but I could see that she was in pain. "Put your foot into my hand and I'll boost you up onto the box."

After a short struggle, I was able to get her mostly up out of the water where she lay groaning and exhausted, but still able to smile faintly as I stayed in the water and steadied the box from one end like a surfer so we could ride up and over the big waves.

I grinned back at her and kept her arms clamped tightly against the smooth surface of the box, at the same time talking to her to keep her spirits up. "If we have to, we can surf all the way to Montauk Point. The tourists eating dinner on Gosman's Dock will wave when we go by."

With her head out of the water and the sun beginning to warm her body, Laura was able to smile and speak in a faint voice. "Whatever you say, Captain. But try to take these waves a little smoother, my ribs feel like somebody's been using them for batting practice."

For several minutes, everything was quiet. I maneuvered to hold the floating box in line with the westward set of the waves and continued to hold my left hand over Laura's wrist to keep her steady as we rolled with the waves. She looked at me through half closed eyes and giggled.

"What's so funny?" I asked.

"It just struck me," she said, "that with that rugged but boyish face of yours, your hair sticking out wildly, and your look of concentration on the water ahead, that you look like a grown-up version of Huck Finn pushing his raft."

I grinned. "Well, I guess that's better than Ishmael pushing a coffin."

Overhead, the color of the sky was deepening to purple, and white clouds were taking on a salmon tint. Nearby, a pair of terns wheeled and swooped.

Laura scowled at me. "Don't talk about coffins. I can't help thinking about Uncle Carl. He once floated, hurt and in pain, in these same waters. But look at the long life he went on to live. We're going to make it out of this alive, too."

I didn't say anything, just smiled and thought to myself, yes, we are going to make it. And, best of all, unlike Carl, we are going to make it together.

For the next few minutes Laura told me how she had cut the raft loose just as we hit the rocks and the first big wave broadsided the boat. I could see the purple bruise on her thigh where she had struck the boat's rail before being flung out into the exploding maelstrom of the sea. The leg was not broken, but her side hurt with every breath indicating at least a couple of broken ribs. She told me how she first saw see the dull, red bottom of the boat with its crushed and twisted propellers awash in white water. But that after her raft dropped into the valley of another sea and rose again there was no more sign of the capsized boat. She had searched desperately for some sign of me, but nothing but flotsam and debris appeared on the surface as the raft drifted quickly away from the site.

For a while she lay in a dazed state, wincing in pain with each breath. Suddenly, something had grabbed onto the raft behind her. She had twisted around thinking it had to be me. That's when she heard a man's wheezing and coughing as the raft shook with someone trying to climb aboard. When she looked down, the pale, cruel face of Kurt Gebhardt stared back at her. There were tears in her eyes as she told me of the struggle to keep him out, of how she succeeded in slashing his shoulder with the knife before he overpowered her. Then he had clubbed her in the back of her head before he pulled her into the water.

I squeezed her hand. "You did good, Bub," I said, and she smiled weakly.

Finally, there was no need for talk. Overhead, a fast moving scud of white clouds swirled by. I looked up at it as I kicked, and at the hills of green water that held us in their grip as we moved slowly towards the sun. The whole scene, I thought, belied the enormous tragedy. It was as though an evil presence had reached out from the pages of history, determined to continue the mindless destruction begun long before. I saw the scene as a tableau: the demented follower of a long-dead madman and the struggling victim of a long-suffering people. The image infuriated me.

CHAPTER THIRTY ONE

"This isn't the first time I've been shipwrecked, you know?" I said as I watched Laura's lips becoming a deeper blue.

Cold, Canadian air had moved in after the storm and the sun had lost most of its warmth as it reddened on the horizon. I was afraid that if we had to spend the night out on the open sea, both of us would be weakened by hypothermia. I also worried about Gebhardt. He was out there somewhere close by, but I hadn't been able to spot the raft since I hauled Laura up.

Laura opened her eyes and managed a weak smile. "Does it get easier after the first time?" she asked.

"Now that you mention it, it doesn't," I smiled back. "The first time, I floated in the waters off Haiti with two of my SEAL buddies after an aborted mission. We had to spend most of one night, an entire day, and part of the next night in the water breathing through snorkels while patrol boats ran sweeps along the coast looking for us. The water was cold, even through the thick wet suits we were wearing. But I did learn a basic lesson about survival."

Laura didn't say anything, only looked through sleepy eyes at me.

I held both of her hands and rubbed them. "I learned that you can survive almost anything as long as you don't give up. As long as you've got the will to go on. Something—or someone—to live for. You'll make it out okay if you do. I know that sounds a little simplistic. Maybe even trite. But it's true."

Laura's eyes flickered open. "Don't worry about me, Captain. I never have been known to give up easily." She looked at me again, still smiling.

"Yeah, that's something I already know about you. I had to learn it about myself the hard way."

"Sometimes the hard way is the only way. Where are we, Erik? How much longer do you think we'll be out here?"

"We're too low in the water to see it, but the Montauk lighthouse should be right over there, not more than six miles away. Even if we don't get picked up by a boat soon, with any luck and a good tide we'll probably drift right up to the beach by nightfall. Maybe I'll take you out to dinner at Gurney's Inn tonight."

"I'm not so sure a great water view is something I'd appreciate right now."

I started to say something, but, just then, a plane's motor came from behind me and seconds later, Zeke Tredia's yellow plane passed over no more than 500-feet up. Instinctively, I yelled out and waved my arms, even though I realized that he wouldn't be able to hear me, nor would he likely see us in the rough sea. The plane continued flying straight out to sea in the direction of Block Island.

"That was Zeke's plane," I said. "If he's looking for Manson's boat, he's not going to find it. But, maybe, he will make contact with the *Prowler*."

Laura nodded weakly and shivered as she spoke. "If he does, I hope it's soon. This shipwreck business is starting to get old."

"Just hang on. Somebody's going to pick us. . ." I cut it off with a curse. "Every time you think you're clear of him, that son of a bitch turns up like a stray cat."

Laura twisted around painfully and looked over her shoulder. Not more than a hundred-feet away, the orange raft rose high on the crest of a swell. As it dropped down, we both could see the gray head and chiseled features of the old Nazi struggling to maneuver the raft in our direction. He was using a small, plastic paddle that must have been in the emergency pocket of the raft to propel the clumsy vessel.

I squeezed Laura's hand. "I might have to leave you alone for a few minutes. Just hang on and I'll see if I can't get us a better boat."

"Please be careful. He's totally deranged and dangerous. He's got the knife."

I stayed low as I breast stroked towards the approaching raft. I was feeling the exhaustion of hours spent in the water. The aching chill had done a lot to weaken me, but, now, the confrontation brought a surge of adrenaline coursing through my body. I squinted into the sun, which was slanting in at acute angle behind the raft. Something on the raft caught the light and flashed it like a signal. I saw the source of this flash as I got closer: Gebhardt had lashed the dive knife to the butt end of the paddle with shoelaces. One end was a paddle, the other a harpoon. From my point of reference—low in the water—raft and man silhouetted against an empty sky lit by a red-glowing sun resembled a primitive image—a prehistoric hunter of the seas.

About thirty-feet separated us when Gebhardt called out.

"Hazen! I don't want to kill you, but you're in my way. You and the woman can swim if you want. I just want the box. It's mine!"

Silence was my only reply. The wind had dropped to a light breeze, the waves were still steep, but they weren't breaking anymore and would soon settle down into long rollers; even the two black-backed gulls that skimmed by low to the water did so in silence. I drew a deep breath and jackknifed under in a silent surface dive.

Ten feet down, I leveled off and swam. I swam with all the power that I could muster, channeling my years of training as a diver into moving efficiently underwater. Without a mask, I could see only blurred shadows, but the black bottom of the raft stood out clearly against the silver surface. I turned and rose below it, quickly accelerating as I came up, my arms held stiff overhead. When I hit the edge of the raft I kicked and heaved as powerfully as my strength allowed, trying to shake Gebhardt loose, then immediately dove and angled off away from the raft.

It didn't work. The raft was heavier and more stable than I had thought. Ten feet away, I came up for air. Gebhardt was still crouched in the raft, brandishing the home-made harpoon and screaming curses at me.

"Hazen, you ignorant bastard! You're just sealing your girlfriend's death warrant. I'll cut her throat—and yours too if you try to stop me." He looked over at Laura where she floated on the box a few yards away. Then he braced himself and began to dip his paddle in the water.

I dove again and came up between Laura and the raft. Gebhardt stood in the raft holding the harpoon aloft as he bore down on both of us. Time seemed frozen for a moment as the distance between us closed. In the background, I could hear Laura shouting for me to dive and save myself. But, in that moment of frozen time, I was staring at something beyond the raft, just above the western horizon.

Then, time speeded up. The black dot on the horizon suddenly turned into a small plane headed directly towards us. Its engine noise came roaring over the quiet water. Startled, Gebhardt spun around to look. I seized the opportunity and lunged across the few feet of water separating us. I got my left arm over the side of the raft just as another roller rose under it. Gebhardt spun forward again, plunging the knife downward piercing my hand. I pulled away knocking Gebhardt off balance. The clumsy harpoon flew into the water and sank as I grabbed my injured hand and squeezed the wrist to stop the blood that came puffing out into the blue water in little clouds of pink. Knocked off balance, Gebhardt fell into the sea on the other side of the raft just as the plane roared past fifty feet overhead.

I began to pull myself up into the raft, but Gebhardt surfaced behind me and pulled me back down into the water. Both of us grappled on the surface for a few minutes but I had lost strength in my left hand. I felt Gebhardt clamp onto my throat with one hand and hold my good right arm in a vice-like grip. With only one good arm, it was impossible to break the older man's grip and I knew that I would have to move the fight someplace else: to a place where I would have an advantage. So I flexed my neck muscles against the chokehold, sucked in some air, and plunged underwater dragging Gebhardt with me. At the same time, I jackknifed my legs up and scissored them around Gebhardt's waist, squeezing with what strength I had left.

If he hadn't been wearing the life vest we would have plunged through the column of water like a dropped anchor. As it was I had to use my left arm to keep us pulled underwater and prevent his head from popping to the surface. Gebhardt's chokehold stabbed red-hot waves of darkness past my eyes as I struggled through the pain to keep from blacking out. I lost all track of time. All equilibrium was gone, and up and down became confused. My thoughts were reduced to primitive instincts—to survive and to kill the thing trying to destroy me.

Then I felt the chokehold relax. I opened my eyes and saw Gebhardt's cadaverous face floating in front of me. The emotionless eyes were now wide in sudden panic, looking up to where the light came filtering through the surface. I felt his hands release my neck and upper arm. Then I watched with a detached interest as the man who had been so intent on killing me seconds before began clawing frantically at the water above his head.

I reached down with both arms stroking now and pulled him deeper. At the same time I continued to squeeze with my legs as Gebhardt kicked frantically and windmilled his arms, reaching for the sweet freedom of air that lay just beyond the heaving ceiling of water. Through years of experience, I was well aware of what he was feeling. I knew that panic had already eaten up what little oxygen that might have been left in the old man's lungs, and that his brain was being poisoned by the build-up of carbon dioxide. In another second or two the overwhelming need to take a breath would be impossible to halt.

Gebhardt's mouth would open and he would suck salt water into his rupturing lungs. There would be a fist of intense pain slammed into his brain, and then all of his organs would shut down.

My own chest was beginning to heave with the same urgency.

Then I felt Gebhardt's body convulse. Once—twice—three times before it went limp. Only then did I release my scissors grip and kick with all my might for the distant surface. Below me, Gebhardt's pale face—mouth and eyes wide in death—rose slowly towards the surface. His eyes were staring upwards through lifeless pupils towards the column of light above.

When I broke the surface and heaved air into my searing lungs, I felt like I was more dead than alive. My windpipe was ruptured and my mouth filled with blood. More blood pumped out of the wound in my hand. I was weak from the loss of blood and getting weaker by the second. My eyes couldn't focus and the rolling surface was a blur of fading blue sky and gray hills of water. There was no raft. It took too much effort to stay afloat. I put my head back in the water and thought about my grandfather sitting in his chair and closing his eyes for the final time as he looked out onto the water that floated him through life. I thought of my father rolled by the surf into the sandy mesh of the seine net. Finally, I thought of Book Johnson, who wouldn't be far away now, drifting above a weedy bottom on the flooding tide.

Suddenly, I was aware that someone was calling my name. I opened my eyes and saw Gebhardt floating in his life jacket, his head hung downwards. Then an arm wrapped around my chest and Laura's face was close to mine as she breathed heavily to swim with me. I tried to oblige her by fluttering my feet but I couldn't tell if I actually did it or if I just imagined it.

A minute later my head bumped something hard and I saw an orange blur that was the raft. I felt hands pulling me. I clawed my way onto the raft to the wonderful feel of a warm, hard surface under my back. Then I was falling, spinning downwards until everything went black.

CHAPTER THIRTY TWO

THE PERSISTENT BUZZING PENETRATED MY CONSCIOUSNESS AND I OPENED my eyes. Less than a hundred feet above the raft, a little yellow plane circled and dipped its wings. It was Zeke's plane again and this time I knew that he had spotted us. Next to me I felt Laura stir, and then saw her face—pale but beautiful—looking down at me. I tried to speak, but my throat was swollen closed and I only wheezed.

"Lie still, Erik. We're going to be OK." She smiled at me but I could see that she, too, was in pain. As she sat up straight I could hear her catch her breath with the effort.

For a minute, nothing happened. The plane continued to stay overhead circling as though it was on a string attached to the raft. The ocean continued to lift the raft in a steady cadence that was hypnotic in its gentleness. The wind had dropped to a breeze, which blew across the open raft with a feathery whisper accompanied by the soft lapping of water.

"There's a boat coming towards us," Laura cried. "I think it's your boat!" She was quiet for a moment and then shouted. "It is! It's the *Finest Kind*!"

I wanted to shout too but I was too weak to even lift my head and look. I closed my eyes for what seemed like a minute, and when I opened them I saw Bill Lester looking down at me from high up over the boat's rail.

"Hey, Captain Erik and Miss Morgan. Just hold on, we'll have you in the boat in a minute." He maneuvered a long boat hook down and caught onto one of the rope hand-holds on the raft. Then he walked the raft down the stern to the diving ramp and hooked it onto the electric winch, which slid it up through the transom door and onto the deck as neatly as a beached fish.

Bill helped Laura stand and supported her across the deck into the cabin. "Please, take care of Erik. I'll be okay," I heard her say.

Lester and my cousin Jack Hazen manhandled me a little to wrap me in blankets but didn't try to lift me out of the raft. I felt a trickle of blood run down the side of my mouth. I picked my hand up to wipe it away and saw white bone inside the jagged knife wound. Some blood oozed out so Lester wrapped it with another compression bandage as Jack sprinted up to the wheelhouse and pointed the *Finest Kind* towards the Montauk Lighthouse.

This time the dream was different. Again, I was deep in the black belly of the Andrea Doria, but now I was looking up from a ruined cabin to one of the portholes far overhead. A face was looking through it down at me. I couldn't tell who it was because it was back-lit by the green glow of deep water. I was filled with an overwhelming weariness and I could barely move my limbs.

Then I was surprised to find myself floating upwards, the face in the portal growing larger and clearer as I moved towards it. Finally, I realized that I was not underwater, and that there was no porthole overhead, and that the face looking down at me was Laura, and that the green glow was the dock lights at Montauk, and that I was lying in the stern of the Finest Kind strapped to a stretcher as Laura stood watching, while Hector Gonzales supported her on the deck next to me.

"Is this heaven, or did we make it back to Montauk," I managed to croak through my swollen throat.

"That's the first time I ever heard this pile of rocks described that way," came a familiar voice from nearby. It was LeClair's voice, and it came from where he, too, lay on a stretcher up on the dock. "Then again, maybe heaven's just a state of mind—and my mind's in a pretty good state right now, even if my ass isn't."

I looked up at him on the dock as he lay face down on the stretcher. An EMT was applying a compression bandage to his buttocks.

On the boat, Laura was wrapped in a blanket as Hector helped her up onto the dock. She groaned a little with the effort.

Then I felt my stretcher lifted and carried up onto the dock where they set me down next to LeClair.

He looked over at me with mock horror. "Jesus! You're not looking too pretty right now, old buddy, so I can understand why the lady left." Then he broke into a broad grin. "Me? I just got shot in the ass. My face is still pretty. But, we'll both live. Yeah, I'd say you're going to live again."

All I could do was roll my eyes at my old friend. I tried to answer but couldn't. So I closed my eyes and thought, same to you, Bub, same to you.

Then Laura came back, knelt next to me and kissed me lightly on the lips.

I rolled my eyes towards LeClair and croaked, "How'd he and Gonzalez get here?"

"Somebody named Calvin Havens—I think he's a neighbor of yours?"

I nodded. "Another Bonacker," I whispered.

"He got the distress call first and he was close by with his lobster boat. He got everyone off the *Prowler*." She looked down at me with a sadness in her eyes. "Everyone except Sean. He … didn't make it. And Book, of course."

I began to say something, even though there were no words to say it.

"Don't try to say anything," she whispered. "We'll have all the time you want to talk when you get better." And then she added, "I love you."

Finally, I opened my eyes and grinned at her. Then I just mouthed the words: "I love you too."

A minute later, as two Coast Guard corpsmen lifted the stretcher to carry me to an ambulance, Laura pointed down to the stern of the *Finest Kind.* I turned my head to follow her gesture. On the deck of the boat, underneath the overhang of the flying bridge, partially concealed by diving gear, and lit by the floodlights shining down from the outriggers, stood Fletcher King. He bit off a new chew of tobacco as he rested one foot on a fiberglass box with an open-mouthed white shark stenciled on its side. He grinned up at me.

I thought how tourists like to call Montauk, "the end", but to us locals it always was the beginning. Then I smiled, dropped my head back on the stretcher, and looked up at the velvet night sky where the stars blinked like diamonds and looked close enough to touch.

THE END

AFTERWORD

I SPENT A WEEK IN THE HOSPITAL GETTING MY VOICE BACK. MIKE LECLAIR was in a room on the next floor lying face down for a couple of days wishing that the nurse who had to change his dressing every day looked a little less like his mother. Sean Roebling's body came back with the *Prowler* and was buried in Greenwood Cemetery, in Brooklyn, not far from the famous bridge that his distant relative had built. Book Johnson was never found. Somewhere offshore his body has probably joined up with the Gulf Stream and gets to drift with that great current around the world every year. Maybe he will eventually make it back home to Bermuda.

None of the men that Laura and I had witnessed being murdered on board the *White Shark II* were ever found. Hank Manson's life-long involvement with sharks had come full circle.

The ocean out by Block Island calmed down a few days after the storm and stayed very placid for another week. The body of Kurt Gebhardt was found floating in his life jacket by a chartered open boat fishing for fluke. A drowning victim.

Also during that time, Fletch King supervised a salvage tug operation—paid for by the Voyage Home Foundation because Manson had let his insurance policy lapse—to raise the wreck of the *White Shark II.* The two bodies that were found trussed up in the cabins brought about an official inquest that I had to answer to. But, between the eye-witness testimony provided by Laura, and the accounts of the incident sworn to by all of the crew of the *Prowler*, no charges were ever brought against me. Even so, I wish it could have ended better for both men.

Also found on the wreck—still in the pilothouse where Gebhardt had left it—was the third attache case of diamonds. Like the other two cases, it contained almost three-thousand diamonds, each one at least three carats in weight. All of the stones range from flawless to very fine. Considering the total number of carats and the quality of the stones, the true value of the infamous collection is in the range of one billion dollars.

Of course, there is some question as to the salvage rights. No insurance company can go after it simply because it was never even supposed to exist. Since it was not found on the wreck itself, no entity of the Italian Lines has a claim to it. And, since the diamonds had come from all over Europe, no single country can lay claim to it. It was, however, found in U.S. territorial waters, so there are some legal issues to get over before a final agreement can be reached. It may take several years, but lawyers for the foundation are confident that, at least, the majority share will be awarded. In that event, large endowments for humanitarian causes are already in the planning stages.

Marcel Feynard's father died a week after the announcement of his son's death. In his final words he asked forgiveness for his service to a criminal government that brought suffering to so many.

As for me, I'm back to running charters for big game, offshore fishing. Bill Lester and I still run into an idiot now and then, but Laura has taught me to be a little more patient and understanding when it does happen—at least I let her think that. We see each other a lot, either at her place in the city or out in the unglamorous "Hamptons" at my little cottage. After the fishing season ends we plan to take a nice vacation out to Arizona, a place that has no ocean—not even any water to speak of—to distract me.

ACKNOWLEDGEMENTS

Years ago, when I was a regional correspondent for the New York Times, I wrote about the commercial fishing industry on Long Island. At that time there were still some traditional, East End fishermen—Bonackers—who hauled seine nets on the beaches from East Hampton and Amagansett to Montauk Point. Some of the characters in this book were inspired by those men. In the early stages of the manuscript, the late writing teacher, Lou Stanek, and the group of writers who gathered at her Manhattan apartment on Saturday mornings gave me guidance and support. Later stages of the book were read and critiqued by my friend Rich Giannotti, and my wife, Jacquie. I thank all of them for helping me to finally bring this book to publication.

AUTHOR BIO

Richard Weissmann has been a teacher, outdoor writer, reporter, naturalist, and fisherman. He lives on Long Island's south shore, not far from the Great South Bay and the Atlantic Ocean.

www.ingramcontent.com/pod-product-compliance
Lightning Source LLC
Chambersburg PA
CBHW031133210626

46816CB00014B/695